G&B Detective Agency
The Welch Avenue Wizards

By R. L. Link

A Max Mosbey and Skip Murray G&B Detective Novel

G&B Detective Agency
The Welch Avenue Wizards
All rights reserved.
Copyright © 2019 by Rollie Link

ISBN: 9781091822221

G&B Detective Agency
The Welch Avenue Wizards

Dedicated to Edlyn and all my friends in Puerto Rico

Prologue

Max sat in the driver's seat of the Ford Taurus patrol car. He and Skip had been driving the same car for five years and it felt like a second home for them. It was a marked car: it had the City of Ames Police insignia on the door, just like any other patrol car in the fleet, however it did not have a light bar on the top. There were flashing red lights in the grill and in the tail lights, but those were only used in extreme emergencies. Technically speaking it was not a patrol car at all, it was a detective car, but for all intents and purposes it looked like a patrol car without a light bar. Max and Skip spent their weekends in the Ford, driving from bar to bar, from downtown to Campustown. Everyone on the department called it the bar car. The bar car was parked in the drive at Fire Station Two on Welch Avenue, pulled up as tight to the wall that stood on the north side of the drive as Max could get it and still allow Skip to get out. If they had to bail out for any reason, they could not let their car impede the fire engines.

It was almost two thirty in the morning on a brisk Sunday, and Welch Avenue was still going strong. The bars had closed at two o'clock, last call had been at one thirty, but the Saturday night crowd was not ready to give it up. The college kids who had been drinking all day Saturday at the football game were still on the streets yelling, screaming and carrying on. Max and Skip were staying warm in their car and watching the show. It would not have been difficult for them to grab up a student for public intoxication and call it a night, there was no lack of eligible candidates, but the two officers let them slide. If they made an arrest it would leave the bedlam that was Campustown bar closing to turn into a free-for-all, so the two sat, a conspicuous deterrent to all but the most inebriated, and one of those had the officers' attention.

"Look at fuckwad over there in the Taco Machine line," Max said.

"Red coat and the goofy cap?" Skip asked.

"Yep, he's going to start a fight," Max remarked.

The young man that they were referring to was standing in line at the food cart across the street. The line extended in front of three or four businesses closed for the night. It wasn't unusual for the owners to show up to a broken window on Monday morning. It was part of doing business in Campustown.

"How many citations do you have?" Skip asked, referring to the citations that he and Max had been writing all evening and night for persons on the premises of a tavern under age, possession of alcohol under age and possession of a false ID.

Max pulled a wad of them from his pocket and counted.

"An even dozen," Max replied.

"I have eleven," Skip remarked. "Plus I still have the paperwork on that drunk we arrested earlier."

"Fuckin' A," Max said in a resigned voice, knowing full well that an affidavit would have to be filled out, signed, filed and a case report dictated for each ticket, plus the extra paperwork for the drunk, before they could go home. Twenty-three tickets would take an hour at least. They got off duty at four o'clock. An hour and a half of shift left, an hour's worth of paperwork, and Welch Avenue was nowhere close to slowing down. Another night where they would go through the drive-up at McDonalds and take their lunch break while they did their paperwork.

Skip cracked his door open and put a foot out on the ground.

"God damn it," Max said as the kid in the red coat and the goofy hat got into a shoving match with the guy behind him in line.

Max swung his door open to get out. A young man who had been working the grill at the cart ran down the line toward the altercation.

"Slo-Mo's gonna get it," Skip said.

The young man was looking at the bar car across the street. He got to the offender, grabbed his arm to get his attention and pointed to the two officers exiting the car. Max and Skip stood outside the car looking as menacing as they could muster at that time of the morning after working twelve straight hours that started the afternoon before at the football stadium.

It looked for a moment like the kid in the red coat and the goofy hat was going to give Slo-Mo some trouble, but he relented and stormed out of the line, staggering south on the sidewalk. Slo-Mo gave Max and Skip a thumbs up and went back to the grill.

"Saved another poor innocent from a night in the heartbreak hotel," Max remarked. "Just call me Slo-Mo, ma'am, the only law west of Ash Avenue."

The two were keeping a close eye on the kid in the red coat and the goofy hat, hoping that he would keep moving and not decide to come back to make more trouble for Slo-Mo. It was a fifty-fifty proposition. If he turned back Max and Skip would intervene. One could only expect so much community service from a guy who cooked tacos for an endless line of drunken college students every weekend night. But they both knew that Slo-Mo preferred to save them all from the jackboots if he could. He didn't like seeing his customers dragged off in cuffs. It was bad for business. So Max and Skip always gave him the first opportunity to find a diplomatic solution before they took things into their own hands, which were never diplomatic. Besides, Max and Skip had a lot to do already.

"Take it easy on the street sign," Skip said more to himself than to Max.

The kid in the red jacket and the goofy cap had jumped up and hammered a no parking sign with his fist with such force that the two officers could hear it from inside their car and Slo-Mo looked up from his grill.

"Fuckwad just cut his hand," Max observed, putting the car in gear and pulling out of the lot toward the kid.

"He's bleeding all over the place," Skip remarked.

Skip took the mic from the radio that sat between them on the floor of the car and touched it to Max's arm to get his attention.

"One-twenty-three, one-twenty-eight," Skip said into the mic, calling the area patrol car that was responsible for Welch Avenue.

"Go ahead one-twenty-eight," a voice answered.

The kid in the red coat and the goofy hat was watching the bar car behind him. He turned onto Chamberlain and walked briskly to the alley that ran south on the west side of Welch. Max looked over and Skip winked at him. Max continued to the alley, keeping visual contact with the college kid who was trailing drops of blood from a hand that he didn't even know was bleeding.

"Yeah, one-twenty-three, we're on Welch and we got some kid, five-ten, slim build, red coat and cap, he's pretty intoxicated, tried to start a fight over in the Taco Machine line. He's on the move now. He tried to vandalize a parking sign and may have injured his hand. We lost him somewhere in the alley behind the two-hundred block of Welch. If you're in the area, could you help us?"

"Ten-four," the area three officer replied. "Seventy-six from Colorado Junction," letting Max and Skip know that he was on his way.

"What the fuck is he doing over on Colorado?" Max asked.

"Just keep him in sight," Skip replied quickly. He brought the mic to his mouth. "Twenty-three, if you can go down to Storm and go north in the alley, I think we can get him between us. He couldn't have gotten too far away."

"Ten-four, just a few blocks away," the area three officer replied.

The two officers could see the kid in the red coat and the goofy hat a block and a half ahead of them. He tipped over a garbage can and started kicking the garbage. He was being silhouetted by a pair of headlights coming toward them three blocks away.

"Pull over and turn off your lights," Skip instructed Max.

"I never turned them on," Max replied, pulling over into a parking area that sat off the alley.

"Twenty-tree, we're over on the three-hundred block of Welch and there is a ruckus going on in the alley west of us. Sounds like someone kicking over trash cans. Might be our man."

"Ten-four, I got him here. Ames, I'll be out with a subject in the alley three-hundred block of Welch," the area three officer reported.

"Ten-four, zero-two-forty-one, one-twenty-eight are you close?" the dispatcher called over the radio.

"Ten-four," Skip said into the mic. "A couple blocks away."

"Fuckwad is trying to fight," Max said, putting the car back into gear and pulling out into the alley toward the area three officer.

Max and Skip arrived quickly to back up the area three officer, but he already had the college kid down, a knee pinning the kid's head to the ground, and was putting cuffs on him.

"Stupid drunk tried to get away from me when I took hold of him," the area three officer announced, hardly out of breath. The college kid was still squirming. The officer put some more weight on his pinned head, causing him to cease movement and cry out in pain.

"I'll let you up when you calm down a little," the officer told the college kid in a calm, even voice. "You want me to put him in your car?" the officer asked Max, who had not gotten out.

"Why don't you go ahead and take him?" Max replied. "We already got a shit load of paperwork to do, and you found him, after all. If you want him, he's yours."

Max knew that the young officer was hot to make an arrest. These young night shifters would arrest their next-door neighbor if they could. They wanted to arrest everyone. It was their goal to put as many people in jail as they could. It was a rookie thing, although some officers never outgrew it. Max and Skip just wanted to get out of the police station and go home at four. The officer stood up, grabbed the kid by the arm and hoisted him to his feet, then propelled him toward his patrol car.

"He's got a nasty cut," Max said to the officer. "You'll need to run him through ER before you bring him down for booking."

"I see that," the young officer said. "Should I call an ambulance out, what do you think?"

Max was getting out of the car and popping the trunk at the same time. Skip showed no indication that he was going to get out of the car. Max got a roll of gauze from his first-aid supplies and walked to where the officer had the kid bent over the back fender of his patrol car and was searching him for contraband. Max walked up and waited. When the officer was done with his search, Max took the bleeding hand that was cuffed behind the kid's back and wrapped the gauze around it. Max was not neat about it. He wrapped the whole roll, until the kid's hand was the size of a softball, then he tied it off.

"There you go," Max said. "That oughtta keep him from bleeding all over the back seat while you take him up to the hospital."

The officer was happy that Max had taken care of that. He had been on the department less than a year, and while he felt like he was getting the hang of everything, he was glad to get help from the likes of Max and Skip. They were the bar car after all, they were legends. Not so much to the rest of the department, but for the young night shift area officers, these guys were kick ass.

Skip was sitting at the table in the detective conference room finishing up paperwork. He could hear Max's voice in the detective sergeant's office dictating cases over the phone. He looked at the clock. Thirty more minutes until their shift ended. Twenty if they bugged out ten minutes early and called themselves off duty over their portable radios on the way home. The phone on the conference table rang and Skip picked it up. It was dispatch.

"One-twenty-three is up at the ER with his arrest and he needs to talk to you," the female voice on the other end told him. "Line two."

"Ten-four," Skip said in a resigned voice. The dispatcher had already ended the call.

Skip pushed the flashing button on the phone.

"What do you need?" he asked.

"I'm trying to do my paperwork on this guy while we are waiting for the doctor to stitch him up and I didn't give him any field sobriety tests. Should I maybe charge him with interference with official acts instead of intox, beings he tried to get away?"

"Why was he trying to get away?" Skip asked. "What act were you officially doing that he interfered with?"

"I was going to arrest him," the officer replied.

"For what?" Skip asked.

"I guess public intox," the officer said.

"Okay," Skip said. "If you don't have a charge of some kind, you got no interference, because he can't interfere with nothing."

The voice was silent on the other end for a moment.

"How about vandalism?" he asked.

"More damage to his hand than to the sign," Skip said. "How about this: 'Observed the above-named defendant staggering in alley on the three-hundred block of Welch Avenue. His stance was unsteady, his speech was slurred, his eyes were bloodshot and blurry. There was a strong odor of alcohol on his breath. Upon making contact, the defendant became uncooperative. Defendant was arrested for public intoxication and transported to the Ames Police Department."

The officer said nothing.

"Are you writing it down?" Skip asked.

"Yes," the officer replied. "What if it goes to court? What do I say? I didn't give him any field sobriety tests."

"You don't need field sobriety tests," Skip said with some exasperation in his voice. "You need to be able to describe a drunk. His stance was unsteady, his speech was slurred, his eyes were bloodshot and blurry, there was a strong odor of alcohol on his breath, the defendant became uncooperative. Doesn't that sound like a drunk to you?"

Okay," said the officer. "How about the interference? Should I file that too?"

"Do what you want," Skip replied. "I usually don't file interference unless I lose the fight, so I've never filed it before. You can pile on whatever you want. He's your arrest. But he tried to run away and you grabbed him before he took two steps. It didn't look like he was giving you anything that you couldn't handle."

There was silence again.

"I think that I'll file the interference," he said.

"Go for it," Skip replied and hung up the phone. He looked up to see Max leaning against the door.

"What's with these guys?" Skip asked. "I mean, they don't know a drunk when they see one? They gotta give them tests to see if they're drunk?"

"Did you tell him everyone is drunk at two thirty on a Sunday morning after bar close?"

"Who the hell trained him?" Skip asked. "They sure didn't do a very good job."

"I think that Milton did," Max replied.

"Who the hell trained Milton?" Skip asked, knowing quite well who Milton's training officer was.

"I trained Milton," Max replied in a matter-of-fact way.

"Yeah, well, his retention isn't very good, then," Skip said.

"You're just grumpy," Max remarked. "You need any help? I'm done."

Skip shoved an affidavit across the table to Max, who was picking up the phone and dialing the number to dictate cases. Max glanced at it while he read off the date, the time and the location of the offense. When he was done with that he went straight into the narrative, "Observed the above-named defendant staggering on the one-hundred block of Main Street. His stance was unsteady, his speech was slurred, his eyes were bloodshot and blurry. There was a strong odor of alcohol on his breath. Upon making contact, the defendant became uncooperative. Defendant was arrested for public intoxication and transported to the Ames Police Department." Max spoke methodically into the phone. He had repeated the narrative hundreds of times, and the drunks were always uncooperative, they had to be. It was how he always finished it off.

Chapter 1

Monday

Max walked across the street from Filo's coffee shop to the offices of the G&B Detective Agency with a ceramic mug of steaming coffee in his hand. He was careful not to look at it. He had learned in navy boot camp that the worst thing a person could do when crossing the parade ground with a cup of coffee for the commanding officer of his company was to look down at the full cup. Better to watch where he was going. His inner balance would keep the coffee from sloshing out of the cup. It wasn't working.

Max walked past Monica's car, which was parked in the space that was reserved for their receptionist/office manager/girl Friday/ confidante/spiritual advisor. Max and Skip had opened the agency when they had won two hundred twenty million dollars in the Powerball. It gave them something to do.

"Hey, what's up?" Max asked Monica as he came through the door and took a seat in one of the easy chairs that sat opposite her desk.

"Nothing much," she replied, not looking up from her computer.

Monica was a strikingly beautiful black woman in her mid-twenties, tall and slender. She had been a stripper at one of the bars that the two patrolled when they won the Powerball, taking a break from college and trying to save up some money to go back. They had asked her to manage the agency and offered to pay her tuition, an opportunity that she jumped on. Now she was married to recently promoted Detective Milton Jackson, Max's best friend still on the Ames Police Department, who some might argue was Max's only friend still on the police department. "I'm trying to concentrate here. I have to get through these e-mails before I leave for class," she added.

"So, how's it going with the ex?" Max asked, ignoring her statement.

"Fine," Monica said in a clipped voice.

"Is he paying his child support?" Max asked.

"Kind of." Monica gave up and sat back in her chair, looking up at Max.

"What does 'kind of' mean?" Max asked.

"Well, he still owes eighteen grand, but he's paying two hundred a month now, so as long as he is paying part of it regularly, they don't push him," Monica said.

"How much is he supposed to pay a month?" Max asked.

"Five hundred," Monica replied.

"And he's paying two?" Max remarked.

Monica shrugged her shoulders and went back to her computer.

"What's he doing now that the comic book store he worked at burned down?" Max asked.

Monica looked up. "He's working at a deli restaurant making sandwiches."

"What's the hubby have to say about the child support?" Max asked.

"Milton?" Monica said.

"No, your other hubby," Max shot back.

"Actually, Milton sides with Brian. It is very obnoxious. However, one would expect that from someone who was trained by you."

"You are a little testy this morning," Max remarked.

"I need to get this done and go to class," Monica said, going back to the computer. "Besides, I was expecting to get started on a project and I'm waiting for something that didn't arrive when it was supposed to. If I get a package, don't open it."

"Do we need to hire someone to help you?" Max asked.

Monica did not answer.

Max turned and stared out the window. Skip was pulling into the parking lot. He parked his car as far away as he could and got out. He inspected both sides of his car before he crossed the lot and entered the agency.

"You're late," Max remarked as he came through the door.

"How can I be late?" Skip asked.

"I'm just saying, usually you are here way before I am," Max remarked.

Skip shrugged his shoulders and took the other seat opposite Monica's desk.

"What's up?" he asked her.

"Don't bother her, she's busy," Max admonished him.

Monica looked up, gave Max a stern look, then went back to her computer.

"Sorry," Skip replied, looking out the window with Max just in time to see Ben Ralston, the insurance agent who had an office next door to the agency, walk by.

Skip tapped the window to get his attention, expecting him to walk on by. But instead, Ben came in.

Monica looked up when he did. "What's up?" he asked Monica.

She smiled but didn't answer and went back to her work.

"I need to talk to you guys," Ben said to the two detectives.

"All ears," Max said.

"Take it somewhere else," Monica said to no one in particular.

Max and Skip got up from their chairs and led the way down the hall to where the conference room stood on one side and a bar sat on the other. Max and Skip turned into the bar and took a seat at a table.

"She seems a little testy," Ben remarked under his breath as they walked down the hall.

"She has to study here now," Max whispered. "With Milton moving into that little townhouse after they got married, and what with her mother living there and Essie, it gets crowded."

"I can hear you guys talking about me," Monica called from her desk.

"Have a seat," Max said.

Ben was looking through the door at the conference room.

"We don't use that room a lot," Max explained. Monica's little girl Essie likes to play in there. We like the bar."

Ben looked around the bar. It was a large room that looked like a bar. He had never been beyond the reception area. Three years their next-door neighbor and he had no idea. There was ornate woodwork on all of the walls and across the ceiling, recessed lighting and a huge teak bar stood on one wall, with walnut shelves filled with bottles of liquor behind it. To one side of the bar sat a wine rack with at least eighty bottles of wine, and next to that a wine refrigerator.

"Jesus," Ben exclaimed. "How do you get any work done?"

"We don't," Skip replied.

Ben took another look around the room. "Hey, I want to hire you guys to do some investigating for me."

"We don't feel like doing an investigation right now," Skip said.

Ben gave Skip a curious look. "Come on," he said. "You owe me, anyway."

"What do we owe you for?" Max asked.

"You guys keep using my business cards. I know you guys come over to visit just so that you can take some cards and then you go and tell people you're Ben Ralston, independent insurance agent. They call me."

"Well, we only do that if we're working a case and we don't want people to know that we are private detectives. And we don't work a lot of cases, so we don't do that very often," Skip explained.

"But you admit that you've done it?" Ben challenged.

"I admit that Max has given out your cards and introduced himself as you, but I haven't," Skip said defensively.

"So you owe me," Ben reiterated.

"What do you have?" Max acquiesced.

"You know that comic book store that burned last month?" Ben began.

"We were just talking about that," Max replied. "Monica's ex-boyfriend was working there. Now he's making sandwiches at some deli."

"Here's the thing," Ben continued. "The arson investigator came back with a report that says the fire was started by faulty wiring."

"Okay," said Skip. "What's wrong with that?"

"Because that is what they always say if they can't determine the cause of a fire," Ben replied.

"Always?" Skip asked. "There's no such thing as a fire starting because of faulty wiring, it's always something else?"

"That's not what I'm saying," Ben said. "Yes, sometimes it is faulty wiring. I'm saying that if they can't figure out the cause, they say faulty wiring."

"What do you want us to do?" asked Skip.

"I want you to take a look at it and see what you think," Ben replied.

"You know, we have absolutely no training or experience in arson investigation," Skip said. "That is a very specialized field."

"I just want you to look at it and see what you think," Ben replied.

"We're going to charge you," Max said. "What's the deal anyway? You got a report from the investigator, why not just pay it out? It's not even your money, what do you care? You're an agent, not an adjustor or anything. You're an independent agent. You write policies."

"I don't like getting jerked around and manipulated," Ben said. "And I think that there is a lot more to this than a comic book store burning down. Don't ask me why, because if I could put my finger on it, I wouldn't be over here asking you guys to look into it. I just think that someone is taking advantage and it is stuck in my craw."

"When's the last time you heard someone say 'stuck in my craw'?" Max asked Skip.

Skip was silent. Max could see the gears in his head turning. Ben started to say something more. Max held up his finger.

"Let him think," Max said to Ben. "You got the seed planted, give it a minute or two to sprout."

Skip looked up at Max with a questioning look.

"What the hell, why not?" Max said, waving his hands in faux resignation.

"Give me some background," Skip said.

Ben began, "Cosmic Comics, small store on Welch Avenue. There is one other comic book store out in that Campustown area, bigger store, they sell games and toys and stuff like that. I don't know much about comic book stores. The other store is a big one. Cosmic Comics was a little one. They sold lots of vintage comics, some books, vinyl records, too. Owned by a guy named Hank Peterson."

"How old is Hank Peterson?" Max asked.

"Forties, I suppose," Ben answered, giving Max a quizzical look.

"Just wondering," Max replied. "I needed an image in my head of him."

"He had three employees," Ben continued.

"We know one of them," Max interrupted again.

"Thursday night four weeks ago, Peterson's manager is working late for some reason that no one seems to be able to tell me. He's just working late, and he locks up and leaves at ten. Midnight, they get a fire call. The place is engulfed. The fire department is right across the street, but they can't get there in time to save the place. It went that fast."

"I'm thinking that old dried up comic books and records burn fast," Max observed.

"Got no problem with that factoid," Ben said. "My problem is with the fact that it burned down at all. That building has been there forever. And the fire inspector was in there three months ago. Fire inspector has not gigged them, ever. I talked to him and he told me that they were real conscientious about staying up to code."

"They have sprinklers?" Skip asked.

"Nope," Ben replied. "They aren't required. But they did have a combination fire alarm and burglary alarm that evidently didn't go off. ADT alarms."

"Why?" asked Skip.

"Something for a private investigator to find out, because no one seems to be able to answer that question," Ben replied. "Another thing, there is a taco stand street vendor right there. The gal working it called the fire in. But the fire was going strong before she did. She had to have looked into the gates of hell standing right there in front of it. She moved the taco stand to keep it from burning along with the store before she called it in. Seriously, it was that big, and she didn't see anything until it was so out of control that the fire department across the street couldn't do anything? That's crazy."

"Got a name for the guy who locked up?" Skip asked.

"Brian Parker," Ben replied.

"Whoa," exclaimed Skip. "That's our boy."

Ben gave Skip a questioning look.

"Brian Parker is Monica's ex-boyfriend. The father of her child," Max explained.

"She's married to that big cop, Jackson, right?" Ben asked.

"Yep," Max replied. "Brian took off four or five years ago. He left as soon as he found out that Monica was pregnant. Was living in KC and not paying any child support. Came up once looking for work, but then he left again. No contact, no nothing. He came back recently and got himself a job at the comic store. Wanted to be closer to his kid all of a sudden. Anyway, he's not our favorite person. He pretty much abandoned Monica and Essie. Now Monica's got married, has a nice house, nice husband, and then he decides to come back up and cause trouble. It wouldn't surprise me if he had something to do with the fire."

"You think that he could have started it?" Ben asked excitedly.

"Well, I'm not going to go that far," Max backpedaled. "But he's a screwup. I wouldn't put it past him to do something stupid, like leave a candle lit or something."

"Why would he have a candle lit?" Ben asked.

"I said, 'or something,'" Max countered.

"Well, I would like you to look into it," Ben said. "Just bill me."

"We'll give it a week," Skip replied thoughtfully. "If we don't come up with any leads in a week, we're done."

"Fair enough," Ben responded. He looked around at the bar again, and across the hall into the conference room with its huge oak table and six leather chairs. A big screen TV was on the far wall. Skip glanced over into the conference room to see what had Ben's attention.

"That's the sports part of our sports bar. We watch games in there. This is like the old timey saloon part. Want a tour?" Max and Skip were standing up.

"So, your detective agency is really a bar?" Ben remarked as he stood up, too.

"Not the whole thing," Skip said.

Skip led Ben to the conference room and let him look around without commenting. When he had his fill, Skip took him down the hall past the men's and women's restrooms. Max held the door to the men's open so that Ben could see that there was a bumper pool table in the restroom, and a shower beyond that.

"Why is there a bumper pool table in the restroom?" Ben asked.

"Not enough room for it in the bar," Skip replied.

Ben looked at the door to the women's restroom.

"The ladies get a pool table too?" he asked.

Max held the door open for him and he saw two pinball machines against one wall.

"That's incredible," Ben remarked.

Skip led the way past the restrooms to the end of the hall where Max and Skip's offices were. Max was following up the rear. Ben looked into Max's office. It was twice the size of Ben's office next door. It quite obviously had been designed to look like a seedy detective office from some forties or fifties black and white film noir movie, right down to the wooden door with the frosted glass and the words "Max Mosbey, G&B Detective Agency" painted on the glass.

"Very nice," Ben commented. He turned across the hall and looked inside Skip's office. Skip's office was nothing like Max's. It was slightly larger, and the entire office looked like one that might be occupied by a CEO of a Manhattan conglomerate. Where Max's office had a somewhat seedy appearance designed into it, Skip's office was spotless. Max's office was dark, while one wall of Skip's had windows facing out toward the Iowa State University basketball practice building.

Max led the way into the back of the building. The space was enormous and there were two garage doors and a walkout door on the back. There were two basketball hoops on either end of the space, one set at a regulation ten feet and an adjustable hoop next to it that was set at four feet. It was a huge space that ran across the entire rear of the building. Some of it actually sat behind Ben's insurance agency. He had always thought that there was another business behind his. He didn't know that it was part of the G&B Detective Agency.

"Skip and Essie like to play full court," Max explained.

Away from the court and on one side of the overhead doors was a playground with an array of equipment. Tucked on the other side was a roll-away tool box, a work bench and an old Triumph motorcycle on a lift in a torn-down condition, the motor sitting on the bench.

"Max's playground," it was Skip's turn to explain.

"So this is how the rich live," Ben remarked.

"This is how we live," Skip replied.

"This is what you did with your Powerball winnings? Start a detective agency, build yourself a recreation center and then avoid taking cases?"

"That pretty much describes it," Skip admitted.

"I had no idea this was all over here."

"You should come over to visit more often," Max said. "We come over and visit you all the time."

"You come over to steal my business cards all the time," Ben corrected. "What is it with that?"

"It's a bad habit of Max's," Skip explained. "When we were on the police department, they wouldn't give patrol officers business cards. If you wanted them, you had to buy your own. So Max would go around visiting detectives and command staff, and when they weren't looking he would steal a couple of cards. He even had a couple of the city manager's cards. Then when he was out on the street, he would hand them out to people. The chief came out one night to check out the bar scene for himself, and he was having coffee with us. Max handed one of his cards out to some college girl in McDonalds and introduced himself as the chief of police. I thought it was hilarious. The chief wasn't that impressed, but the next week we got business cards. The only problem was that by then Max was a business card kleptomaniac and couldn't break the habit." Skip shrugged his shoulders as if to say that there was nothing that could be done about it at that point. Max just grinned.

"Alright," Ben said, turning toward the front of the agency. "Unlike my neighbors, I gotta make some money. You guys keep me up on what you find out?"

"Sure," Skip replied, picking up a basketball and dribbling it around in circles. "We'll get right on it."

Chapter 2

Monday

Max walked Ben to the front of the agency while Skip stayed in the back, shooting hoops. When they got up to the reception area Ben noticed that Monica had left. Max watched him look toward her desk and then around the reception area. The desk was a huge piece of solid oak furniture. Two leather chairs with a round matching oak end table formed the waiting area. The office chair behind the desk was leather. A large painting of a ballerina hung on the wall.

"She used to be a dancer," Max commented.

"Someone said she was a stripper before she went to work for you," Ben replied.

"Like I said," Max responded. "She was a dancer."

"You can tell me to mind my own business if you want, but I'm curious how much a desk like that costs," Ben looked toward Max.

"I don't know," Max replied. "Ten grand, maybe."

"Jesus," Ben exclaimed.

"I'll bet Skip's cost more than that," Max said.

Ben shook his head. "Okay," he said. "I gotta go back to work. I really appreciate you guys looking into this case for me. I know that cheating on your taxes and screwing the insurance company is the American way, but sometimes a guy just gets tired of it."

"We'll ask around," Max said earnestly. "We'll see what comes up and go from there. We keep in touch with Monica and she usually knows what we are up to, so if you want to check in with her, she should be able to keep you up to date."

Ben held out his hand and Max shook it. He went out the door and Max watched him walk past the window toward his own offices. Skip walked up from the back of the agency.

"Where we going to start?" he asked, still bouncing the basketball on the carpeted floor and looking out the window toward the street.

"Find the fire investigator," Max suggested.

"You didn't think to get a name and number from Ben, did you?" Skip asked.

Max turned toward Skip and hung his head. "I'll go over and get it," he said.

Skip turned and rolled the basketball down the hall like a bowling ball toward the rear of the building.

"I'll sit and wait," he said, taking a seat in one of the leather chairs.

Max left the agency and walked past the window. He could see Skip grinning through the window. He extended his middle finger toward the window and mouthed the words "fuck you" toward his partner in crime.

Max came back five minutes later with a handful of papers. He came through the door and handed Skip the pile as he went by, taking Monica's chair behind her desk and touching the screen of her computer to bring it up.

"Copy of the fire investigator's report," Max told him.

Skip knew what it was that he was looking at as soon as Max handed it to him and didn't comment.

"Want to call him up and talk to him, or you want to go looking for him?" Max asked.

"Let's just call him up," Skip replied. "Because it looks like it was someone from the fire marshal's office. Why didn't one of the Ames fire investigators do it? Don't we have our own arson investigators?"

Max shrugged his shoulders.

Skip threw the papers onto Monica's desk. Max pulled them across to himself and proceeded to punch the phone number on the header on the first page into the phone. He hit the speaker button. Skip listened to the beeps as he hit the numbers, then the ring tones.

"Fire marshal's office," a woman's voice answered the phone.

"Max Mosbey from the G&B Detective Agency," Max said to the woman. "I'm trying to get ahold of an arson inspector named Peter Gilmore."

"Just a moment, I'll transfer you," the woman said.

Skip and Max waited while the phone rang again. They heard the phone being picked up and a man answered, "Gilmore."

"Hi," Max said into the phone. "Max Mosbey, G&B Detective Agency in Ames. We're calling about a fire that happened about a month ago. Cosmic Comics. We have your report here."

"Okay," said Gilmore. "How can I help you?"

"We were hired by the insurance agent to look into it," Max replied.

"I already talked to the adjustor and he didn't mention any problems with my report," Gilmore said. "What's the deal?"

"We weren't hired by the company itself," Max explained. "We were hired by the agent who wrote the policy."

There was silence for a moment. "I guess and that I don't understand," Gilmore said.

"Look," Max replied. "The agent just hired us to follow up on your report from our perspective and see if there is something that might have gotten missed. We're just doing our job. We're not trying to make anyone look bad or to undermine your investigation, it is just routine."

"Okay," Gilmore said in a resigned voice. It wasn't the first time that someone had hired a private investigator because his investigation didn't come up with the results that they thought it should or hoped it would. "What do you need?"

"Well, the report says faulty wiring," Max said.

"Right," Gilmore replied before Max could say anything else. "The wiring was old, lots of aluminum wiring, lots of old copper. Looked like some old knob and tube wiring up in the joists that was supposed to be disconnected. It had both a breaker box and a fuse box right beside it. Just sort of all cobbled together. The walls were lath and plaster. I determined that one of the wires in the wall got hot and started burning the lath. Once it went up, it went fast."

Max took advantage of a break in the conversation while Gilmore took a breath. "Any possibility that there was an accelerant present?"

"No," replied Gilmore. "If there had been, I would have mentioned it in the report."

"Did you happen to talk to the person that called it in?" asked Max.

"Yes," Gilmore answered. "I'm pretty sure that she didn't have anything to do with the wiring shorting out and getting hot. It was a young lady who happened to be outside the building and spotted the fire. She didn't have much else to say about it."

"It just seems that it took her a long time to do anything," Max explained. "The agent thinks that she might have been aware of the fire for a while before she called it in."

"Doesn't have any bearing on the cause of the fire," Gilmore replied. "The fire was caused by faulty wiring. There is always a lot of contributing circumstances. The length of time that it burned before it got called in and the response time certainly contributed to the fact that the fire had engulfed the entire building before firefighters arrived, but it does not change the cause. But her statement is in my report. You can read it."

"Why did it take her so long to call it in, though?" Max asked again. "The fire station is right across the street."

"As I remember, she moved her food cart away from the fire before she did anything else," Gilmore explained. "I can understand that. I'm not saying that she couldn't or shouldn't have abandoned her cart and run across the street as soon as she saw flames, but also you gotta understand that she is young and she is making a decision to save her employer's property first. Then she called dispatch from her phone. I'm sure that she wasn't even thinking that the fire station was right across the street. She did what she did. I can't fault her for any of it. She didn't cause the fire."

"Another question," Max said. "Why did the state fire marshal's office take this case and not one of the city's fire investigators?"

"Conflict of interest," Gilmore replied. "Evidently there is a connection between the employee that locked up the store that evening and a detective on the APD. Anyway, I don't think that it is a conflict, but you know how it is. No one wants even a hint of impropriety. I mean, why should they? They called and asked if we could come up and do an investigation, so they sent me up. It happens."

"We talking about Brian Parker?" Max asked.

"That's him," Gilmore affirmed. "He locked up around ten, maybe a little after, if I remember right. It's in the report. Girl working the food cart called it in at midnight, or thereabout."

"I guess it is pretty cut and dried," Max remarked.

"It is all in the report," Gilmore replied. "I'm assuming your client wants to think that it was arson. If he didn't, we wouldn't be talking right now. He would have read the report and that would be the end of it. He isn't the first one I've come across who wanted a fire to be something that it wasn't. It was faulty wiring."

"Okay, thanks," Max said. "We aren't trying to bust your balls, we're just following up for our client. That's what he hired us to do."

"I understand completely," Gilmore said. "But it is what it is."

"Thanks," Max said again and ended the call.

"What do you think?" Max asked Skip.

"I think that Gilmore was pretty decent for someone who is just doing is job and then gets a call out of the blue from a couple of private investigators questioning the results of his investigation."

"What now?" Max asked.

"Let's see if our half of that conflict of interest knows anything about it."

"Milton?" Max asked.

"I'm not talking about Brian," Skip replied.

Max got out his phone and found Milton's phone number in his contacts and punched the number into the phone on Monica's desk. It rang twice.

"Hey baby, why aren't you in class?" Milton's voice answered the phone.

"Oh, I missed you so much because I haven't talked to you since breakfast, I had to skip class and call you," Max said in a girlish voice.

"Fuck you, Max," Milton replied tersely.

"I'm going to report you for using naughty words," Max said. "You're not supposed to swear."

Milton did not reply.

Hey," Max continued. "What is the deal with the Cosmic Comics fire? Are you and Brian the reason that they had the state come up and do the investigation?"

"Yes," answered Milton.

"What's the deal with that?" Max asked.

"There is no deal with that," Milton said. "Sarah went out there to do an investigation and the first person she interviewed was Brian. She called up the sergeant and told him that Monica's ex was involved and he told her to back off and he would call the state to do the investigation. That's all there is to it. Pretty routine."

"Sarah's an arson investigator?" Max asked.

"Yes," Milton answered. "She's bucking for detectives. She got passed over this last time for promotion, so they threw her a bone. They sent her to arson investigation school."

"Do you think that Brian had something to do with the fire?" Max asked.

"No," Milton replied. "The fire marshal ruled it faulty wiring."

"Well, he doesn't know Brian like we do," Max said in a conspiratorial tone.

Milton was silent for a moment. "I got no problem with Brian," he said.

"Come on," Max said. "You got no problems with Brian?"

"No," Milton replied. "I got no problem with Brian."

"The guy owes your wife back child support. He's paying less than half of what the court ordered, getting farther and farther behind every month. Plus, he shows up out of nowhere and wants to reestablish his connection with your wife and kid," Max chided him. "Sure, you got no problem with that."

"He's been nothing but polite with me," Milton replied. "He's making payments. You can't get blood out of a stone. He is following the rules for visitation, and I am not at all threatened by Brian Parker."

"How does Monica feel about him?" Max asked.

"She thinks he is an A-number-one piece of shit," Milton replied. "But I'm pretty sure that even she doesn't think that he had anything to do with Cosmic Comics burning down."

"Wow," said Skip from across the room. "I can see why Sarah thought it would be a conflict of interest."

"There isn't a conflict of interest," Milton said defensively. "Brian is Essie's father. That's something that we all four have to deal with. I don't like Brian, but we get along. We have to. That's all there is to it. I'm glad that the state came up and investigated the fire. We got enough to deal with."

"So you don't think he had anything to do with it, even accidentally?" Max asked. "He didn't leave a candle burning or something?"

"Why would he leave a candle burning in a comic store?" Milton asked.

"I said, 'or something,'" Max replied.

"You got anything else you need?" asked Milton.

"You know where he's working now?" Max asked.

"Slo-Mo hired him," Milton replied. "He's working at the deli on Welch Avenue, making sandwiches."

"You don't happen to know his hours?" Max asked.

"Ten to six," Milton replied.

"I suppose you stop in for lunch," Skip called out from across the room.

"Sometimes," Milton shouted back at Skip.

"Okay," said Max. "I think we're going to have to have a talk with Mr. Parker."

"What the hell are you guys up to, anyway?" Milton asked. "Why are you so interested in Cosmic Comics burning down?"

"Ben Ralston hired us to look into it," Max replied.

"Oh, that's just great," Milton said. "That is going to make everyone happy, you guys nosing around."

"Just doing our job," Max replied.

"Well, don't get all shitty with Brian," Milton said. "We got enough to deal with, without you sowing discontent."

"We'll see," Max said.

Milton ended the call.

"What do you think?" Max asked Skip.

"I don't know," Skip replied. "Honestly, he's right. We don't want to cause Milton and Monica a bunch of grief over this."

Max shrugged his shoulders and leaned back in Monica's chair. "Let's talk to Sarah."

Chapter 3

Monday

Max hung up the phone, then took it back out of the cradle. He looked over at Skip.

"What?" Skip asked him.

"Do you have her number?"

Skip got out his cell phone and swiped the screen with his finger. He read a number off the phone to Max, who punched it into the phone on Monica's desk. It rang twice.

"Hello," a woman's voice answered.

"Sarah, Sarah, Sarah," Max said into the phone. "What are you up to?"

"Max Mosbey, Max Mosbey, Max Mosbey. Cruising around in a patrol car," Sarah answered.

"How did you know it was me?" Max asked.

"Because every time you call me you say, 'Sarah, Sarah, Sarah, what are you up to?'"

"Where are you patrolling?" Max asked.

"Area four," Sarah replied. "Why?"

Max thought for a moment. "If you aren't busy, would you want to cruise on by the agency and talk to us about Cosmic Comics?"

"Is Monica there?" Sarah asked.

"Not at the moment," Max replied.

"Sure," said Sarah.

"You weren't going to come over if Monica was here?" Max asked her.

"I was just asking," Sarah said defensively. "I was going to come over if Monica was there."

"Okay," Max said. "I guess we'll see you in a little while."

"You'll see me in thirty seconds," Sarah said.

Max and Skip looked out the window to see Sarah pulling her patrol car into the lot in front of the agency and parking in Monica's space.

"That was fast," Max said into the phone. He could both see Sarah in her patrol car and hear her over the phone calling out on the radio. The phone went dead and Sarah got out of her car, stuffing her phone into the breast pocket of her vest.

"What about Cosmic Comics?" Sarah said as she came through the door and took one of the chairs opposite Monica's desk.

"We heard that you got the call for it and then passed it off," Skip remarked.

"I got to briefing that morning and the sergeant told me that Cosmic Comics on Welch had burned, and that I needed to get my gear and go over there to investigate it. I went over to detectives and got briefed. Then when I got out there, the first guy I ran into was the manager of the place and he told me his name was Brian Parker. Well, fuck me, I asked him if he knew Milton and Monica Jackson, like I didn't know what the answer was going to be. So then I called the sergeant and told him we had a problem. He called the fire marshal's office. End of report."

"Did you just turn around then and leave?" Max asked.

"No," Sarah said. "I thought that I would screw the pooch for a while. I didn't want to go out on the street. I walked around a little. The building had burned pretty good, considering that the fire station is right across the street."

"What do you think started it?" Skip asked.

"I'll say faulty wiring," Sarah answered.

"No accelerants or anything?" Skip asked.

"If you're talking about petroleum-based accelerants, no," Sarah replied. "But the whole place was a tinder box. There were boxes and boxes of old comics in the basement."

"Did it start in the basement?" Skip asked.

"Probably started up in the joists in the basement. There was a breaker box and a fuse box on the north wall. Lots of old wiring up in there. Then it got up in the walls," she said. "That north wall is common with the store next door. There wasn't any insulation or anything. Probably just got a draft going like a chimney up through there once it burned through. It burned fast."

"Any chance that it was purposely set?" Max asked.

"I doubt it. I mean, it was an electrical fire. And there wasn't anything to gain from it. The owner was way underinsured, and he knew it."

"Prime property," Max remarked. "Probably worth some money."

"He didn't have to burn it if he wanted to sell it," Sarah observed.

"And Brian was the manager?" Max said.

"I guess so," Sarah replied. "Guy named Hank Peterson is the owner. I guess the building has been in the family for generations. His grandparents had a smoke shop there in the fifties and sixties. I can tell you that what little I saw of him, Peterson was genuinely distraught about the whole thing."

"We heard that Brian was working late that night," Max remarked.

"They close at eight on Thursdays, but people can make an appointment to come in after closing. For some reason that is a popular thing to do. Brian said that he seldom gets out of there before ten on Thursdays. Even if there aren't customers, he stays late to catch up."

"Catch up on what?" Max asked.

"Work," Sarah shrugged. "Why are you guys all concerned about Cosmic Comics?"

"Ben Ralston next door is the insurance agent who wrote the policy. He wants us to look into it. He thinks there's something suspicious going on."

"Well, Pete Gilmore is a pretty well-regarded fire investigator. If he says that it was faulty wiring, it was faulty wiring," Sarah said. "He taught some of the classes at the fire investigator school."

"What about the girl that called it in?" Skip asked.

"I didn't talk to her," Sarah replied. "I didn't do the investigation. I walked around, talked to Parker and Peterson a little bit, got tired of waiting around and went back on the street. End of report."

The three sat for a moment in silence.

"The insurance agent thinks there is something fishy going on?" Sarah asked.

"I guess so," Skip replied.

"Why?" asked Sarah.

"He says that whenever they can't determine the cause of the fire, they say it was faulty wiring. I guess he's fed up with being told that it is faulty wiring all the time. He thinks that it was something else and he picked this one to piss on."

"That's so much BS," Sarah said. "Fire investigators do not say faulty wiring just because."

"It isn't me saying it," Skip replied. "I'm just doing my job."

"Since when?" Sarah remarked.

"Since Max has been stealing his business cards and going around the county handing them out to people and introducing himself as Ben Ralston."

"He's got something on you?" Sarah asked.

"Kind of," Max replied. "He's a nice guy and a good neighbor. We like him. We're helping him out."

Sarah stood up. "I need to get back on the street, I'm not one of those fat-ass detectives that can sit around all day," she said, tripping over Skip's foot on her way to the door.

"Wow," Max said. "Do I hear a note of resentment?"

"It's cool," Sarah replied. "He has time on me, he deserved it. Tell Monica hi from me, we'll have to get together sometime."

"I'll tell her," Max said.

They watched Sarah through the window get into her patrol car, pick up her mic and call back in service.

"What do you think?" Skip asked.

"I think that the fire was caused by was faulty wiring and Ben is pissing up the wrong tree," Max replied. "Why do you think that Sarah didn't want to come over if Monica was here?"

"When did she say that?" Skip asked.

"When I called her and asked if she could stop by, she asked me if Monica was here."

"Maybe she wanted to know if Monica was here so that she could see her," Skip said. "She and Carlisle are going out with Monica and Milton all the time."

"Well, she used to be Milton's girlfriend," Max remarked.

"Like a long time ago she and Milton went out," Skip replied. "She had moved on and was dating Carlisle before Monica and Milton ever met."

"I'm just saying," Max pushed back.

"You're just saying nothing," Skip replied. "What now?"

"We told Ben that we would give it a week," Max said.

"Let's find Brian and see what he has to say," Skip suggested. "You're driving."

Max got up from Monica's chair. He looked at his watch. It was nine thirty. By the time he and Skip got around to leaving it would be close to ten and they could catch Brian at work. Max followed Skip down the hall toward their offices to check their emails.

"Did we play the Powerball Saturday?" Skip called across the hall from his office.

"Did you give me any money to play the Powerball?" Max called back.

"I just figured that you might buy a ticket and put it on my tab," Skip replied.

"Yeah, I did," Max replied. "We didn't win, and you owe me five bucks."

"Put it on my tab," Skip told him.

"We probably wouldn't have won it anyway," Max said.

"That's probably what we said the last time we won it," Skip replied.

Max had clicked on a link for Martin guitars in one of his emails and had immediately gone down a rabbit hole. He was looking at a seven-thousand-dollar Martin.

"I'm thinking about playing bluegrass," Max said.

Skip did not respond.

"I'm going to play at Filo's Saturday night; you guys wanna come over and we'll go out afterwards?" Max asked.

Skip did not respond. Max did not notice.

"Going to do a couple of sets, sixties and seventies protest songs," Max said.

Max looked up to see Skip standing in his door.

Skip asked. "You ready to hunt down Brian, or are you going to play on the internet all morning?"

Max got up from his chair, taking one last look at the Martin.

The two walked out of the agency. Max went toward his car, Skip locked the door. Skip caught up to Max as he was starting the engine of his Camaro. Skip got in on the passenger side and buckled up. Max pulled onto Mortensen and drove east toward Welch Avenue in Campustown. Max turned off Storm Street and onto Welch Avenue. As he neared the deli where Brian worked, Skip spoke up.

"Go on down to the one-hundred block and do a drive-by so we can check out the store," he said. "We must have sat there staring at it for years, and I don't even remember seeing it."

Max drove past the deli. Both looked at the building a block down the street. The windows and the door were boarded up with plywood.

"Not much to see," Skip observed.

Max stopped for the light at Linclonway, waited for it to turn green, then turned right and drove around the block and back to Welch Avenue. He pulled into the deli parking lot and got out.

"Barlow's Welch Avenue Deli," Max read the sign over the entrance. "Who's Barlow?"

"Barlow Hicks, aka Slo-Mo," Skip replied.

It was a few minutes before ten. Max cupped his hands to block the glare on the glass door and looked through them inside. He could see the familiar figure of Brian Parker behind the counter. Max tapped on the window and waited. Brian looked up but did not recognize the person at the door peeking through his hands at first. Skip moved toward the door and tried to see past Max's head.

Max tapped the window again, and Brian looked up. He recognized Skip standing behind Max and came around the counter with a key in his hand to unlock the door and allow the two detectives to enter. He locked the door behind them.

"What's up?" he asked with a bit of trepidation. The two always made him nervous.

"What's up with you, Brian?" Skip asked. "How's the new job?"

"It's okay," he answered. "Hoping that it's temporary."

Both detectives were looking around, getting the lay of the land. Old habits died hard. Max automatically found the back exit and looked to see if someone was trying to make a fast escape, even though the only other occupants were Skip and Brian.

"I assume you aren't here for sandwiches," Brian said.

"We want to talk to you about Cosmic Comics," Max replied.

"Yeah, too bad," Brian remarked. "That was going to be a pretty good job, I think. I was hoping the owner would rebuild and I might get my job back, but it sounds like he's going to sell it, now."

"We heard that you were the manager," Skip said.

"Yep," Brian replied. "First job I ever had that I actually got promoted and got a raise."

"So you weren't very happy when it burned down?" Skip asked.

Brian thought about his answer for a second.

"You guys are investigating the fire and think that I might have wanted the store to burn down?" He seemed somewhat astonished that they would think that.

"You catch on quick," Max remarked.

"Listen," Brian said defensively. "I was making fifteen bucks an hour over there as manager of the store, and now I'm making eight putting together deli sandwiches for college kids on their way to and from classes and cleaning up after them. I'm not happy at all with the situation."

"Eight bucks an hour?" Skip asked. "That's what Hicks is paying you?"

"Not really a skilled profession," Brian answered.

"And selling comic books is?"

"Yeah, actually, it was," Brian replied. "The customers are really into comics. They read them, collect them, trade them, it is a big business. I was putting a lot of time into learning the business. When I wasn't selling them or stocking them or sweeping the floor, I was reading them, trying to get to know the product. It was a good job. It was interesting. There was a future in it. I don't feel the same about slicing cold meats and putting them on a hoagie bun."

"What about the fire?" Max asked, getting back to the subject of their visit.

"There isn't much to tell," Brian began. "We stay open until eight on Thursdays. There was a group of four still there at closing, going through some of the boxes of old comics. That isn't unusual. I locked the door and sat behind the counter reading a comic myself and let them look. They bought half a dozen comics, I think one of them bought a record, and then I let them out. Probably twenty after. Then I stayed there and read the rest of the comic I had started, did some tidying up after that, and when I saw that it was ten, I decided to call it a night. I went home, ate some supper, watched part of a movie, then went to bed. Hank called me at two in the morning and told me that the place burned down. That's about it."

"After the customers left, anyone else come in?" Max asked.

"My girlfriend Serenity came in. She works the Taco Machine cart on Thursday nights. She's the one who called in the fire," Brian explained. "She always stops in on Thursdays to say hi. That's all."

"Were you using candles or anything like that?" Max asked.

"No," Brian said a bit sarcastically. "We had lights. At least we had lights that night, we don't use candles unless the electric gets cut on us," Brian laughed. "Just kidding, we haven't been cut off, we just talk about the possibility a lot."

"I just know that candles start a lot of fires," Max explained.

"How about the owner?" Skip asked. "How did he take it?

"Devastated," Brian replied. "First of all, that store has been in his family for generations and he was sick that it burned down while he was running it. Second, he had just bought a ton of inventory at a comics expo out in Vegas and we got it in the week before. It was all in the basement. We were planning to do a big week-long event to generate some sales. He was sick about it."

"You say that now he is selling out?" Skip asked.

"That's what he said," Brian replied.

"What is he planning to do?" Max asked. "I mean, for a living now."

"He's been working at Sauer Danfoss for a couple of years," Brian said. "Honestly, that's what kept the bills paid, and barely. I was running the place, and he was putting everything he could spare into the business."

"What will you do now?" Skip asked. "There's another comic store, you could work there, maybe."

"I've been thinking about that," Brian said thoughtfully. "But the next day after the fire, Hicks offered me this job. I thought that I would see what Hank is going to do. I guess that if he's going to throw in the towel, I'll probably go over and apply. I'm not staying here if I can get something else."

Brian stepped around Max and Skip to the front door to unlock it and let a college-age girl in. She went behind the counter and picked up an apron.

Brian came back. "Look, guys," he announced. "I need to get to work and open up here in five. If you got anything else, maybe we can do it later."

"Sure," said Skip, heading toward the door. Brian ran ahead and unlocked it again to let them out.

"We'll get back if we have anymore questions," Max said as he went through the door.

"I'll be here," Brian answered. "I got no other options at the moment."

Chapter 4

Monday

Max and Skip got back into Max's car.

"What now?" Max asked as he started the engine.

"I was thinking that we should talk to the city inspector who did the fire inspection three months before the store burned down."

Max shrugged his shoulders. "If you think so," he said.

"You don't want to talk to him?" Skip asked.

"I'm just thinking that it is probably someone we know from when we were on the police department. Sarah and the fire marshal got defensive about being questioned. I'm thinking that we're pushing it. I mean, why piss off everyone? They are all going to have the same story, that the place burned because of faulty wiring, end of report, as Sarah likes to say."

"We're not doing much of an investigation if we don't talk to the people connected to it," Skip remarked.

Max didn't say anything for a moment. "Why did we take this case?" he asked.

"Because you keep stealing Ben's business cards," Skip shot back.

Max drove out of the parking lot and turned toward Lincolnway. At the intersection he waited for some students to get through the crosswalk against the signal and proceeded toward city hall.

"What do you think?" Max asked.

"You mean Brian?" Skip asked him back.

"Yep," Max said.

"He seemed genuine. I didn't get the feeling that what he had to say was rehearsed."

"He's an experienced liar," Max observed.

"What's there to lie about?" Skip said. "He isn't lying that the job he had at the place that burned down was probably a lot better than the one he has now. That's pretty plain to see."

Max didn't reply.

"His story was pretty solid," Skip continued. "I didn't see anywhere that I could poke holes, did you?"

Max thought about it. "You're not starting to think PB, are you?"

"Poor Brian? Hell, no," Skip replied. "I just don't think that he burned down his place of employment."

"But you do believe someone else did?" Max asked.

"I'm not there, either," Skip replied. "I'm doing an investigation. I'm not going to come to some determination about it and then try to make the evidence fit. We just got started. I have no opinions at this point in the investigation."

"Except you are convinced that Brian didn't have anything to do with the fire," Max noted.

"At this point it doesn't look like it to me," Skip clarified. "Tell me what's fueling your suspicions of Brian at this point."

Max didn't answer him and continued driving east on Lincolnway past the intersection with University Avenue.

After a minute Skip spoke up, "That's what I thought."

Max pulled into the parking lot on the west side of city hall and parked in a ten minute visitor's space.

"Brings back old memories," Skip remarked.

"No kidding,'" Max agreed.

The two went through the rear door of the city hall building and wound their way down the halls to the east end of the building and the stairs that led to the courtroom and the second-floor city offices. They made their way to the inspections offices and went in. Max recognized the woman sitting behind the counter, but he could not recall her name. He looked around for a name on her desk, but the only thing he saw was a nameplate that said, "City of Ames Inspections."

"Mr. Mosbey and Mr. Murray," the woman said cheerfully.

"Hey, how are you doing?" Max replied. "Looking for the fire inspector."

"You're in luck," she said, reaching for her phone. She punched four numbers and waited a moment. "Larry, there's a couple of Ames's finest retired here to see you."

The woman placed the phone back down and looked up. "Down the hall." She pointed to a door.

"Really good to see you," Skip said as they both went through the door. Larry Chee, the Ames Fire Inspector was standing in the hall.

"What the hell?" he said, holding out his hand. "I'm surprised to see you guys lurking around city hall."

"We're not lurking," Max said. "We came to see you. We got a private detective agency now, and we were hired to look at the Cosmic Comics fire."

Larry led them to his office and took a seat behind his desk. The two detectives sat in a couple of upholstered institutional chairs that sat along the wall of his very small institutional office. A few pictures of Larry and his family sat on a book shelf against one wall. A bulletin board with fliers about fire safety pinned to it hung on the wall above the book shelf, a couple of awards and framed citations on the wall behind him. One of the awards was for years of service. Max was thinking that it was probably the award that he deserved the most; putting in time working for the city was an accomplishment in itself.

"You seen one, you seen them all," Max remarked, looking around.

Larry gave him a questioning look.

"City offices," Max clarified.

Larry laughed. "What do you want to know about the Cosmic Comics fire that you think I can answer?"

"First of all, how is it that the building was passing fire inspections for years and then suddenly burns down from faulty wiring?" Skip asked bluntly.

Larry was not the least taken aback. "Lots of reasons," he replied. "The building has been standing there since before World War One. The wiring was shit."

"How does that get past inspection?" asked Skip.

"Well," began Larry. "There's been dozens of remodeling projects on that building over the last century. Every time they do a remodel, they have to bring whatever they do up to code. Every time they bring it up to code, some of the old stuff gets tore out or disconnected, some of it gets grandfathered and some of it gets updated. You have a building that old and all the wiring is cobbled up together. No one knows what the hell is behind those walls anymore. The only sure way would be to make them gut the place and rewire the whole thing every time they remodeled or worked on it. But then you have the whole infrastructure that is cobbled together the same way, so…" Larry shrugged his shoulders.

"You're saying nothing is up to code out there?" remarked Skip.

"I'm saying that everything out there is up to code," Larry replied. "I inspect it according to code, and code says that a lot of that wiring out there was up to code when it was put in, and it doesn't have to be upgraded. If you build new, then you have to build it to the new code." Larry shrugged his shoulders again. "That's the best that I can explain it. The code is always changing, but it doesn't affect what is already there."

"So this knob and tube wiring, whatever that is, that's code?" Max asked.

"I guess under certain circumstances it could be," Larry said. "But I doubt the Cosmic Comics building was still hooked up to any of the knob and tube."

"You don't think the old knob and tube wiring caused the fire?" Skip asked.

"No, but that's the knob and tube. Supposedly that was all disconnected a long time ago. But there was a lot of old wiring in that building. Like I said, we don't tear down the walls and pull down the ceiling to inspect the wiring every time we come through."

"Do you think that's what caused the fire, faulty wiring?" Max asked.

Larry gave it a moment before he spoke. "I'll warrant that it was wiring, but I think that people are assuming it was the old wiring."

"What's that mean?" Max asked.

"Just between you and me, they had some electricians put in new lighting a couple of months ago. Seems coincidental."

"So?" Max asked.

"So I told Pete that, and he looked at it. I do inspections, not investigations."

Max and Skip didn't say anything.

"Look, new wiring, old wiring, it doesn't make a difference, Pete's a professional. Sometimes you just can't narrow it down to a specific cause. You make an educated determination based on the information and evidence that you have."

"You're saying that it could have been something else, other than faulty wiring, then?" asked Max.

"That's not what I'm saying at all," Larry replied. "I said that sometimes you can't pin a fire down to a single wire. It could have been that some of the old knob and tube was still hot—I doubt it, but it is possible. It could have been the wiring put in after that, or the wiring after that, or it could have been in the last wiring that they did, but I doubt that would be the case. That's all I'm saying. Don't try to make this fire something that it isn't."

Skip laughed. "We're not trying to bust your ass," he said.

"It feels like you're trying to bust my ass," Larry replied.

"Okay, we'll quit busting your ass and let you get back to your work," Skip said. "We have to check everything out. If we're not questioning, we're not doing what we were hired to do."

"No problem," Larry said. "Can I ask who hired you to investigate the fire?"

Max looked at Skip, who shrugged his shoulders. "Ben Ralston, the agent that wrote the insurance policy."

"I was talking to the owner the other day, and he said that the insurance company already signed off on it."

"Ralston is the agent," Max explained. "He hired us. He has his own reasons."

Larry didn't look like he was convinced that Ralston had a valid reason, but he let it go. It wasn't his business to tell the two detectives what cases to take up, but he felt like they were soaking the poor guy. There wasn't anything to investigate as far as he could tell. He knew from Mosbey and Murray's reputation when they were on the police department that they could be unpleasant if they wanted to be. They worked the bar shift together for years, and it was no secret that, at least on the street and around city hall, they did as they pleased and were not afraid of the consequences.

"Here's the thing," Larry said as the two were standing up to leave. "That place passed inspections, but it wasn't like they were doing anything special. They did what they had to do. That's what everyone does, just what they have to do to get through the inspection. But that place was packed full of combustibles. Once it got started, there wasn't any way that a fire was going to get put out easily. It can smolder for days. Those stacks and boxes of books have to be separated and soaked to get all of the burning embers out. What I'm saying is that fire could well have started a long time before it got some air and really got to burning. Could have started days before. Wires short out, they get hot, it takes time for them to start something smoldering and then it takes time for it to break out into a fire."

Skip stopped to listen. "Were there smoke alarms?" he asked after a moment.

"One on every floor," Larry replied.

"Even if a fire is just smoldering for a while, like you say, wouldn't there be smoke? Wouldn't the alarms go off?"

Larry shrugged his shoulders. "They like to call it 'fire science,' but some things in science aren't always predictable. Fire's one of them."

Skip held out his hand and Larry took it. Max did the same.

"Thanks," said Skip. "We are learning a lot today."

The two men left the office and walked down the hallway.

"Seems to me that if a fire starts in a wall somewhere, it isn't going to smolder in a pile of comic books for a couple of days," Max remarked when they left the building.

"He was just trying to explain," Skip said. "Ben might be right. Maybe they do say faulty wiring when they can't find anything else. But wiring or not, no one is saying that this fire looks like it was intentionally set. We've talked to three people who have some experience and training in fire, and all three agree that it wasn't intentional, that it was probably faulty wiring. Ben Ralston, independent insurance agent, someone who doesn't have any fire inspection training, has a feeling it wasn't."

Max thought about what Skip was saying. "Point taken," he replied. "Like you said, we talked to three experts in the field, one ex-comic book salesman and an insurance agent. Who else do we need to talk to?"

"Probably the owner," Skip replied. "And see if we can hunt down the girl that called it in, Brian's girlfriend. Owner's probably at work, and I don't want to go bother him at work," he mused. "We could go back by the deli and get Brian's girlfriend's name and number."

"We could talk to Barlow," Max said.

"About what?" Skip asked.

"I don't know, he's out here all the time at night. He sees a lot. He always seemed to know what was going on out on Welch. It might not hurt to talk to him. Maybe some of the other stores, see what they think about the whole thing?"

"That's not a bad idea," Skip replied.

The two got into Max's car. He looked at his watch; it was getting close to noon. "I'm starting to get hungry," he said. "You wanna go back out to Welch and eat at the deli? Talk to Brian?"

"Let's go somewhere we can talk," Skip suggested. "It's right at rush hour for the deli. Brian isn't going to talk to us with a line of customers at the counter. I get the feeling he doesn't want to talk to us at all."

Max shrugged his shoulders. "How about that fancy place down at the research park?"

"You're driving," Skip answered.

Chapter 5

Monday

Max and Skip came out of the restaurant and walked across the parking lot to Max's car.

"Let's go back to the office and make some phone calls to see if we can talk to that girl who called in the fire and the owner of the store," Skip suggested.

"Sounds like a plan," Max replied, picking the remnants of his lunch from his teeth with a toothpick and spitting them on the pavement.

"That's gross," Skip remarked.

"That was one tough piece of meat," Max responded.

The two got into Max's car and started toward the agency.

"I'm beginning to think that Ben's gut instincts might be off," Skip said thoughtfully.

"We just got started," Max replied. "Give it some time."

"Do you really think there's something more to it?" Skip asked.

Max didn't say anything. Skip gave him a questioning look, while Max glanced over toward Skip through the corner of his eye.

"Not really," Max finally agreed.

"So what do we tell Ben?" Skip asked.

"I say we go through the motions," Max replied. "We took the case, we might as well follow it up. I got nothing else to do."

"How hard do you want to hit it?" Skip asked.

"You got something else going on?"

"I was thinking of a round of golf," Skip replied.

"Nine or eighteen?" Max asked. "I'll tell you right now, I'm not playing Veenker."

"Why not?" Skip asked, knowing quite well that Max didn't like playing the Iowa State University golf course. He always complained that he lost too many balls.

"I'll do the country club," Max said. "I hate Veenker."

"We'll play best ball," Skip suggested.

"I'm not playing Veenker, period," Max said with a tone of finality.

"Homewood?" Skip resigned himself.

"When?" Max liked playing the city course. They could easily get through it in an hour and a half, and Max could find more balls than he lost, which was the only thing that he kept score of.

"I'll call right now and see if I can get us a tee time this afternoon," Skip said, picking up his phone and going through his contacts before Max could say anything else.

Max listened to the conversation.

"Three-ten?" Skip looked at Max.

"Get a cart," Max said.

"I'll take the three-ten and I need a cart," Skip said into his phone. He listened for a moment. He thanked the person on the other end then closed the connection. "Stop by the office, make those calls, get our clubs and head to Homewood," he said to Max. "Quick nine holes and we hit the case hard tomorrow."

Max pulled off of New Highway 30 onto Dakota, then turned on Mortenson Road toward the agency. When they got to the parking lot they observed Monica's car parked in her space.

"Do we tell her that we took a case?" Max asked.

"I don't know," Skip replied. "I suppose we better. Milton will probably say something to her about it tonight."

Max parked the car, turned off the ignition, and both detectives got out of the car.

"What's up?" Max asked as he and Skip came through the door.

"Homework," Monica replied. "What are you guys doing?"

"Making a few phone calls then going to play golf," Skip said.

"What about Ben Ralston's case?" she asked.

Skip was taken by surprise and didn't answer immediately.

"He's been over here twice wanting an update," Monica said, looking up at the two. "It would be nice if I had something to report, considering you told him that you would keep me in the loop."

"We talked to the arson investigator and the fire inspector. Talked to Sarah," Skip replied.

"Talked to Milton," Monica added.

"Man," said Max. "You get around."

"It's my job to keep track of you two. It would be nice if you wouldn't make it harder than it has to be," Monica commented, handing Skip some papers and going back to her homework.

"I get your point," Skip replied defensively. "We are pacing ourselves with this one. We don't want to get done too fast. We need to pad the bill."

"Whatever," Monica replied absently, not taking her attention from her homework.

Skip went back to his office with the papers that Monica had given him while Max stopped off at the bar to mix them a couple of drinks. When he got to Skip's office, Skip was on the phone. Max put his screwdriver on the desk in front of him and took a seat next to the desk with his own rum and Coke.

"Here's the thing," Skip was saying into the phone. "We just want to talk to her about that comic book store fire that she called in."

Skip sat with his phone cradled against his ear while he took a sip of his screwdriver. He looked at Max and gave him a thumbs up.

"Look," Skip said into the phone. "We're not going to harass or stalk her, okay? We want to talk to her. We were hired to do an investigation. We need to talk to the person that called it in, right?"

Skip sat a moment listening.

"Could you give her my number?" Skip asked. "Would that work for you?"

He was scribbling some notes on the legal pad in front of him on the desk. Max leaned over to look at it but couldn't understand what he had jotted down.

"Okay," Skip said, giving the person on the other end his cell number. "Tell her to call me anytime."

There was a moment of listening.

"Thanks," Skip said, hanging up the phone. "For nothing," he said as he put the phone back into the cradle.

"Slo-Mo?" Max asked.

"Yep," Skip replied. "He won't give me her number. He'll get ahold of her and give her our number. She's going to call us."

"The gal that called it in?" Max asked. "Brian's girlfriend?"

"Yep," Skip replied. "The callback number on all of the reports comes back to a cell phone that belongs to Slo-Mo. It looks like Gilmore tracked her down and talked to her, but he didn't put down any other number for her." Skip looked up for a moment. "I don't know." He paused. "I got numbers here for the owner of the comic store as well, a home number and a work number. You think I should call him at work?"

Max shrugged his shoulders and took a drink. Skip dialed the phone and waited.

"Mr. Peterson," Skip said into the phone. "This is Skip Murray, G&B Detective Agency. We were hired by the insurance company to check into the fire at your store. Is this a good time to talk?"

Max wished that Skip would put the phone on speaker.

"Yes sir, I know that the insurance company already signed off on your claim," Skip said into the phone. "We were hired by the agent to dot the Ts and cross the Is. That's all, standard procedure."

Max waited while Skip listened again. He tried to get Skip's attention to push the speaker button, with no success. He reached toward the phone and Skip batted his hand away, fearing that he was going to knock over his drink.

"Yes sir, tomorrow at five-thirty. We can meet you there," Skip said into the phone. "Sir, is there any way that we might get inside and take a look at the damage?"

Skip listened. "Thank you so much. If we can get in there and look around, that would really help us. Appreciate it." Skip hung up the phone.

"Five-thirty tomorrow evening you and I are going to Welch to meet the owner and take a look inside," Max said. "I figured that out from your side of the conversation."

"Yep," was all that Skip said.

"We could go by the deli and see if we can get that gal's phone number from Brian and do an end run on Slo-Mo," Max suggested.

"I wanna play golf," Skip replied. "If she doesn't call today, we can run her down tomorrow."

Max and Skip walked to the front of the agency where Monica was working on her homework and took the two leather easy chairs across from her desk. Monica looked up.

"What are you up to now?" she asked.

"Gonna play a round at Homewood," Skip replied.

"Not going to work your big case?" Monica remarked.

"No, we need to learn how to pace ourselves," Skip answered her. "We work too hard."

"You don't work at all," Monica admonished him. "You worked two cases this whole year, and this is one of them."

"But when we work them, we work them hard," Max defended Skip and himself.

"So you guys are going to play golf," Monica said. "Good exercise; you guys need some exercise."

"We don't need exercise," Max said.

"Well, Marjorie and Gloria were talking to me last week, and they said you guys are eating too much junk food and not getting enough exercise," Monica said.

"When were you talking to our wives?" Skip asked.

"Last week," Monica said again. "And they said that you two are eating too much junk food and not getting enough exercise." She raised her hands as if to ask them if they wanted her to say it again.

"I ride my bicycle to work," Max replied to her gesture.

"You rode your bike to work last summer," Monica corrected. "And it is a mile and a half. That isn't exercise. How long does it take you, six minutes?"

"Maybe a little more," Max answered.

"Well, I'm glad you're going out to play golf," Monica said. "What else is new?"

Just as Skip was about to tell her nothing else was new, the UPS truck pulled up in front of the agency and stopped.

The young driver jumped out with a box the size of a shoebox and made a beeline to the door.

"Howdy, howdy," he said to Monica as he came through the door and tossed the box on her desk. "Nice day."

"It sure is," Monica said smiling. "I was expecting this to show up last week."

The driver shrugged his shoulders. "Sorry, I don't have any control over that." He didn't seem to be in any hurry to leave. He looked at Skip and Max sitting in the chairs and nodded. "Nice day," he said to them. Neither replied.

The driver turned back to Monica. "I don't know what to say. You doing homework?"

"Well, I was until these two came up here," Monica replied. "Now I'm just sitting here wondering when I'll get back to it."

The driver didn't know what to make of her remark, but she was smiling at him, which meant that she was probably just messing with him.

"How's school going?" he asked.

"Pretty good," Monica replied. "Over the hump. I'm studying hard, trying to get a jump on it for finals. When you have a husband, a kid and these two to deal with all day, you gotta plan ahead."

The driver laughed. No one said anything.

"Well, I have to get going, lots of deliveries today," he said to Monica, ignoring the two detectives sitting to the side of him. "Sorry that your package didn't get here as soon as you expected."

"That's okay," she replied. "Don't work too hard."

The driver laughed at her remark and went out the door to his truck.

"I think he likes you," Max said as they watched him drive away.

"I know, I have that effect on men," Monica said.

"Okay," Max said. "You didn't win the humility category in the beauty pageant, I'm thinking."

"If ya got, it flaunt it," Monica said.

"What's in the box?" Skip asked.

"Something for you guys," Monica replied.

"Give it to me, Max will open it," Skip said.

"You guys can see what you got tomorrow," she replied.

"It's addressed to us," Max said.

"It's addressed to me," Monica said.

"You got us something?" Max asked.

"Yes," Monica responded.

"What is it?" Skip asked again.

"You can see it tomorrow," Monica said with finality in her tone.

"That's not fair," Max said.

Monica looked back down at her desk. "I have homework to do, if you are done harassing me," she said, not looking up.

"I can take a hint," Skip said, getting up and walking toward the back of the agency where his and Max's golf clubs were sitting in a corner. Max walked behind him.

"Glad you didn't mention that we're getting a cart," Max said. "Her whining about us getting exercise and all."

"I wonder what's in the box," Skip replied.

"Why are the girls talking to her about us anyway?" Max asked.

"They talk," Skip replied. "They are like three bees in a hive, they just talk all of the time."

"That makes no sense," Max said. "Three bees in a hive. I've never heard anyone say that before. And when are they being three bees in a hive? I never see them all talking together."

"They all three go shopping together," Skip remarked.

"They do?" Max asked, surprised.

"Yes, they went Christmas shopping a couple of times."

"That was last winter," Max said.

Skip shrugged his shoulders and passed Max's clubs to him before picking up his own. The two made their way back the way they had come, toward the front of the agency. Max went into the bar to get some beers to take with them. Skip continued to the front where Monica was working on homework.

"So you guys got a cart to do nine holes of golf at Homewood," she said without looking up. "That is pathetic."

Skip didn't reply.

"I hear everything you two say," Monica responded to his silence.

"It was Max's idea," Skip said defensively.

"And you didn't argue," Monica remarked.

Max came up with a soft-sided six-pack cooler stuffed with Miller Lites.

"What's up?" Max asked, looking back and forth between Monica and Skip.

"Have fun driving your golf cart around," Monica sneered.

"Yeah, the way I play golf it is the only fun I have out there," Max said as he headed out the door. Skip quickly followed him.

"I look forward to seeing you two tomorrow," Monica called to them as the door closed. "We will see how it goes," she said out loud to herself.

Monica took her cell phone out of her purse and went through her contacts, finding the number that she was looking for. She punched the screen and waited. It rang several times before a male voice answered, "Hello, Monica."

"Brian," Monica replied. "I need a number for Serenity."

"This for your cop buddies?" Brian asked.

"No, this is for my employers, who are not cops anymore. They're private detectives."

"Same difference," Brain said. "They came in here and talked to me this morning before opening."

"The number," Monica said.

There was hesitation.

"Brian," Monica said sternly.

"Man," Brian whined. "I don't want those assholes harassing Serenity."

"Too bad," Monica said. "The number."

Brian gave Monica the number and she wrote it on a sticky note.

"Thanks, you're a peach," Monica said sarcastically.

"What's the deal?" Brian asked. "Does the insurance company suspect arson or something?"

"The insurance agent isn't satisfied with the fire investigator's report," Monica said. "He has the guys going over it to take another look, that's all."

"Shit," said Brian. "Just what I need is those two breathing down my neck."

"You got something you're hiding?" Monica asked. "They're just following up on the investigation. You nervous for some reason?"

"Those guys make me nervous, just being in the same city as them," Brian replied. "And no, I got nothing to hide.

But those guys can make a guy look guilty when he's not, and it ain't a secret that they don't like me."

"It isn't anything personal," Monica said. "You just aren't a likable kind of guy. A lot of people don't like you."

"Well you got the phone number that you were looking for," Brian responded. "If you are going to insult me some more, I got to go back to work."

"Have a good one," Monica said. "And don't tip off your lady there, so she doesn't answer when they call her up."

She ended the call and got up from her desk to make her way to Skip's office, sticking the note in the middle of the screen on his laptop where he was sure to see it, then she went back to her desk and continued with her studies.

Chapter 6

Tuesday

Max woke up to Gloria shaking his arm.

"Get up," she said. "Monica is expecting you, you're going to be late."

"Late for what?" Max asked in a groggy voice.

"For your walk," Gloria replied, as if Max should know what she was talking about.

"Walk?" Max said, sitting up.

"Yes, she didn't say anything? She is going to go for a walk with you and Skip every morning. She bought some Fitbits for you to wear."

"What's a Fitbit?" Max asked.

"You wear it on your wrist, it tells how far you've walked," Gloria held up her wrist to show Max a slim black bracelet he had never seen before.

"Are you walking, too?" Max asked.

"No, I have my own workouts that I do," Gloria said patiently. "This is something that you guys are going to do with Monica. It is a team building thing. Quit asking questions and get up."

Max swung his legs over the bed and sat up. "No one told me about this," he grumbled.

Gloria shrugged her shoulders. "We were talking one day, and Marjorie and I were saying that you and Skip hadn't wintered well and that you were going to have to buy all new shorts this summer, a size or two bigger. Monica said that she thought it would be fun for you all to go walking in the mornings to get yourselves going and to work on your beach bodies."

"Our employees conspiring against us," Max said. "Next thing we know they'll be trying to unionize."

Gloria laughed at Max, pushed him backwards on the bed and jumped on him, pinning him down.

"You only have one employee, and she doesn't need to unionize because you guys don't negotiate, you just give her what she wants, and rightfully so. Now she's going to go above and beyond by walking with you two every morning."

"Every morning?" Max groaned.

"Until you hit your targets," Gloria said.

"What are you doing on top of me like that?" Max said with a grin. "You looking for a little early morning delight?"

Gloria laughed, climbing off Max. "That's 'afternoon delight,' not 'early morning delight,' and you need to get up, get dressed and get going."

Max got out of bed and started digging around in his dresser.

"Wear some shoes that you can walk in," Gloria said as she went through the bedroom door and down the hall.

Max put on a pair of tight-fitting cargo pants that he could still button and his jogging shoes. It was still a little cold in the mornings. He put on a Rolling Stones tee shirt and pulled a fleece over the top. He went downstairs to the kitchen and opened the cupboard to get out a cereal bowl. Gloria was sitting at the dinette eating her breakfast.

"You don't need to eat," Gloria said. "Monica is going to feed you guys. You just need to get going so that she isn't late for class."

"Man, this just sucks," Max said, exasperated that his routine was being interrupted.

Gloria was not sympathetic. "Hurry up and quit crying," she said, looking up and puckering her lips.

Max gave her a kiss and went out the door to the garage.

When Max got to the agency he saw Monica's car parked in her reserved space. Skip's car was parked across the lot. Max pulled his own car into the space beside Monica's and got out. He looked across the street at Filo's coffee shop.

"Don't even think about it," he heard Monica call from the door.

Max went into the agency and saw Skip sitting in one of the easy chairs examining the new Fitbit on his wrist.

"Sit down and give me your wrist," Monica said to Max, standing with another Fitbit in her hand.

Max sat down and held out his hand. Monica attached the device to his wrist and started instructing him and Skip how to use it. Both men went through the motions as Monica went over all the features, settings and options. When she was satisfied that they had the basics down she asked them if they had any questions.

"Let's go for a walk," Monica announced when neither asked anything.

"I got a question," Max said as Skip was getting up out of the chair to go through the door that Monica was holding open for them.

"Save it," Monica said.

Max followed Skip out into the early morning sunlight, Monica coming behind him and locking up.

"How about we start with two miles," Monica suggested.

Neither responded, but they followed behind as Monica led the way across the parking lot and toward the sidewalk that turned into a bike path at Dakota.

"Beautiful day for a walk," Monica said pleasantly. She turned around and saw the two lagging behind. "You two get up in front and lead the way," she told them.

"What about Milton," Skip asked her as they walked. "Isn't he getting a little tubby?"

"Yep," Monica said. "We bought him a Fitbit, too, and he and I already did two miles before he went to work."

"You're doing two-a-days?" Skip exclaimed.

"Yes, I am," Monica said. "I gotta stay in shape to keep up with all of my dashing and handsome men. We're going to be trimmed down looking good by the time Skip takes the cover off his pool. We're looking forward to it, aren't we? This is going to be a bikinis and speedos summer."

Neither of the two were particularly impressed with Monica's enthusiasm.

"Come on guys, let's make this fun," Monica admonished them.

"I am not wearing a speedo," Skip said.

"Me neither," Max replied.

"No, but in a month you could if you wanted, and not look like a sausage," Monica said.

"I don't think it's right, you body-shaming us like this," Max complained. Monica just laughed.

The three crossed Dakota at Mortensen and continued walking on the bike path.

"What was with the secret yesterday?" Skip asked. "You could have told us that we were getting these fit watches, and that you and the girls decided to force us to exercise."

"I thought that it would be a fun surprise," Monica replied. "I honestly thought that you guys would like them. I'm kind of disappointed that you don't. It makes me feel bad that I've gone to all of this trouble and you don't want to go walking with me in the mornings."

The two didn't say anything, but both were thinking the same thing, that they didn't want Monica to be disappointed in them and feel bad, but that they also didn't want to get up and go for a walk every morning. They walked in silence.

"One mile, boys. Let's turn around and go back," Monica announced after they had gone past the middle school and were almost to State Street. She made an abrupt about-face and led the two back toward the agency. "Keep up," she told them.

Monica picked up the pace a bit.

"Are we taking up jogging, now?" Skip asked.

"We're taking up walking a little faster," Monica said. "We need to get that heart rate up."

The three continued walking. It seemed to Max that the walk back was going much faster, and they reached Dakota quickly. They had to wait at the intersection for the light to change, and when it did, Monica hustled across the street at a jog, her two charges right behind her.

"Wanna keep jogging?" she asked, looking back to see that the two were walking again. She slowed down to let them catch up.

"You guys lead the way," she told them, herding them in front of her.

They quickly got back to the agency and caught their breath while Monica unlocked the door.

"Let's go back to the bar and we'll have a little breakfast before I need to get out of here and head for class," Monica told them.

Max and Skip followed her into the bar and took seats at one of the tables. Monica went to the refrigerator and took out a canister of yogurt and put it on the bar, along with a box of granola. She dished out a bowlful of yogurt for each of them and sprinkled the granola on top. From the refrigerator she took some fruit to put on top of it all. She stuck a spoon into each bowl and admired her work.

"There we go," she said, coming around the bar and putting a bowl in front of each of them. She went back to the bar to get her bowl of yogurt and brought it back, taking a seat at the table. "How's that?" she asked. "This is nice. I feel good after a little exercise, don't you guys?"

"Looks like snot," Max complained.

"Don't look at it then," Monica replied. "Just eat it."

The three sat eating their breakfast together.

"We're shooting for ten thousand steps a day," she said, holding up her Fitbit. "Look at yours," she instructed.

Skip started to say something, but then decided not to. He thought about it a moment and then spoke up. "I read that ten thousand steps is an arbitrary number and that there isn't any data to prove that ten thousand steps resulted in optimum results."

"Might be arbitrary, but that's the number we're using as our target," Monica said.

"I don't think that it is fair that you are walking with Milton, and then with us," Max noted. "I mean, you get a head start before we even get here."

"You two are welcome to join Milton and me," Monica said. "Or you could go take a walk with your wives in the evening instead of sitting down on your ass to watch Netflix. I'm sure that they would both enjoy that."

"You always got an answer, don't you?" Skip remarked.

"I speak the truth," Monica responded. "That's all."

Monica got up and took her bowl to the sink, rinsed it out, then put it and her spoon into the dishwasher behind the bar.

"I'm going to class," she said. "Clean up after yourselves, okay? I don't want dirty dishes sitting around here attracting bugs."

"Aye-aye," Max replied.

"By the way," Monica turned to Skip as if she had not heard the sarcasm in Max's voice. "There is a post-it note on your computer with Serenity's phone number."

"Where did you get that?" Max asked.

"I called up my ex yesterday after you left and got it from him," she said. "I also told him not to tell her you were going to call. I wouldn't bank on that, but it is what it is, you got a number now."

"Thanks," said Skip.

"Don't mention it," Monica replied. "That's what I get paid the big bucks for. I'll be back after noon, maybe I'll see you then. If not, same time tomorrow."

The two did not acknowledge her.

"We're walking again tomorrow," she said sternly.

The two nodded in unison.

"Come on, guys," she stopped as she was leaving the room. "Let's just have fun with this. It's good for us to have a little self discipline. I'm serious, you can't get complacent and just sit around. I care about you guys. I want to hang around with you guys even after I've graduated with my doctorate and I'm as rich and famous as you are. Except I'm going to have to actually work to get there. But I still want you guys around to amuse me. You're my favorite pastime. So smile a little. Let's do this. We're a team."

"Let's do this, coach!" Skip shouted.

"That's the spirit!" Monica shouted back. "Go G and B!"

She looked at Max.

"What?" Max asked.

"Some team spirit?" Monica asked him back.

"Go G and B," Max half-heartedly shouted.

Monica came back and gave Max a high five, then turned to Skip and gave him the same.

Monica left the room, gathered her books in her backpack and went out the door.

"It wasn't so bad," Skip remarked.

"Don't encourage her," Max said.

Skip just smiled. "What do you think? It's early, should we wake up Miss Serenity and see if she'll talk to us?"

"Why not?" Max replied. The two got up from the table, leaving their dirty bowls, and headed for Skip's office down the hall. When they got there, Skip took a seat at his desk and Max slouched in the chair next to it. Skip dialed the number on the note attached to his computer screen. He hit the speaker button and the two listened to the ringtone. Just as they thought that the phone was going to go to voicemail a woman's voice answered. It sounded like she just woke up.

"Hello."

Max sat up in the chair and leaned in toward Skip's phone. "This is Max Mosbey of the G&B Detective Agency," Max said. "Did we wake you up?"

"No, I was about to get up, anyway," she said in the voice that people use when they just got woke up by a phone call.

"We are investigating the fire at Cosmic Comics for the insurance agent who wrote the policy. We understand that you were the one that called it in. We were wondering if there is a time today that we might sit down together and you could tell us about it."

The line was silent for a moment. "Yes, I called it in. I don't know anything else about the fire though," she said guardedly. "I have class and I'm pretty busy today."

"You don't have class all day, do you?" Max pressed. "We are pretty flexible; we could meet you any time, any place."

Serenity didn't answer.

"Lunch can be on us, wherever you want to go." Max tried to encourage her to meet with them.

"What do you want from me?" Serenity asked. They could tell by her voice that she was waking up and getting her bearings.

"We just want to go over the events of that night, get some sort of timeline, see where your call fits in relation to everything else that took place," Max explained.

"I gave that information to some investigators already," Serenity replied.

"We are private investigators hired by the insurance agent to look at the official investigation to see if we can identify any information that might have been overlooked," Max explained again.

"Listen," Serenity replied. "I'm pretty busy right now and I don't have time to talk about it. Like I said, I gave a statement to the investigator. I honestly don't know anything more than that about the fire, I just saw it and called 911."

"But you are familiar with the store itself and the manager, Brian Parker. We understand that you are Brian Parker's girlfriend, and that you stopped in to visit with Brian there earlier that evening. We thought maybe there might be something you could recall that you might have noticed that would clarify some things it the report. We would just like to go over it all and see if we can get a better understanding of what transpired that night. I'm sure that some of your insights, considering you are familiar with the store and with Mr. Parker, would be very helpful."

There was silence on the other end of the phone. Max and Skip both knew that Serenity was thinking about how she was going to answer.

"Isn't that true?" Max asked, trying to get her to say something.

"I would not call myself Brian Parker's girlfriend, and I do not recall visiting Brian that night inside the store," she said in a measured tone. "I don't know where you got that information, but it is not accurate."

"We got it from Brian," Max replied.

"He must be mistaken, then," Serenity answered. "Look, I gotta get ready for class, and I would appreciate it if you would not contact me again. I gave my statement to the investigator and I don't have anything to add."

"I feel like you are getting defensive," Max replied. "I'm not accusing you of anything, we just want to get a timeline established."

"I said that I have nothing else to say," Serenity interrupted. "I'll thank you not to contact me again." She ended the call.

Max looked over at Skip. "Okay, I guess that is that," he exclaimed.

"That girl's been around the block," Skip observed, placing the receiver back on the phone.

"What do you think?" Max asked. "She hiding something, or is she just anti-social when it comes to someone questioning her?"

"I don't know," Skip said. "What's to hide? She went in to talk to her boyfriend and then a couple hours later the place burned down."

"What if she was smoking dope with her boyfriend and she dropped a roach in a pile of comic books?" suggested Max. "Later the place burns down and she starts thinking about that roach."

"You have to have a fertile imagination to come up with that scenario," Skip answered. "She's a little hostile, but maybe she didn't go in to talk to Brian. When it gets down to it, you gotta think about whose story we're going to hang our hats on. Brian thinks she's his girlfriend, she's saying she isn't. He's saying she stopped in, she's saying she didn't. Maybe Brian needs an alibi, she doesn't. I mean, all of a sudden are we taking Brian's story over someone else's? Before we try to pin her down, I think that we should see if we can pin Brian down. After all, Brian doesn't really have a track record of being honest and open, and that we know. Maybe we talk to him again and see if he changes his story before we start in on a hostile witness."

Max shrugged his shoulders. "Good points," he agreed.

Chapter 7

Tuesday

As soon as Serenity got off the phone with Max, she swiped through her contacts until she found the number that she was looking for. The phone rang twice and a male voice answered.

"Hello, Serenity," the voice said.

"I just got a phone call from some private detective who is investigating the Cosmic Comics fire."

There was silence at the other end.

"Bee-something Detective Agency. I don't remember the guy's name. He woke me up. Maybe Bumble Bee Detective Agency or something."

"G&B Detective Agency."

"That might be it," Serenity answered.

"What did they want to talk about?"

"The fire," Serenity answered.

"Specifically," the voice on the phone asked.

"We didn't get that far," Serenity explained. "I just kept telling them that I didn't know anything about it."

"What else did they say?"

"They tried to say that I was Brian Parker's girlfriend and that I was in the store that evening before the fire."

"And what did you tell them?"

"I told them that I am not Brian's girlfriend and that I didn't go visit him in the store that evening," Serenity answered.

"What else?" the voice asked.

"That's it. I told them that I had given a statement to the fire investigator and that I didn't have anything else to say."

"How did they take that?"

"Probably not well, but I ended the call, so it didn't go any farther," Serenity answered.

"How did they get your number?" the man asked. "I thought that you gave the investigator your work cell."

Serenity thought for a moment. "Probably Brian, they said that they had talked to Brian. He must have given it to them."

"That really doesn't sound like Brian," the man responded. "I couldn't really see Brian cooperating with the authorities. I wonder if they are looking at him for some reason."

Serenity didn't reply.

"I think that you did right," the man said. "Maybe you need to find yourself a new boyfriend. Be seen with someone else. I don't want you getting dragged into this investigation because of Brian. We don't want to find ourselves under the microscope."

"I'll do that," Serenity replied.

"So where are you on the schedule? Are you working tonight?"

"Thursday," Serenity answered.

"Okay, if Brian calls you up or tries to contact you, just blow him off," the man said. "If he comes out there on Thursday, just tell him you are busy. Don't break it off with him, just act like you are losing interest."

"He has his daughter this weekend," Serenity informed him. "I told him that I would hang out with them on Saturday."

"Tell him you can't, something came up."

"What came up?" Serenity asked.

"You don't have to tell him what, just tell him that something came up," the man on the phone answered. "If he doesn't like it, maybe he'll break up with you. Save you the trouble."

Serenity thought before she replied. "What do I tell other people? Won't it look a little suspicious that all of a sudden this investigation comes along and I'm breaking up with him?"

There was a moment's pause. "If anyone asks, tell them that there is just something strange about the fire, and you think that Brian might know more about it than he is letting on."

"Throw some suspicion on him," Serenity said, smiling.

"See where that goes."

"Sounds good," Serenity replied.

The call ended.

Serenity gathered up her books and put them in her backpack. She went out the door without breakfast, but she was running late because of all the phone calls. She needed to get to class. Every night that she worked that damned greasy stinking taco stand reminded her why she was going to college. She ran out the door of her apartment and down the stairs instead of waiting for the elevator.

Max and Skip heard the front door open and then Milton's voice ask if anyone was home.

"Back here in Skip's office," Max shouted.

Skip got up from his chair and went out into the hall. Milton waved as he went into the bar. Skip started in that direction with Max right behind him. When they reached the bar they found Milton sprawled in a chair drinking a Coke that he had helped himself to from the refrigerator.

"What's up with you?" Skip asked, taking a chair at the table. Max sat down with him. Max still had not gotten used to Milton in slacks and a sport coat, wearing a tie. His posture in the chair allowed his coat to fall open and Max could see the Sig Sauer .40 caliber pistol in his shoulder holster. A badge was clipped to his belt.

"Just taking a break," Milton said.

"Monica's at class," Max said.

Milton didn't reply.

"I hear that you and Monica are into walking now," Skip said.

"Yep," Milton replied. "She wants to run, though. Two miles every day. Started yesterday."

"Are you hitting the gym, too?" Skip asked.

"Yes," Milton sighed. "Going in on my lunch break Mondays, Wednesdays and Fridays."

"I forgot that the dicks get an hour for lunch," Skip replied.

"I'm not into running and walking," Milton said. "I'm a weights guy. Guys my size don't run."

"Then what's the deal?" Max asked.

"She wants to run, and she wants me to run with her," Milton answered. "I'm doing it because she wants me to. It doesn't hurt me, I guess."

"She lifting weights with you?" Max asked in a commiserating tone that made it sound like it was unfair for Milton to run with Monica if she wasn't lifting weights with him.

Milton just gave him a frown for an answer.

"I'm not recording you," Max said. "You can talk."

"Getting anywhere on your big arson investigation?" Milton asked, changing the subject.

"Who can run faster?" Max asked.

Milton gave Max the same look as before.

"Haven't done a lot yet," Skip replied. "Talked to you, talked to Sarah, the state fire investigator, city fire inspector." He paused for a moment. "Talked to Brian and some girl he claims is his girlfriend."

"Serenity?" Milton asked.

"Yeah," Skip said. "She says that she's not his girlfriend; he says she is."

"I see her with Brian all the time," Milton said. "She sure looks like she's his girlfriend. She's bossy," Milton added.

"You think she makes him jog with her?" Max chided.

"What's your problem today?" Milton shot back. Milton directed his attention back to Skip. "I would call her his girlfriend."

"Well, she doesn't want to talk to us," Skip replied. "Like when someone is lawyering up. She advised me not to try to contact her again."

"She's kind of a strange one," Milton observed. "She has this hippie free spirit thing going, but I get the feeling she is more with-it than she wants to appear."

"She works for Slo-Mo," Skip said. "I mean, Slo-Mo sort of attracts that kind."

"Hippies?" Milton replied. "Or kids who have their shit together?"

"Hippies, skateboarders, you know what I'm talking about," Skip answered.

"Hipsters," Max added.

"Not hipsters," Skip said back to him. "Hipsters work in coffee shops."

Max shrugged. "I think that you shouldn't stereotype people."

Skip ignored his comment.

"Hipsters sit on stools in coffee shops and play their guitars," Skip had to get in the last word.

"Neither of you guys know what a hipster is," Milton interrupted the banter. Skip gave him a questioning look. "Anyway…" Milton did not finish his sentence.

"Just that we talked to her and she didn't want to talk to us," Skip explained.

"We're supposed to meet the owner of the store that burned this afternoon, after he gets off work," Skip said. "I'm going to be interested in what he has to say."

"You really think that Ben is right?" Milton asked.

Skip thought for a moment. "Honestly, I would have to say that on the surface I see no reason to believe that the place didn't burn down because of faulty wiring, just like the investigator said. But it is kind of like being a goddamned lawyer, you start believing your client, even though everything is telling you that he's full of shit."

"So you do believe that he's on to something."

"Until I see something that tells me different," Skip replied.

Milton thought about it for a moment. "But if everyone is saying that it wasn't arson, what do you mean you believe Ben until someone proves different?"

"Ben never said that it was arson," Skip corrected Milton. "Ben said that they always say faulty wiring when they can't pin a fire on something else. He is questioning that the cause of the fire was faulty wiring."

"What difference does it make, then?" Milton asked, exasperated. "What difference does it make if the fire investigator couldn't find a specific cause and attributed it to faulty wiring? If it wasn't arson, it was accidental. Who cares?"

"I guess our client cares," Skip replied. "He hired us to check it out. So that's what we are doing. We don't particularly like taking on cases, but when we do, we take them seriously."

Milton finished his can of Coke and started to get up. "What's with the dirty bowls?" he asked, looking at the two bowls on the table.

"Breakfast," Max said. "Monica made us eat some sweet snot with granola on it."

"Yogurt," Milton said. "She's got me on yogurt breakfast, too. What is she trying to do to us?"

"Welcome to married life," Max said.

Skip was picking up the two bowls and heading toward the back of the bar where the dishwasher was. Max walked toward the front and took a seat at Monica's desk, watching Milton get into his city car and back out of Monica's space.

Skip came up just as Milton was driving out. "He's just got a lot of gall, parking in Monica's parking space. Just like a cop," Max observed.

Skip watched Max, who had pulled a piece of paper from the printer and found a sharpie in Monica's desk. "Your hubby left this for you to throw away," he wrote on the piece of paper and handed to Skip. Skip took the piece of paper and went back to the bar, picked up the empty Coke can and placed the piece of paper under it.

Skip came back up front and sat down in one of the overstuffed chairs opposite Monica's desk. "What's the plan now?" he asked.

Max was leaning back looking out the window at Filo's across the street. He couldn't think of anything, so he stayed silent.

"I wish that Milton wouldn't come in here and demoralize us like that," Skip said. "I really felt like we were making some headway until he came in and threw a wrench into it."

"Well, there is Serenity," Max observed. "Brian thinks she is his girlfriend, Milton thinks she is Brian's girlfriend."

Neither spoke for a moment, thinking about Serenity. Max looked up at the clock. "I wonder if Monica is in class right this moment."

Skip shrugged his shoulders. Max pulled his cell phone out of his pocket and went through his contacts. When he got to Monica, he touched the screen and brought up her number. "Serenity, girlfriend, *si o no*?" he typed a text and hit send. "Call if not oo," he typed and hit send again. He put his phone on the desk and looked back out the window. Skip was staring outside as well. Max's phone buzzed, vibrating on the desktop. Max picked it up, swiped the screen and put it up to his face. "What's up?" he asked.

"What does oo mean?" Monica asked.

"Otherwise occupied," Max replied.

"What do you want?" she asked.

"Are you busy?" Max asked.

"I'm between classes," Monica replied.

"Is Serenity Brian's girlfriend?" Max asked.

"I guess so," Monica replied. "Why?"

"Well, we talked to her on the phone a little while ago and she said that she wasn't Brian's girlfriend. Brian told us yesterday she was. Seems like Milton thinks she is. We thought we would ask you what you thought and get a consensus."

"She sure acts like she is," Monica replied. "She's with him every time he picks up Essie."

"That's interesting," Max observed. "Why would she tell us she isn't?"

"Beats me," Monica said. "She wants to distance herself from him for some reason?"

"Brian was in the store late that evening that it burned," Max said. "He told us that Serenity came in to see him before she went to work at the taco cart. She told us that she didn't go to see him."

The phone was silent for a moment while Monica was thinking. "That's kind of strange. Why would Brian say that she did if she didn't, and why would she say that she didn't if she did?"

"Brian needs an alibi?" Max suggested.

"Or she wants to distance herself from him for some reason," Monica suggested again.

"Why do you keep saying that?" Max asked her. "Why would she want to distance herself from him?"

"Because he was the last person in the store before it burned. She thinks that she knows something and doesn't want to get dragged into it."

"Do you think that Brian burned the place down?" Max asked.

"I don't know what Brian did," Monica replied. "But why else would she all of a sudden claim that she isn't his girlfriend and that she wasn't with him that night? Seems to me like there has to be a reason to distance herself. Why would that be? You put it together and see what you get."

"You've got a point," Max replied. "But we still don't have a motive. What does he get from it? A job at a deli for a lot less money and a lot less prestige?"

"Maybe it wasn't on purpose," Monica replied. "Maybe something else happened. Negligence."

"Dang, woman, you got all the answers," Max said.

"I know Brian," Monica replied. "I might not be ready to believe that he set the fire on purpose, but I'll bet he had something to do with it."

"Okay, gotta go." She ended the call before Max could reply.

"You hear that?" Max asked Skip.

"Nope," Skip answered, "but you can fill me in on the way to lunch."

Max got up from the desk and went back to his office to check his email before they left. Skip was waiting for him at the door when he came back.

"Let's walk," he said, looking at the Fitbit on his wrist and then pointing toward Dakota and the Westend Grill that sat at the intersection. "Get in some steps."

Chapter 8

Tuesday

Max and Skip were parked in the Campus Plaza lot behind the burned-out Cosmic Comics waiting for the owner, Hank Peterson, to show up. The detectives had walked to the Westend Grill for lunch and continued discussing the case the entire time. Max filled Skip in on his conversation with Monica while they walked the three blocks to the restaurant. He told Skip that it sounded like Monica was convinced that Brian had something to do with the fire, and that Serenity knew what it was. Monica thought that Serenity was distancing herself from Brian so that she wouldn't get dragged down with him if the truth became known. The two continued to mull it over while they ate.

When they were done eating, they had walked back to the agency and busied themselves with the one thing that they did better than anything: goofing off. Skip did some searching on the internet, trying to find information on Serenity Stephens. He was having no luck in the student directory. He wondered if she was even still a student. Maybe she had just told him that she had classes to end the call. Skip looked for a while, then let it go. He started reading the financial sites. The market was tanking for no reason that he could determine, so he read other people's theories on it, looking for a definitive answer. But he knew before he started reading that no one understood the stock market. The whole economy was built on the unknown. Trying to outsmart the markets and failing to do so was the only thing that kept it running. Good investors made their money off of other people's losses. When the market tanked, like it had been lately, someone was making a lot of money, and it wasn't the guy who had his retirement investments there.

Max had been surfing the net as well. First he looked at Martin guitars and almost bought one. But then he went to the Taylor guitar site and decided that he didn't want a Martin, he might want a Taylor. Then he went to the Fender site. Max was not a Fender fan. He was more of an acoustic guitar player. To him Fenders said electric, even if they were acoustic. He went to the Gibson site. They had gotten fined for using banned woods in their guitars and had a bunch of their wood confiscated by the feds. Max started reading articles about that. For some reason it made him want a Gibson.

Each in their own world, the two had whiled away the whole afternoon accomplishing nothing, until Ben came in to get an update. The two detectives sat in the bar drinking rum and Cokes while they went over everything. Ben was working and drank a ginger ale instead. He was getting used to hanging out at the agency. It beat his spartan office space next door.

Ben wasn't any help. He just listened, interrupting every once in a while wanting to know the "bottom line." Skip told him there was no bottom line yet. After an hour, Ben went out the door and toward his office, obviously disappointed that the detectives had not found something, anything, other than faulty wiring and some unsubstantiated conjecture as to the cause of the fire.

"Lots of tagging," Max observed, looking around the Campus Plaza area from the parked car. Campus Plaza was essentially a parking lot situated behind the businesses on the west side of the one-hundred block of Welch, the south side of the twenty-five hundred block of Linconway, and the east side of the one hundred block of Hayward, one square block that defined the area. It was bound on the south by Chamberlain Avenue. The plaza was dominated by the rear doors to the businesses that lined the blocks that formed the perimeter, housed in a combination of old and new buildings. The last decade had been a battle between the two as developers bought up the prime Campustown properties, tore them down and built new high-rise buildings with retail business on the first floor, many with apartments above. It was hit and miss, which gave a haphazard mixture of building styles and designs that had come to define the area across from the Iowa State University campus.

"Notice how all of the old buildings are tagged, but none of the new ones are?" Skip asked. "I wonder what WAW is? See all of the WAWs?"

"Waw," Max said. "Waaaw," he said it again, drawing it out to see if he could make it sound like something, like one would sound out personalized license plates on cars while they waited in traffic.

An older Mercedes convertible pulled into the lot and parked. A man got out and looked around. He spotted the two detectives sitting in Max's car and waved.

"Peterson," Max remarked as he opened the door of his car and got out. Skip was doing the same. "Mr. Peterson," Max addressed the man as he walked up and shook hands. "Max Mosbey, and my associate, Skip Murray."

"We've already met," Hank said as he shook their hands. "Citizen Police Academy about eight years ago. I had just come up to take over my parents' store and I got invited to attend. You guys gave a talk."

"Sorry we didn't recognize you," Max replied. "We talked to a lot of people in the citizen academy over the years."

"I'm sure," Hank said. "I was also out here on one of my ride-alongs and you guys were mopping up the street with some college kids that decided to take you on when you arrested them for drunk and disorderly."

"I'm assuming we won that one and got them arrested," Skip remarked.

"Yeah, very much so," he said laughing. "I think that a couple of them had to go to the hospital."

"Wasn't us then," Max remarked. "We used to pride ourselves in taking it right up to that point, but not all the way. We never hurt 'em bad enough that they had to go to the hospital."

Hank didn't know what to say.

"Just messing," Max said. "Let's take a look."

Hank led them through the short alleyway that connected the plaza lot with Welch Avenue, and then around the corner until they stood in front of the Cosmic Comics building. There was a door in the center, with two large plate glass windows on each side of it. The building was one of those long, narrow ones that were built in the early nineteen-hundreds to cater to the students from the campus and dorms across Lincolnway. They could look down Welch Avenue from where they stood and see Lake LaVerne, a pond that lay between the Friley dorms and the Memorial Union.

"Remember when you were chasing that kid and he jumped in Lake Latrine?" Skip asked Max.

"There's one we might should have taken up to the hospital once we got him arrested," Max said. "I'm surprised he didn't end up with the bubonic plague or something from wallowing around in that shit pond."

Skip and Hank laughed.

The two front windows were covered with plywood, the glass door was blackened by smoke and fire so that they could no longer see in through it. Max was looking at the trash in the entry. He recognized the wax paper wrappers that the people working the Taco Machine put around the tortillas that they filled for the college kids at bar closing on the weekends from their cart of flavors and ingredients.

"They were keeping it picked up," Hank said, looking at the same thing. "I had some words with Hicks about it, and he said that he would get on them. But it looks like they aren't worried about it now that we burned."

"What kind of words?" Skip asked.

"Just that his people would set up right here every weekend. The kids would throw their garbage in the doorway. My people would come to work on Friday, Saturday and Sunday mornings and there would be a lot of garbage. Nothing serious, and I would call up Barlow and complain. They would clean it up pretty good for two or three weekends, then it would get bad again. It went like that. I'd call him up once a month or so.

"I thought that Barlow was all about keeping the streets clean," Max remarked.

"Barlow himself is all about cleaning up, but some of those kids that work for him aren't so much so. Over the last couple of years, Barlow has been out here less and less at night. The kids working for him aren't as particular about it as he is." Hank was looking at the burned-out building and didn't say anything for a minute. "Worst thing," he continued, "those kids come over here and congregate at bar closing and they like to get in the doorway here. Especially if it is cold. They don't just throw their wrapping on the ground, they puke and piss in there. One time I even found someone had pooped in my doorway. I'd call up

Barlow to complain and he would tell me that he couldn't control the kids, that he would pick up the garbage, but he couldn't stop them from puking, pissing and pooping." Hank laughed. "Anyway, we went back and forth. No big thing, he's easy enough to talk with. He's really good at listening," Hank remarked with a wink and a nod. "I just wanted him to move it down the street a ways, and he said that if he did it would just be someone else's doorway. I told him that was fine with me. I got the feeling that he thought that I should be more considerate of my neighbors and be glad that they were doing it in my vestibule and not in someone else's. I'm a neighborly guy, but I could never really embrace that thinking when I was out there cleaning it up."

Max and Skip had been listening, remembering when they worked the bars, watching the kids in line at the Taco Machine piling into the doorways as Peterson described. They had seen plenty of them throw their garbage on the ground, they had seen their share of puking and peeing college students, but they had never seen anyone taking a dump right there on Welch. Maybe back in the plaza they had seen a few.

"Ever get any vandalism?" Skip asked.

"Couple times I came in and a window was broken," Hank replied. "Funny thing, broken windows don't have a deductible. But yeah, I got a couple of them."

"Any tagging?" Skip asked.

"Not a lot," Hank replied. "Most of the tagging went on back behind those Lincolnway businesses. I got a couple of Wizards tags, but nothing more."

Skip gave Hank a questioning look. "Wizards?"

"W-A-W," Hank explained, saying each of the letters. "Welch Avenue Wizards."

"What are the Welch Avenue Wizards?" Skip asked.

"Maybe three or four years ago the kids started this little group out here, called themselves the Welch Avenue Wizards. It's a club. Most of them hang out at Meteor, the other comic book store. I think they started there. I'd get a few of them come through my store."

"A comics club?" asked Skip.

"Comics, but mostly gamers," Hank replied. "I didn't cater to gamers. I was vintage comics and records, not games. I mean, I had some old board games, but nothing worth attracting a lot of those kids. Nothing like Meteor over there."

The two did not say anything.

"I used to think the Wizards were pretty harmless, but the last couple years they've gotten kind of nasty," Hank remarked.

Skip gave him another questioning look.

"Just that they put pressure on businesses around here. Speaking of broken windows, crossing the Welch Avenue Wizards is a good way to get a window broken."

"You mean they're shaking you down?" Max asked.

"Not really shaking us down in the sense that they are extorting money, but more like the Teamsters, you know? Like if you're hiring and you don't hire a Wizard, you might find yourself with a broken window, or maybe a mob of kids come through after class, and when they leave you find some of your merchandise left with them. I one time hired the wrong person and a few days later I found chewing gum stuck inside a dozen or so of my best comics."

"Did you have any of these Wizards working for you when your place burned?" Max asked.

Hank shrugged his shoulders.

"You don't know?" Max asked.

"They aren't like Hell's Angels; they don't advertise," Hank replied.

"Your manager, Brian Parker. Is he a Wizard?" Skip asked.

Hank shrugged his shoulders again. "Maybe. I mean, he never told me that he was, but let's just say that my inventory losses were minimal when he was working for me."

"Except your business burned to the ground while he was working for you," Skip exclaimed.

Hank thought for a moment. "I had a very good working arrangement with Brian. Wizard or not, I don't think Brian would have anything to do with my place burning down. He was pretty much running the business for me, almost like a partner. I owned the business and he was investing his time. It was a very good relationship. I can't see him burning my business down. Besides, the inspector said that the fire was caused by faulty wiring, not arson."

Hank stopped speaking for a moment. "Are you investigating this because you think someone burned my store down? Because I don't believe that someone purposely burned it down," he said in an adamant tone.

"The insurance agent thinks that it might have been something other than faulty wiring. That's all," Skip answered. "He doesn't think it was arson, he just doesn't buy the faulty wiring. That's why he hired us to look into it. He's not trying to pin it on anyone."

Hank looked a bit relieved.

"Do you think that we could get a look inside?" asked Max.

"Sure," Hank replied. "We gotta go around back."

Hank led them around to the back, where the charred back door was secured by a hasp and a padlock. It was new and contrasted with the charred door. Max was surprised that the back door was still wood. Hank took the padlock and gave it a slight tug. The screws pulled from the door.

"Can't get them to stay," he explained. "I might as well just do it like this, they will pull loose just opening the padlock with the key."

Max gave him a dubious look.

"There's nothing in there worth anything," Hank said in response. "At this point it's a liability thing. The padlock discourages people from randomly walking in to look around."

He pulled the door open and they went inside. Max pulled his phone from his pocket and turned on the flashlight. Skip did the same. Hank had a small LED flashlight in his jacket.

"Always prepared," he said.

The three started walking through the building, Hank leading the way. There was some light getting through the front door and around the edges of the plywood over the windows, but not enough to see clearly without the flashlights. The walls were lined with shelving containing burned and charred comics and records. Many of the records had melted inside the jackets and resembled a Salvador Dali painting.

"Surrealism," Max commented.

"Yeah," Hank answered back.

The three looked around and saw nothing that would indicate a source of the fire. Hank was perceptive. "In the basement," he went to an open door that led to a steep stairway.

The three made their way carefully down the stairs into the dark basement. Hank turned on a battery powered lantern that hung from a blackened nail pounded decades before into a now charred joist in the ceiling.

"I've been down here seeing if I can find anything worth salvaging," Hank explained.

Max and Skip looked around the room. It was dark, damp and reeked of smoke. The beam of the flashlight in Skip's phone passed over a breaker box and a fuse box. He stopped it there and took a closer look.

"I would say from the burn patterns that is where it started," Skip remarked.

"That's what the investigator said," Hank replied.

Max examined the breaker box, then looked at the fuse box. The fuse box contained a bank of four old twist-in fuses. They were black and burned.

"You think this is the culprit?" he asked, trying to twist out one of the fuses and failing.

"Could be," Hank said. "Who knows? But I'm pretty sure that the electricians who were in here a couple of months ago told me that none of those circuits were hot. I think most of the wiring was long ago routed through the breaker box.

Max had managed to get soot all over himself in his unsuccessful attempt to remove one of the fuses. He gave up and shined his flashlight over both electrical boxes and up into the ceiling. Hank was showing Skip the boxes of comics and other merchandise he had bought in Las Vegas.

"This is what really did us in," he was telling Skip.

"I spent a lot of my savings on this stuff. We were going to have this big week-long event and sell it all. Pie in the sky. Brian and I were so excited about it." Hank was shining his flashlight over the boxes. "None of this was insured. I mean, you just do the math in your head," he said wistfully. "I should have done some kind of inventory along the way, but I just had a policy for a hundred grand for the store contents. I thought that would cover it." He shined his flashlight over the boxes again as if he still could not believe what he was seeing. "A hundred grand doesn't even cover the inventory upstairs on the shelves," he sighed. "I'm on the hook for all of this."

The three stood silent, looking at the pile of charred dreams.

Chapter 9

Tuesday

Skip and Max walked out into the sunlight as Hank secured the door. Max had worked up a sweat rummaging around the breaker and fuse boxes trying to track the progress of the fire, but realized that he had no idea what he was looking at. Neither of the detectives had any experience in fire investigation and both of them were flying by the seat of their pants.

Skip wiped some sweat from under his eye, leaving a black mark on his cheek. All three of them smelled of smoke.

"So, what now?" Skip asked Hank.

"I guess I sell out," he replied. "Rogers Enterprises approached me about buying me out last year. I wasn't interested. They've been doing a lot of the development around here. I talked to him last week, and he is going to look at it again and make an offer. I've put out a couple of feelers."

"Got a real estate agent?" Max asked.

"I'm going to see what kind of offers I get first," Hank replied.

"You got this free and clear, or do you owe on it?" Max asked, wondering at what point Hank would tell him it wasn't any of his business.

"We own both the building and the business outright," he replied. "My brother, my sister and I inherited it. My brother had been running the store, but he got sick and I came up to take over. Our sister doesn't want anything to do with it; she lives in Maryland."

Hank looked at the back of the building. "It's prime real estate. I mean, at least it has that going for it." He paused for a moment. "My grandparents bought this building in the fifties. They opened up a smoke shop. They sold tobacco, pipes, cigars, cigarettes and magazines. Dirty magazines," Hank laughed. "My grandpa used to bring them home and my grandma was always telling him to put them up where us grandkids wouldn't get into them."

Hank paused in reflection. "Then they got old and couldn't keep up with it. Times changed. In the eighties my parents took it over."

Max and Skip stood listening. Hank was going somewhere with his story, and the two detectives wanted to hear where it went. They had been through this before and didn't want to interrupt his thoughts.

"Over the years, the store went from a smoke shop to a book store. They sold those little Hallmark figurines, cards that the kids could pick up and send home to wish their parents a happy birthday or happy anniversary. My parents would sell them a stamp and chuck the cards in the mail for them. The store barely broke even, but they kept it going. Came a time my brother didn't have anything going for him, he was that guy living in his parents' basement. Dad passed, and Mom was tired. My brother took over the store and turned it into a comic book store. Except there was already a comic book store around the corner by then, so he sold old comics and old records. Then he got sick about eight years back and couldn't work anymore. I was living in KC and working a dead-end IT job. I don't know what the hell I was thinking. I moved my family up here and took over the store."

Hank looked at the two detectives, who were listening intently to his story.

"Biggest mistake I ever made," Hank continued. "I hate that it dies under my watch, but I also feel like a big weight is off my shoulders. I just can't keep the business going. I tried. If Rogers or somebody comes back with an offer that I can get out of this with my shirt, I'm out of here. I got a good job at Sauer Danfoss and if I don't have this anchor around my neck, I'll be good."

Max and Skip didn't reply right away. They waited to see if Hank had any more to say.

"You said that you were underinsured," Max said when Hank did not continue. "Do you think that you can come out of this ahead some way?"

"I don't know," replied Hank. "I'll have to see what Rogers offers me for the building. Location, location, location, that's all I got left. I'll collect my insurance, see what I can get for the property, and then try to dig myself the rest of the way out of the hole I've dug myself into. If I'm lucky, it won't be that deep. I suppose my brother and sister will want their cut."

Hank was lost in thought again. "You know," he said wistfully. "I honestly think this place could have struggled through another generation if my sister wasn't taking a third of my profits and if I didn't have to take care of my brother's medical bills." He was quiet again. "Wouldn't that have been a curse on my kids?" He laughed. "I'm glad that it burned. I just feel sorry for Brian. He hasn't been here long, but he was really putting a lot of sweat into the business. He was always telling me that if we hung in there, eventually we would make the turn. I don't know. I never saw that light at the end of the tunnel that he saw."

He was quiet again, lost in thought. "Okay," he said abruptly. "I gotta get home. It's getting close to supper. You guys need anything else?"

Max and Skip both shook their heads. The three turned toward their cars and started walking. "Hey," Max said, stopping Hank. "What about Serenity? Do you know if she was in the store the night that it burned? Brian said she was, she said she wasn't. Do you know?"

"I don't," Hank said. "It wouldn't surprise me, though. She was in there a lot. I think that Brian's living situation is not conducive to privacy. He has two roommates. I think he used working late as an excuse for Serenity to come over after closing, if you know what I mean."

"You were good with that?" Max asked.

Hank shrugged his shoulders. Max started to turn.

"You know you asked me about Brian being one of the Wizards?" Hank asked.

Max nodded his head.

"I don't know for sure, but if I was to guess that someone was a Wizard, it would be Serenity, not Brian."

"Really?" Max replied.

"You ever read Suicide Squad?" Hank asked.

"Nope," Skip said at the same time that Max was nodding affirmative.

"I saw the movie," Max said.

"Harley Quinn," Hank said. "That's Serenity."

"Interesting," Max said.

Hank raised his eyebrows and shrugged his shoulders, turned and walked toward his car.

"What's that about? Who's Harley Quinn?" Skip asked while they walked to Max's car.

"Comic book character," Max said. "I think that she's had a couple of personas, but in Suicide Squad she's like a psychotic ass-kicker. Beats the shit out of her adversaries with a baseball bat."

"Okay," exclaimed Skip. "Brian's girlfriend can kick his ass."

The two got into Max's car. "Did he just confess to us?" Skip asked as Max drove out of Campus Plaza and onto Hayward, where he turned south toward Mortensen Road.

"You think that's what it was?" Max replied.

"I don't know what it was. His family history?" Skip remarked. "But by the time we parted company he'd done a good job of convincing me that he had plenty of reason to burn the place down."

"What about being underinsured and all that? What does he gain, buying all of that expensive inventory in Vegas and having it shipped back here so that he can burn it?"

"Throw everyone off?" suggested Skip.

"Official report is faulty wiring, no question about it. What is there to throw everyone off of?" Max replied.

Skip thought about it a moment. "Was it expensive inventory that burned?"

Max didn't answer.

"Just saying," Skip said. "There's more kinds of insurance than what Ben sells. How's Peterson know what the fire investigator is going to report? Nice to have some insurance planted in the basement just in case. And everyone's taking his word for it that he had a sizeable investment go up in flames. Everyone is thinking that Hank lost his ass in the fire. That's his alibi. Anything to back it up?"

"Brian seemed to think it was a sizable inventory," Max said.

"So Brian said," Skip retorted. "Since when is Brian a reliable source? Hell, it sounds to me like those two were working pretty close together. Maybe all three of them were working together."

Max pondered what Skip was saying for a minute. "You make sense sometimes," he said. "You think Serenity was in on it, too?

"Maybe," Skip replied. "According to Brian, Serenity is his girlfriend. According to Peterson, Serenity was coming in after closing, and it wasn't to read comics. Sounds like a girlfriend to me."

Max didn't reply.

"We got two who are saying she's his girlfriend and one saying that she isn't," Skip continued. "Two against one. Why is she telling us she isn't his girlfriend?"

"What's her motivation?" Max asked. "And it might be two against one, but the one is the supposed girlfriend. I would think that she would know, if anyone."

"It's a discrepancy," Skip replied. "If she is Brian's girlfriend, why is she all of a sudden distancing herself?"

"You just asked me that," Max said.

"You didn't answer me," Skip replied.

"How about she isn't, and those two are trying to throw some suspicion at her, take a little bit of it off themselves, send us off track?" Max suggested. "What do you do if you want to put some distance between yourself and someone else, and you got no place to run? You put something between you and them. Maybe that something is Serenity. What is the last thing Hank wanted us to leave with? Serenity is a Wizard. She's the Welch Avenue Harley Quinn."

Skip thought about it. "Sometimes you make sense, too," he said.

"Sometimes?" Max replied.

Max pulled his car into the parking lot at the G&B Detective Agency. Skip opened the door to get out. "What about tomorrow?"

"I guess we have to walk," Max replied. "How many steps do you have?"

Skip looked at his Fitbit. "You know how to read this thing?"

Max looked at his own Fitbit and started pushing buttons.

"It's getting late," Skip commented, watching to see if Max could figure it out.

"I'm going to go home and see if Gloria wants to go for a little walk," Max said. "I think that she knows how to work this thing."

"Don't do that," Skip complained. "If you go for a walk, I'm going to have to go for a walk."

"No one is telling you that you have to go for a walk," Max said.

Skip got out of the car. "I'll see you tomorrow," he said through the open door. Max pulled away as soon as he shut it.

Max thought about Peterson's words and Skip's take on them. Skip was very methodical and very perceptive. He liked to connect the dots. Max buried his head and plowed through everything. Skip was driven by reason; Max was driven by emotion. They made a good team. Over the years Max had learned to trust Skip, and Skip had learned to trust Max. If Skip thought that there was something suspicious going on, he could tell you why. Max on the other hand went by his gut, and if you asked him, he would say that he just had a gut feeling, and right now his gut was telling him that Skip's suspicions were on target. When they both felt the same about something, that was a good indication that there was something there.

Serenity's phone was ringing in her back pocket. She pulled it out and looked at the screen. It was Brian. He would be getting off work about this time. She almost didn't answer, then changed her mind. She swiped the screen just before it went to voicemail.

"Hello," she answered without enthusiasm.

"What are you up to?" Brian's voice asked on the other end. "You don't have to work tonight, you want to go get a pizza?"

"I gotta study," Serenity replied, putting a bit of inflection in her voice to make him feel like she was wishing otherwise.

"I'll come over and help you study," Brian suggested. "We can order pizza in. Maybe have a little smoke? Help you concentrate."

"Oh, yeah," Serenity said sarcastically. "That would help me concentrate. I think that I better say no for tonight. I really need to get some studying done."

Brian didn't answer for a moment. "Listen," he said, just when Serenity thought to end the call. "Yesterday morning a couple of private detectives were asking me about the fire."

"Okay," replied Serenity, waiting to hear what brought up the subject.

"Well, they were asking me about everything that happened that night before, and they asked me who all was in the store after closing."

"And you told them that I was," Serenity said.

"Well, I did," Brian replied. "So they might want to talk to you, but don't worry about it, they're just going over the reports to verify the information in them."

"And you gave them my phone number," Serenity challenged.

"No, not really," Brian backpedaled. "Well, actually I gave it to my ex. She works for them, the detective agency that is. Sounds like maybe they already talked to you?"

"Why did you tell them that I was there?" Serenity asked. "I mean, why drag me into it? I don't need this."

"What am I going to say?" Brian was defensive. "They asked me and I told them. I told them that there were some customers that stayed late, that you stopped in, and then I locked up and left."

"Jesus, Brian, you could have left out that I stopped by," she said. "And what do you mean that your ex works for this detective agency? I thought that she was married to that cop, and that's the reason that someone else had to investigate the fire in the first place. Now your ex is investigating it?"

"She's not investigating it. She is married to the cop. The detectives used to be cops. Now they're private detectives. My ex is their office manager," Brian explained. "She called and asked for your number, so I gave it to her. Look, they aren't going to not talk to you because they don't have your phone number. That isn't how they work. I figured that the faster they talked to you the faster they would move on. The more you try to hide from them, the more suspicious they get. Trust me, you got nothing to hide. Just talk to them. You don't want to get them all suspicious about you because they think you are trying to avoid them."

Brian listened for a moment. Serenity did not say anything. "If we start lying to them, especially when we got no reason to lie, that's just like waving a red flag in their face. I know these guys."

Serenity still didn't respond.

"We on for Saturday? Brian asked, trying to change the subject. "I got Essie. I was thinking about taking her down to the mall in Des Moines. I thought that I would buy her some clothes or shoes or something."

"I don't think so," Serenity replied. "I have a lot of studying to do."

"Come on," Brian whined. "You said that you would come with me on Saturday when I have her. I want her to like you. Let's go down to the mall. It will be something to do. We'll have fun. Essie will love it."

Serenity didn't answer.

"I know you're pissed at me," Brian said. "I didn't do nothing that you need to be pissed over. Just let's go to the mall on Saturday. Forget about those detectives and their stupid investigation. It doesn't have anything to do with either of us. We didn't do anything."

"I'll think about it," Serenity replied, realizing that Brian wasn't going to give it up.

"I'll talk to you tomorrow," Brian said.

Serenity ended the call. She was not happy with the recent turn of events.

Chapter 10

Wednesday

Max woke up in the morning the same as he had the previous morning, with Gloria shaking him until his eyes opened, and then shaking him more for good measure.

"Get up," she said. "You don't want Monica and Skip to have to wait for you."

"Does this mean that I'm never going to get to sleep in late again?" Max asked her sleepily.

"No, you can sleep in on Saturday and Sunday, just like everyone else," Gloria told him good naturedly.

Max sat up and swung his legs down to the floor. "This sucks."

"It does not suck," Gloria chided him. "It's good for you. You have all kinds of time to do whatever you want, you can set aside a little time to pay attention to your health."

Max knew that there was no use in arguing. He got up out of bed and went into the bathroom to take a shower.

"Why don't you take a shower after you work out?" Gloria asked. "Don't you have a shower at the agency?"

"I'm not going to work up a sweat," Max replied. "We're walking."

Gloria shrugged her shoulders and left the room. When she got to the kitchen, she picked up her phone off the counter and texted Monica. "Max is moving slow and thinks that he needs a shower."

Seconds later she got a reply. "Tell him he can procrastinate as long as he wants, not going anywhere without him."

Gloria went back to the bedroom and to the bathroom door. "Max, I don't want to be a nag, but they are waiting for you and you don't want to make Monica late for class."

Max stepped out of the shower and took a towel off the rack. "I'm going," he said, resigned.

Gloria stepped up to him, put her arms around his wet body and gave him a kiss.

"You trying to get something going again?" he asked, reaching around and holding her.

"I would if you weren't so busy," she said, twisting away. "But you have to get going right now."

"Dang," muttered Max while Gloria left the bathroom.

Max pulled into the parking lot at the agency to find Monica and Skip stretching.

"Max, you're missing out on the stretching," Monica said.

"I'm good," Max replied. "I'll loosen up when we start walking."

"We're working on our flexibility," Monica said. "Team G and B needs to be in fighting shape, and that means both strength and flexibility. No slackers on team G and B! Come over here and stretch."

Max walked up on the sidewalk where the other two stood and started reaching down in rhythm with Monica's lead. She was counting as they stretched from one side to the other, bending over to touch their toes, which Monica was having no problem doing. Skip was giving it everything he had, turning red in the process, and touching the toe of his shoe with the very tip of his finger. Max was two inches from matching Skip.

"Look at Skip," Monica said to Max. "Don't let him beat you," she challenged. Monica quit counting and began to make a "hoo-ah" grunting sound that she thought sounded like something the ISU football players did during warm-ups for games. "Hoo-ah, one; hoo-ah, two," Monica was trying to create a cadence. The two detectives began to make the same sound, but not counting. Monica kept going.

"Okay," she finally said. "Two miles, boys, Team G and B, let's make this one count!" The two looked ready to go. Monica paused for a couple of seconds. "Listen up," she said. "Skip, Max got in six hundred more steps yesterday than you did."

"How do you know that?" Skip asked.

"On my computer," Monica explained. "The Fitbits report to my computer."

"They're spying on us?" Max asked.

"No," Monica replied to him. "They report how many steps you took," she paused. "Stuff like that."

The two didn't look convinced that they weren't being spied on.

"Did you go for a walk last night?" Skip accused Max.

"No, but I thought about it," Max replied.

Skip was glaring at Max.

"Thinking about it doesn't count," Max said in his own defense. "So don't give me your stink eye."

"Okay, enough. Let's go." Monica took off at a brisk stride, hoping that Max and Skip were following. After the first couple of blocks the two quit arguing, saving their breath. Monica picked up the pace at the one-mile point. Skip caught up to her and was walking at her side, taking rapid short steps, huffing and puffing.

"What are you doing?" she asked.

"Maximizing," Skip shot back. "Getting in extra steps."

A moment later she heard Max behind her doing the same thing. When they got back to the agency, she got them to do some more stretching.

When they were done, they went inside. Monica went back to the bar to prepare the breakfast of yogurt and granola for the three of them while Max and Skip collapsed into the easy chairs. Monica came back to her desk balancing the three bowls. Max and Skip had worked up a bit of a sweat.

"What do you think?" Monica asked. "It feels good, doesn't it?"

"No," replied Max.

Monica dug into a box that sat on the floor behind her desk. She pulled out two olive green tee shirts and tossed one across to each of her employers. "Here," she said. "Tomorrow we're officially Team G and B."

The two looked at their shirts. The words Team G&B were stenciled across the front, giving the shirts a military look. On the back the words, "A few Lead, The Rest Follow," was stenciled in the same military script. Max checked the size on his shirt. "This is an extra-large, must be yours," he tossed his shirt in Skip's lap.

Skip checked his and tossed Max's back. "They're both XL," he said.

"You think we're extra-larges?" Max asked Monica.

"When I asked them what size to get you guys, your wives said you two had outgrown all of your larges," she replied. "I got you extra-larges."

Max frowned at her.

"You get yourself down to where you can wear a large again, I'll get you a large," she said. "In fact, I'll order them today. That's our goal: to fit in large tee shirts again."

The two seemed satisfied. They watched out the window as Ben Ralston came walking past the window, looking in at the three looking out at him. He waved as he went by, then came in.

"Where we at on the case?" Ben asked.

"We have three suspicious people that we don't know why they are suspicious, but they are," Skip remarked.

"I'm guessing one of them is Brian Parker?" Monica said, not shy about bringing up his name in front of Ben.

"And his supposed girlfriend, Serenity," Skip said, "And Hank Peterson, the owner."

"So, basically, everyone you've talked to?" Monica remarked.

"Everyone except the fire inspector," Max said in a definite tone. "But we aren't sure what it is they have done. There isn't any evidence that the fire was anything but what the fire investigator reported. We don't have any physical evidence to tie anyone into."

Skip laughed. "What he is saying is that we don't know what we have. I honestly want it to turn into something more than it probably is, and that's not good."

Ben was leaning back against the wall, looking around for a place to sit, but there wasn't anywhere. "So you do think that there is something suspicious going on?" he asked.

"I would like to go down in that basement again, without Hank," Max said. "I would like to take a closer look at that wiring. The fire investigator says faulty wiring. Maybe instead of interviewing people and trying to find a way to make them fit into our suspicions, it might be more productive to look at the wiring and see if we can somehow identify something that will support his findings, or not."

No one said anything for a moment.

"I think that if we really want to do an investigation, we need to let the evidence dictate to us, and not let our suspicions dictate what evidence we look at," Skip remarked.

"Isn't that what I just said?" Max asked with an annoyed tone.

"I think that you were more specific," Skip replied. "You were talking about wiring. I was talking in more general terms."

Max shook his head and did not reply.

"So right now, you don't have anything to report?" Ben asked.

"These things don't just solve themselves," Skip replied. "We still need to do some more digging."

"Okay," Monica said, getting up from her desk. "I'm hitting the showers and going to class. You guys made me work up a sweat. Good workout. You guys are pushing it. That's good. Team G and B! We're serious about what we do!"

"Rah, rah," Max said as Monica went down the hall toward the women's restroom and showers. "I worked up a sweat, too," Skip remarked, looking at his tee shirt and getting up.

Ben was eying the chair that Skip was about to vacate. "What's with the shirts?"

"Monica has us on this workout thing," Max replied. "She's in cahoots with our wives. We gotta come in every morning at a god-awful hour, without breakfast, and exercise. We gotta stretch, then go for a two-mile walk. It's like army bootcamp." Max held up his tee shirt for Ben to see. "Then she gives us some sweet snot with granola on it to eat after we're done. He nodded toward his empty bowl on the end table between the chairs.

"What do you know about army bootcamp? You were in the navy," Skip remarked, still standing in front to the chair that Ben was perched to jump into as soon as Skip got out of the way.

"I watch reruns of Gomer Pyle," Max said.

Skip walked toward the men's restroom across the hall from the women's, and Ben took his seat.

"So, you don't think that the fire is suspicious?" Ben asked Max.

"I think that we have some suspicious characters," Max replied. "But honestly, I'm pretty sure that the fire investigator would be the one to determine if it was a suspicious fire."

"They always say faulty wiring," Ben said.

"Maybe so," Max replied. "Maybe you're right, maybe they do say faulty wiring when they don't know what else caused it. But if it were suspicious, then the fire inspector would say that. He wouldn't call a suspicious fire faulty wiring, because he would know that it is suspicious." Max shrugged his shoulders.

"So that's it?" Ben asked.

"No," Max replied. "We are still following up leads. But at this point, nothing is indicating to us that this was anything but faulty wiring. That's up to this point. If something changes, then we will follow it up and see where it leads us."

Ben did not look satisfied with Max's answer.

"Wanna go across the street and get a cup of coffee to bring back?" Max asked.

"Sure," replied Ben in a resigned voice.

Max threw his tee shirt in the chair and the two left the agency to walk across the street to Filo's coffee shop. When they returned with their mugs of coffee, they found Monica at her desk, wearing her new olive green tee shirt.

"Nice shirt," Max remarked.

Monica looked up. "I didn't expect to take a shower this morning. I might have to bring some clothes in with me if we keep this up."

"You wearing that shirt to class?" Max asked.

"Yes," Monica replied. "I don't have anything else."

Ben had taken up the easy chair that he had been sitting in earlier.

"Skip's done if you want to hit the shower," Monica said, making a face like she could smell something.

"Pretty funny," Max said, grabbing his shirt and going down the hall, shirt in one hand, coffee in the other, leaving Monica and Ben in the reception area.

Chapter 11

Wednesday

Max took his shower and put on his new tee shirt. The front of the agency was empty. Monica must have gone to school and Ben back next door. As he walked to his office across from Skip's, Max looked over to see Skip in his tee shirt surfing the net.

"We're twins," Max remarked.

Skip looked up and snickered. "Maybe she should have gotten you a double-XL."

Max feigned a hurt look.

"What's the plan, man?" Max asked.

"We need to corner this Serenity," Skip said. "I've been going through the student directory and I didn't find a Serenity Stephens, so now I'm looking for anyone named Serenity. Not a one."

"You've been searching the ISU student directory for someone named Serenity?" Max asked. "How many names are in the student directory? Like maybe thirty or forty thousand?"

Skip shrugged his shoulders. "I'm thinking about calling up Brian," he said.

"Got a better idea," Max replied. "Call up Milton. I'll guarantee you that he's done a thorough background on her. I don't see him letting her get close to Essie without digging up everything that he can on her."

Skip smiled. "Good idea," he laughed.

Max was smiling, too, proud of himself that he had thought of it.

Skip picked up his landline and punched in Milton's cell number, then put it on speaker. The phone rang three times and then a cautious Milton answered.

"Who is this?" he asked.

"This is your cute little wifey," Skip said in a falsetto voice. "I miss you so much, I wish you would come by here to see me."

"Grow up," Milton said.

"Got a question," Skip said in a hoarse voice that he thought sounded like an old man. "What do you know about Brian's girlfriend Serenity?"

Milton ignored Skip's impersonation. "What do you want to know?"

"Last name," Skip replied.

"Stephens," Milton replied. "And her first name is not Serenity, it's Pamela."

"*Interestante,*" Max said.

"What else you got on her?" Skip asked.

"Senior at ISU, majoring in electrical engineering," Milton said. "On the four-and-a-half-year plan. Apparently, she skipped last semester. From West Des Moines. Her pappy is rich, a developer. He owns a third of Campustown right now, working on owning half. Evidently the two don't get along very well. She's kind of a flake. She's all into comic books and animation stuff. I think that she must be a step kid or something, because her name is Stephens, his name is Rogers. No priors. She lives at those apartments on Lynn."

"Which apartments?" Skip asked. "There's thousands of apartments on Lynn."

"Right behind where the old bookstore used to be," Milton said.

"You got an address?" Skip asked.

"Yes," Milton replied.

"Can I have it?" Skip asked.

"No," Milton said. "Last thing I need is you two getting some college girl's address from me and harassing her. That's doesn't look good for a guy who is hoping to stay in the detective division for a while."

"She's a suspect in our case," Skip said.

"Suspected of what?" Milton asked. "The place burned down because of faulty wiring."

"You're sure of that?" Skip challenged.

"No," Milton answered. "I didn't investigate it, the State Fire Marshal's office investigated it and they're sure that it was faulty wiring. What are you trying to prove, that is wasn't faulty wiring?"

"We are investigating to see if there are any inconsistencies," Skip replied.

"Well, good luck with that," Milton said. "Anything else you are wondering about?"

"You feel confident enough about her that you let her be around Essie?" Skip asked.

"She's Brian's girlfriend. I can't see a good reason to tell Brian who he can see and who he can't see. She's just a college kid."

Max had been thinking. "What about the Wizards?" he shouted into the phone. "She one of those Welch Avenue Wizards?"

"Could be," Milton replied. "I don't know that she is."

"That doesn't raise a flag?" Max shouted again.

"The Wizards are just a bunch of college kids running around playing comic book characters. They are kids. They are weird, that's all. They dress up and go to Comic Con."

"Seems like they've vandalized most of Campus Plaza," Skip suggested.

"Probably some of them are art majors. Going to grow up to be comic book illustrators. Campus Plaza is a pit.

Everything but the parking meters is private property, and no one is complaining about the Wizards decorating the place. It is an improvement."

"Wow," Skip exclaimed. "You're pretty liberal in your thinking."

"I'm a realist," Milton replied. "I got enough real crime to investigate without chasing kids who are spray painting the walls of a bunch of rundown buildings that the owners don't even care about and that Serenity's dad is going to tear down in the next couple of years anyway."

"What else do we need to know?" Skip asked.

"Nothing," Milton said. "She is just another kid that is rebelling against her parents. She's got purple hair, wears fishnet stockings under short shorts and Converse tennies. And she works a food stand on Welch Avenue with a bunch of other weird kids. I'm sure her dad wishes that she would conform to societal norms, and she probably will, eventually. Don't they all?"

"We tried to talk to her about the fire and she was downright…" Skip was trying to think of a word to describe her.

"Petulant," Milton helped him out.

"Petulant," Skip repeated.

"Yes, Serenity is petulant," Milton said. "She called in the fire; what's the big deal?"

"She was in there hanging out with Brian after closing the night of the fire," Skip replied.

"Okay," Milton said. "And that proves what?"

Skip and Max did not reply.

"Exactly," Milton said. "You know guys, someone has to have been the last people in the building before it caught fire because the wiring is so old most of it was installed by Fred Flintsone. Reasonable people would consider them lucky that it didn't catch fire while they were in there."

"Not a suspicious bone in your body," Skip remarked. "You're quite the detective."

"Smart enough detective to know that the case was investigated and closed," Milton replied. "Cause of fire: faulty wiring."

No one said anything for a moment.

"My training officer told me one time that you can't make a case where there isn't one," Milton interrupted the silence.

"That's true, he did," Max replied.

"Okay," Skip said. "Thanks for the info, we'll get back in touch with you if we need anything else."

"Hey," Max shouted into the phone. "How's the morning walks gong?"

"They're okay. What with Shawna living with us in the tiny townhouse all winter, it is nice to finally get out in the mornings and take a walk, get some fresh air."

"She got us tee shirts," Max shouted.

"Tee shirts?" Milton asked. "What for?"

"Team G and B," Skip said. "We're Team G and B. Two miles every morning, stretching before and after."

"She's walking with you guys, too?" Milton asked.

"Yeah, she's doing two-a-days," Skip replied.

"I didn't know that," Milton said.

"Don't you two talk?" Max shouted.

"We talk all the time," Milton replied. "And you guys got tee shirts because you're walking?"

"Yeah, Team G and B shirts. We're styling when we're out there," Skip replied.

Milton didn't say anything.

"We're wearing them now," Max shouted. "All three of us. Monica wore hers to class. Take a look at it when you get home. They're good."

"Okay, we'll let you get back to your real investigations," Skip said when Max was done shouting at the phone, ending the call.

"So, Serenity is not her real name," Skip remarked after he hung up the phone.

"What do you think?" Max asked.

"I think that I would still like to talk to her again," Skip answered.

"Me, too," Max said. "And I'm thinking that we need to run down Slo-Mo and talk to him."

"I want to talk to whoever owns that other comic book store, too," Skip added. "Let's just say, for conversation's sake, that Cosmic Comics burned down because of something other than faulty wiring. Might be that there is some connection with the other comic store."

"You mean like they burned down the competition?" Max asked.

"More like whatever reason Cosmic Comics burned, maybe the other comic store is susceptible to the same thing."

Max pondered it for a moment. "That's a thought."

Skip was on his computer. After a minute he reached for the phone and dialed a number. The phone was still on speaker. It rang several times before it was picked up.

"Meteor," a voice said.

"How's it going?" Skip asked. "My name is Skip Murray, and I'm a private investigator with G&B Detective Agency. Is the owner or manager handy?"

"I'm the manager, Rod," the voice on the other end replied.

"We're wondering if we can talk to you today about the Cosmic Comics fire," Skip said.

"I guess. I don't know much about it," Rod said defensively.

"We didn't think that you did," Skip said, trying to relieve some of the trepidation that he heard in Rod's voice. "Look, we're just trying to get a handle on what is going on out there in Campustown and maybe get a little better understanding of what is going on in the comic book business. We don't know anything about it. We just hoped that we might talk to you and get some of your insight."

"Sure," said Rod. "I'm here until five-thirty."

"Thanks," Skip said. "We'll be over there in a half hour or less. That work?"

"That would work," Rod replied.

Skip hung up the phone.

"Let's talk to him, go over to the deli and chat a little with Brian, then maybe see if we can find Slo-Mo," Skip said.

"You're driving," Max said quickly.

Skip grabbed his keys from his desk drawer while Max went into his office to do a fast check of his email to see if there was anything important for him to look at. As usual, there wasn't. The two went out the door and Max locked it behind him. Skip had walked across the parking lot and was getting into his Audi.

"Don't birds shit all over your nice car sitting over here under the tree?" Max asked as he got into the car.

"I park it under here so it doesn't get so hot sitting in the sun."

"It's spring," Max observed. "It doesn't get that hot."

"Habit," Skip replied.

"Bird shit?" Max asked again.

"Ginco tree," Skip said. "It repels birds."

"They attract birds," Max corrected him.

Skip didn't remark.

Skip took the direct route to Campustown, Dakota to Lincolnway and Lincolnway to Welch. Max would have taken the back way on Mortensen. Skip found an open parking space right on Welch and took it.

"Don't get lucky like that often," Max noted.

The two walked to Lincolnway and made their way to Meteor Comics and Games. When they went through the door they were greeted by a man standing behind the counter at the side of the room.

"You're at the right place," the man said.

Skip gave him a confused look.

"I'm assuming that you two are here to see me, and not to buy comics or games."

"Rod?" Skip asked, approaching the counter.

"I hope that I'm not being offensive by stereotyping you guys, but you just don't look like one of my customers," he laughed.

"No offence taken," Skip replied, holding out his hand.

Rod reached across the counter and shook Skip's hand, then Max's. He seemed amiable enough to the two detectives. He looked to be close to the same age as Hank.

"You're the manager?" Skip asked.

"Part owner, full-time manager," Rod replied.

Max was looking around. There was no one in the store.

"It's early," Rod said, noticing Max looking around. "Our clientele are not early risers."

"We wanted to talk to you about the fire over at Cosmic Comics," Skip said, getting right to the point.

"Like I said," Rod replied. "I don't know much about it. We had some customers in here until late that evening. My assistant manager called me up in the middle of the night and told me that someone had called him to tell him that Cosmic Comics was burning. Next day I came in early and walked over to take a look at it. Talked to Hank a little bit. That's it. Hank was in here the other day and said that the fire investigator thought that it was bad wiring. I asked him what he was going to do, and he told me next step was dealing with the insurance company. He had boxes and boxes of comics in the basement that he just bought that weren't covered. That's about all I know."

"I take it that you and Hank are on pretty good terms?" Skip remarked.

"Hank's a good guy," Rod replied. "His family has had a store there forever. He had a guy named Brian running it for him. Hank has his job at Sauer Danfoss. I think that he'll come out of it okay, but I don't think that he plans to rebuild."

"You two have a friendly competition, then?" Skip suggested.

"Yeah," Rod replied. "Not so much of a competition. I mean, I do sell some vintage stuff, but mostly I sell the new stuff. And he sold some of the new comics, but mostly vintage. We were always sending people back and forth. Then he had his records. I sell games. I sell more games than comics right now. Games are big."

"Sounds like you two got along," Skip said. Max had wandered away and was looking at comics, but staying in earshot.

"I think that Hank spent more time in my store than he did in his own," Rod said. "Brian was pretty much running the place and I think that suited Hank just fine. His heart was never in that store."

Skip thought for a moment. Max looked around to make sure there was no one that he had missed. "Just a point of clarification," Max asked across a couple of rows of comics. "You say that his heart wasn't in it; you think that he might not have been too heartbroken that the place burned to the ground?"

"I see where you are going with that question," Rod said seriously. "No, I don't think he was heartbroken. But I also don't think that he was that desperate. Hank has his job, he has a wife and kids. Cosmic Comics—the building, anyway—was in his family for generations. He had someone he trusted running the place. Hank was along for the ride. Brian talked him into going out to Vegas to buy a shitload of vintage comics and Brian was going to organize this big vintage comic event. Hank wasn't going to have to do anything, Brian had it covered. I was out in Vegas at the same time. Hank was all excited about it."

"So you saw all of these vintage comics that Hank bought?" Skip asked.

"I helped him go through them and pick out the ones we thought would sell," Rod replied. "We were on the phone with Brian for two days straight."

Max had wandered back to the counter. "Changing the subject," Max said. "It looks like the Welch Avenue Wizards have done a number on the back of your store."

Rod laughed. "That they have."

"What do you think of that?" Max asked.

"It is what it is," Rod replied. "The Wizards rule the roost. You live with 'em."

"What's that supposed to mean?" Skip asked.

"The Wizards showed up four or five years ago. Just a bunch of kids. They started right here. Most of them were my customers. But then they got territorial. If they didn't get the recognition that they thought they should, well, things happened, if you know what I mean."

"They are shaking you down?" Max asked.

"Well, not in the sense that they are taking money, but let's just say that if you are looking for help, you go to the Welch Avenue Wizards first and make sure that they don't have someone looking for a job, before you go hiring an outsider."

"Seriously?" Skip said.

"Seriously," Rod replied. "They sort of run the show out here."

"That go for Cosmic Comics, too?" Skip asked.

"Goes for everyone," Rod replied.

"Brian is one of these Wizards?" Skip exclaimed.

"No, but he's connected," Rod replied. "He's a little old for the Wizards, truth be told. Not to say there aren't Wizards his age, or older, but they've been Wizards. Brian isn't Wizard material, that's the easiest way to explain it."

"What's the connection that you mentioned?" Skip asked.

"Serenity Stephens," Rod said. "Serenity got him that job."

"You're saying, then, that you know Serenity is a Wizard? Because we heard that she might be, but no one has actually said so," Skip said.

"She is THE Wizard," Rod replied.

"You mean she is the president of the club, or whatever? The grand poobah?"

"She is," Rod said with a bit of a smile.

"Serenity Stephens, daughter of a developer out here, who works a taco stand for Slo-Mo at night, is calling the shots in Campustown?" Skip exclaimed.

Rod thought for a moment. "I wouldn't say that she calls the shots," Rod said reflectively. "It would be more accurate to say that she has a lot of influence on the kids out here. And those kids are our customers. So indirectly she has some weight when it comes right down to it, but it isn't like she is running Campustown."

"This Welch Avenue Wizards and Serenity Stephens, and this whole thing is just weird," Max said. "I mean, do people really take them serious? Are they serious? We talked to a cop friend of ours before we came out here and he wasn't taking them very serious."

Rod thought again before he answered. "They are not a criminal organization, they are a social group. If they didn't call themselves the Welch Avenue Wizards they might be taken more seriously. If they called themselves the Campustown Consumer's Coalition. I think that the name Welch Avenue Wizards is where outsiders get their first impression and they don't get taken seriously. They are kids. They like calling themselves the Welch Avenue Wizards better than Campustown Consumer's Coalition."

"They are leaning on you enough that you feel obligated to hire them to work for you, but they are just a social club?" Skip asked dubiously.

"I think that you are looking at this from a private detective perspective," Rod said. "From a business standpoint, they bring in business. They have influence with the students. Why would I not hire a Wizard?"

Max started to say something, but he noticed that Skip was glancing at him. Max decided to let it go.

Skip held out his hand to Rod, and Rod took it. "Thanks," Skip said, shaking hands. "You've been a lot of help. I think that we have a much better understanding of the dynamics out here, with the students and the businesses and all. If you hear about anything that might be helpful with our investigation, give us a call." He handed Rod a business card.

"No problem," said Rod, glancing at the card. "One thing," he said as the two detectives were getting ready to leave. "When you were talking about Serenity working at the taco stand, it made me think. I'm pretty sure that if you looked closely enough, you could find a connection between Barlow Hicks and the Wizards. He pretty much only has Wizards working for him, and in his case, I don't think that it is just to attract customers."

Skip paused. "Thanks," he said, then led the way out of the store.

Chapter 12

Wednesday

"Let's go up and see if Brian is working," Skip suggested.

Max just nodded his head.

The two walked the block and a half to Barlow Hicks's deli and looked through the locked glass door. There was no movement inside. Max knocked on the door with his knuckles. They could see a head peek around the corner of the counter and down the hall at them standing outside, but they couldn't make out who it was. Max knocked harder. Someone came out from a room and down the hall toward them. It was Barlow Hicks. He unlocked the door and let them in, locking it behind them.

"What's up?" he asked.

"Looking for Brian Parker," Skip said. "But you'll do."

Barlow gave the two detectives a resigned look and led them to the dining area of the restaurant. The three took seats at a table.

"What's up?" he asked again.

"Pamela Stephens, aka Serenity Stephens," Max said. "What do you know about her? And don't be giving us your employee-slash-employer confidentiality bullshit, you're not her lawyer. And I got her phone number, so you don't have to do your tap dance to protect her by not giving me that anymore."

"She works for me," Barlow replied. "She's been working for me for probably four years."

"And her dad is a developer, owns a third of Campustown?" Max said.

"He's bought up some property in Campustown," Barlow replied.

"How does he feel about his daughter working a taco stand out on Welch Avenue on the weekend? If he is such a high roller and all, why is it that his daughter is working for you?"

"They don't get along very well. I don't think that he's supporting her or paying for school, or anything like that," Barlow explained. "She's on her own."

"How about you, how is your business?" Skip asked. "You doing pretty good?"

"I'm doing good," Barlow replied.

"How you getting along with the store front businesses? You still fighting with them about parking your cart in front of their places? I heard that Hank Peterson and you had some words."

"I wouldn't call it 'having words.' He had some concerns. I addressed them and we have a mutual agreement, we respect each other's businesses," Barlow said. "Hank's concerns were about trash. I understand that and I have addressed it with my employees out there."

"Trash and puke and people pissing in his entry, you come to a mutual agreement on that, too?"

"There's only so much I can control," Barlow replied. "I don't think all that happens because I park my stand on the street there. Kids coming out of the bars are going to do that. It has nothing to do with me or my business. I explained that to Hank and he understands."

"So, what's with you and the Welch Avenue Wizards?" Max asked.

"I don't have anything to do with the Welch Avenue Wizards," said Barlow defensively.

"Word is that the Welch Avenue Wizards are pretty influential in Campustown and that you have the head wizard working for you. Word is that everyone you have working for you is a Wizard."

"Well, that's not true," Barlow replied.

"Not true that you only have Wizards working for you, or not true that you have the poobah working for you?" Max asked.

"Both," said Barlow.

"You saying that you didn't know that Serenity is the boss lady of the Wizards?" Max looked back and forth between Skip and Barlow. "What do you call her? The poobah, the president, the boss lady?" He paused for a moment. "The Grand Wizard?"

"Probably not the Grand Wizard," Skip remarked. The two looked back at Barlow.

"I was not aware that she is," Barlow said.

"You know who the Welch Avenue Wizards are?" Skip asked. "If you don't, you're the only businessman in Campustown who doesn't."

"They are a comic book club," Barlow replied. "For all I know she could be the president of the Spanish club, too. What does that have to do with anything?"

"We just heard that in Campustown, you don't hire someone to work for you that isn't part of the Welch Avenue Wizards. That's what everyone else is saying. I would think that someone like you would know a little more about it than you're pretending to," Skip said. "Everyone else is also saying that you have something to do with the Wizards. Some people say that there is a reason that Serenity works for you, and it isn't the high wages, the benefits and the matching contributions to her 401(k)."

"Okay," Barlow said quickly. "I do have some Wizards working for me. But other than that, I don't have anything else to do with them."

"You're a moving target, aren't you?" Max exclaimed. "Like to dodge around."

"Why are you guys busting my balls?" Barlow asked.

"Not trying to bust anyone's balls, I'm trying to investigate a suspicious fire, and one of your employees keeps popping up in the discussion. Just trying to eliminate her from the suspect list. Nothing more," Max replied. "I might ask the same thing. Why are you trying to bust our balls?"

"I'm not trying to do anything," Barlow exclaimed.

"Barlow," Skip said. "We go back a long ways. We're trying to have a two-way conversation here with you. You seem to be a little less than forthcoming. Why is that? I thought that we are friends. So, what's the deal with Serenity and the Wizards? If Serenity doesn't have anything to hide, why are you trying so hard to help her hide it?"

The three looked up when they heard someone at the door with a key. Moments later Brian came down the hall toward the dining area. He saw his boss and the two detectives sitting at the table. A look of resignation came over his face, as if he realized he was trapped in an uncomfortable situation. Barlow seemed to be relieved that Brian had shown up and interrupted the interrogation.

"Brian, have a seat," Max said, patting the chair next to him at the table.

Brian took the chair.

"We're talking about your girlfriend and the Welch Avenue Wizards. We were discussing her official title. What do they call her, the Prime Minister?" Max asked.

"I don't think that they call her anything," Brian replied.

"Are you denying that she is the leader of the pack?" Max asked.

Brian shrugged his shoulders. "I guess you could say that she is, but it isn't a club, it is just a bunch of college kids who are into the same things. They don't have meetings and vote for officers, or anything organized like that. They all look to Serenity, she's been in the group for a long time, nothing more to it. They are friends."

"Look to Serenity for what?" Skip asked.

Brian thought for a moment. He was aware of who he was talking to and he wanted to pick his words carefully.

"Speak up, Brian," Max said. "What do you have to think about?"

"Frankly," Brian said. "I'm trying to think about how I can explain it without you two twisting it around and making it sound bad."

Brian paused a moment longer.

"Serenity is a very smart person. She has her shit together. The rest of the Wizards recognize that and look to her for advice and leadership. She wasn't elected to the position, she comes by it naturally."

"So what's she doing with you?" Max asked. "And why is she working for Barlow here, if she's so smart and all?"

"Hey," Barlow spoke up. "I'm a legit businessman. I employ a lot of students. I don't deserve these insults. I think that you guys are getting a little out of line." He looked at both men. "You're right, we go back a long ways, and I never did anything to deserve being treated like this."

The two detectives didn't respond. Barlow waited.

"Fair enough," Skip finally said. "I apologize for my associate." He gave Max a glaring look. Max shrugged his shoulders and looked out the window.

"One question," Skip asked. "Did Serenity have anything to do with you hiring Brian the day after the business that he was working at burned down?"

Brian spoke up before Barlow could answer. "I'm not as financially well off as a lot of people around me," he said. "I need to make money to support my daughter and myself. I asked Serenity if she would talk to Barlow and see if he had a job for me. She did, and Barlow was kind enough to put me to work the next day. I appreciate that."

No one responded. "I gotta get to work," he said, standing up and making his way into the kitchen.

"Us too," Skip said, getting up from his chair. Max got up as well.

Skip turned to Barlow. "If you hear anything, let us know, us going back so far and all."

Barlow nodded as the two turned toward the door. Barlow got up and followed to unlock it for them. Customers were already waiting outside for the doors to open.

"Popular place," Max observed, going out the door.

"What do you think?" Skip asked when they had reached the sidewalk.

"I kind of feel bad beating up on Slo-Mo like that," Max reflected.

"But not Brian," Skip smirked.

"He deserves whatever he gets," Max said. "I'm surprised that they both pushed back like that. It doesn't seem to be in their characters."

"Let's take a look at what we got," Skip said as they walked toward the car. "Think about this: Serenity is the boss of the Welch Avenue Wizards. Mysteriously, the place where her boyfriend works burns down. Fortunately, said boyfriend gets a job the next day working for Serenity's boss at his deli. Is that coincidental?"

"Is it fortunate that Brian loses his comic book gig and gets a job slicing deli meats and making sandwiches?" Max asked. "Seems like a big step down to me."

"Is it?" Skip replied. "One would think that the Wizard honcho who controls who gets hired out here would have a better job than working the taco stand at bar closing. Maybe there is something about those jobs that we aren't aware of. Maybe there's more to it than slicing deli meats and filling up tortillas."

Max was thinking about what Skip had said when they got to the car. Skip walked around and got in the driver's side. Without unlocking the passenger door, Skip took out his phone, swiping the screen.

"What are you doing?" Max asked impatiently.

"I'm looking up Slo-Mo on the internet to see what all he has his mitts into," Skip said.

Max waited a bit longer. "You going to spend the whole morning doing that?" he asked.

Skip didn't answer.

"I'm going to walk back to Campus Plaza and take a look around while you're otherwise occupied," Max said. He turned and walked the half block to the drive that went off of Welch Avenue to the parking lot behind the businesses in the one-hundred block. It was quiet. There was no reason for students to be there at this time of the morning. He saw a couple of young men who looked like they were cutting through the lot on the way to class. Both were big kids. They looked like football players. He didn't give them any more thought. Max looked around at the graffiti on the walls. A lot of it looked well done. He had to admit that it was an art form. He looked across to the north, at the rear of Meteor Comics and Games. It was particularly well decorated. Max was thinking that Rod might be right about hiring Wizards if the rear of his building was any indication of the benefits. It looked like a comic store from that perspective.

Max walked to the back of the burned-out Cosmic Comics building and shook the lock. The hasp fell out of the door as it had when Hank had taken them through the building. He carefully put it back, pushing the screws into their holes with his thumb. He could tell that they were getting loose enough that eventually they would not hold the weight of the padlock. Max heard footsteps behind him and turned to see if Skip had come looking for him. His eyes momentarily took in a glimpse of a young man in a plaid jacket standing directly in front of him and another, in a navy blue jacket, standing to the side. Before Max could ask them what they needed, the kid in the plaid shirt lifted both of his hands up and slammed them into Max's chest, driving him backwards into the brick wall next to the door. At the same time as the wall abruptly halted Max's rearward motion, his internal organs continued on their course, colliding with his back, driving him deeper into the wall. Max felt like they were going to keep going through the wall and into the interior of the building. Instead, his internal organs came to an abrupt halt as well. Max's entire upper body felt hollow. He could not breathe. His head felt about to explode and his knees buckled. He could barely make out the difference between light and dark. He could sense the presence of the two kids, but he could not focus on them. His ears were ringing. He slumped to the ground and lay in a fetal position. He felt his body jar as he took a kick to the ribs, but he felt no pain connected to it. He gasped for breath. Through the haze he heard a voice shouting at him.

"Time to go home, old man," the voice said. "You got no business here."

Max was starting to make out the facial features of the person bent over him. He was unable to speak.

"Do you hear me?" the man asked, standing up. Max was unable to nod his head. He closed his eyes, expecting another kick. When he opened them again, the two were gone. He was able to breathe again. He moved slowly, rolling onto his stomach. He got his hands under himself and was able to pull himself up to a seated position and lean his torso against the wall. He looked around. He was alone. He sat quietly, trying to decide if he should try to stand up. Suddenly he heard Skip next to him. Skip had ahold of his arm, keeping him upright.

"Jesus Christ," Skip was saying to him. "What happened? Are you going to be okay? You need an ambulance? You having a heart attack?"

Max shook his head negatively in response to Skip's rapid-fire questioning.

Skip was kneeling beside him. Max looked over and saw the concern in his eyes. It was the first thing that he had been able to focus on. He took a couple of deep breaths and tried to talk. He was unable to say anything. He took another couple of breaths.

"I'll be okay," he croaked. "Someone bounced me."

Skip did not reply. Max was starting to get his senses back.

"Help me get up," Max said.

Skip helped him to his feet.

"Are you okay?" Skip asked as Max wobbled a bit and leaned against the wall.

"If they hadn't kicked me in the ribs," Max said a bit more clearly, "I would be fine."

"Who kicked you?" Skip asked, looking around the parking lot.

"Two college kids," Max said, standing up on his own. "One was wearing a red plaid jacket, like one of those old plaid shirt jacket things we used to wear back in the seventies. A CPO jacket. I think that he was wearing a PBR cap. Big kid, I mean big."

Max shook off Skip's hand on his arm and started twisting to see where it hurt.

"The fuckhead bounced me," he said, looking at Skip. "You know, moving body slams into immovable object, internal organs rattle around for a while, your life flashes before your eyes but you don't die. You just wish that you had."

"You got bounced?" Skip said.

"Didn't I just say that I got bounced?" Max asked.

"Where did the fuckers go?" Skip asked, looking around for anyone who even looked like they might have attacked his friend. "Someone's going to get hurt," he said.

"They're long gone," Max said, bending over and vomiting on the ground.

"You sure you are okay?" Skip asked. "I'm calling an ambulance."

Max stood up. "I feel better now that I puked," he said, putting his hand out and stopping Skip from getting on his phone. "I'm fine, just give me a minute."

Skip stood with Max for a minute or two while he recovered. "Let's go back and have another talk with Brian and Slo-Mo," Max said, walking back toward Welch with Skip at his side.

"You sure?" Skip asked. "I think that we should maybe go back to the agency."

"I'm actually fine," Max said.

"What happened?" Skip asked.

"I was just checking things out," Max explained, almost back to normal. "I was checking out the padlock on the back door of the comic store when these two big kids that I saw earlier cutting through the lot came up behind me. When I turned around, one of them bounced me off the wall. You know, like we used to do when someone got frisky, classic bounce. Where the fuck does a college kid learn to do that? Then he kicked me in the ribs and told me to 'go home old man, you don't have any business here.' Then they left. Then you showed up."

"This is serious," Skip said. "We need to report it. I'm going to call the PD."

Skip was pulling his phone out of his pocket again.

"I don't want to call the cops," Max said. "I'm fine. Please, let it go. Last thing I want is explaining to some cop how I got bounced."

Max stopped at the car and sat on the trunk for a minute.

"Are you sure you're okay?" Skip asked again.

"I'm fine," Max insisted.

"I'm back there looking around," Max said. "No doubt they were targeting me. So the question is, who planned it? Rod?"

"Or Slo-Mo, or Brian, or Brian and Slo-Mo," Skip said. "Those three knew that we were out here asking questions."

The two sat thinking for a while. "Or someone else could have seen us out here, who knows?" Skip said finally.

The two were silent while they pondered who might have targeted Max.

Chapter 13

Wednesday

Serenity was standing with her father in his newest building, looking through the glass that faced Lincolnway. Six stories, the whole ground floor storefronts, with offices on the second and third floors, apartments on the top three. Workers were scurrying around them setting up metal studs for walls.

"There's your two detectives," Carl said.

"What?" Serenity asked, her mind elsewhere when he said it.

"Right there, walking down the sidewalk," Carl said, pointing at two middle-aged men talking while they walked past the front of the business, oblivious to the man and the young woman standing on the other side of a pane of glass from them.

"You know them?" Serenity asked.

"I know of them," Carl said. "Used to be cops. Had a rep as bad-asses. They won the Powerball some years back and started a detective agency."

"Yeah, evidently Brian's ex works for them," Serenity told him. She walked to the window and watched the two detectives enter Meteor Comics and Games. "I wonder what they're up to?" she asked absently, as much to herself as to Carl, who stood behind her watching, too.

"When did you find that out?" Carl asked.

"He told me yesterday. He wants me to hang out with him this weekend. He has his girl. I put him off, like you said."

"Maybe I got second thoughts on that," Carl said. "How well does Brian get along with his ex? Maybe he can feed us some information on what these detectives are doing."

"She hates his guts," Serenity said. "I've only talked to her once, and he doesn't talk about her. Hell, I didn't even know where she worked until yesterday. Her husband is usually the one who hands the kid off. He seems easier to get along with. She's a bitch."

"It just seems that this whole thing is getting crowded," Carl remarked. "Brian, his ex, the cop husband, two private detectives. What the hell? They're all connected? How the hell did that happen?"

Serenity didn't answer.

"Who hired them?" Carl asked.

"The insurance company," Serenity answered.

"I thought that the insurance company signed off on the fire investigator's report," Carl exclaimed.

"I don't know," Serenity answered absently, still looking at the door of the Meteor Comics store.

"Well, we need to either feed them something to convince them to close their case and tell their client to accept the fire investigator's report, or somehow get them to lose interest in the investigation until I can buy that property and tear it down."

"Which one?" Serenity asked.

"I'll let you decide that," Carl said, and turned away. "As long as the latter is part of the solution."

Carl purposely walked away, leaving Serenity to do what needed to be done without his involvement.

Serenity pulled out her phone and dialed a number. The phone rang three times and a voice answered.

"Xavier," Serenity said. "Where are you at?"

"The cafeteria at the dorms," he answered.

"You have Paul with you?"

"Yep," Xavier answered.

"Can you get over here to Campustown? I need you to get an eyeball on two guys, middle age, both wearing blue jeans. Both about six foot, one of them is wearing an ISU baseball cap. The other one has a full head of grey hair. The guy with the hat has on a light grey fleece. I can't remember the other one. You got that?"

"Yep," replied Xavier. "We're walkin' now."

"Okay, they went into Meteor just a few minutes ago. I don't know what they are doing, but whatever it is, we wish that they would quit. I want you guys to get one of them alone and shake him up a little. Nothing serious, I don't want to make a big scene. Just shake him up and let him know that snooping around Campustown is not healthy. Can you do that?"

"Yep," Xavier replied.

"Listen, low key, okay?"

"I hear ya," Xavier answered.

"When you're done, don't call me back. I don't need to know the particulars, just do it."

"You got it," Xavier answered.

Serenity ended the call and remained at the window.

Xavier and Paul made their way through the Friley dorms and onto Lincolnway across the street from Meteor Comics and Games. Xavier spotted Max and Skip coming out of the store.

"That's gotta be them," Xavier said. "Hang back."

The two followed the detectives on the opposite side of Welch as they made their way toward Barlow's Deli. They watched while the detectives knocked on the door and peered through the glass.

"Let's just go over and fuck 'em up," Paul suggested. "No one around."

"Let's go," Xavier said, starting across the street.

As they got to the sidewalk, the door of the deli opened and the two detectives went inside. Xavier pulled up. Paul waited a minute, then walked up to the door and tried it. It was locked. He went back to where Xavier was standing.

"Serenity said to get one of them alone and shake him up," Xavier said. "She didn't say kick the shit out of them both."

Paul shrugged his shoulders. The two walked back across the street and found a table to sit on outside where they could see the door to the deli.

Xavier was a big boy. He had been a star linebacker in high school and his ambition had always been to be an ISU Cyclone football player. In his senior year he got scholarship offers from a couple of small Iowa colleges, but Xavier held out for the brass ring, an ISU scholarship. When it didn't come, he enrolled at ISU anyway. He tried out as a walk-on but didn't make the cut. He was determined to try again the next year. But before he got another opportunity for the football team, Xavier met a third-year sophomore in one of his Phys Ed classes who had been a manager on the track team. He recognized Xavier, not from football, but from high school track, where they had competed against each other in shot put and discus. Paul talked Xavier into trying out for the track team, and that spring Xavier found himself one of three discus throwers on the ISU Cyclones track team.

In the late summer of Xavier's sophomore year he tried out again for the football team, and for the second time he did not make the cut. Discouraged, Xavier's grades fell too low to maintain his track scholarship and he was replaced by the forth-string discus thrower. That fall he met Serenity. He thought that she was beautiful and exotic. Serenity was full of fire, hot to the touch. Xavier fell in love; Serenity did not, at least with him. But she teased him with it nonetheless, and if that was all Xavier could have, he would take it. Xavier loved Serenity.

When Xavier lost his scholarship, his parents tried to take up the slack. It was hard for them, but they did the best that they could. His father co-signed a college tuition loan for him, then another. But it wasn't enough money. It barely covered his tuition, room, board and books. Xavier needed a job, and Serenity came through for him. She got him on at Buddies, a popular Campustown bar on Welch Avenue. Xavier worked every Thursday, Friday and Saturday night, eight in the evening until two thirty in the morning. He checked IDs at the door, broke up fights and kicked rowdies out of the bar if need be. His mentor was an on-again-off-again senior who had much the same background as Xavier. The money was good. Xavier did his job, and no one got past him without an ID. That was what they taught him the first week on the job: he didn't have to be good at reading IDs, he just had to read them. Being stupid was not against the law. He could let as many underage drinkers into the bar as lined up outside the door, as long as they had an ID that said they were old enough, and Xavier hustled them through the door, down the stairs and bellied-up to the bar as quickly as he could. If the cops were going to pull a sting on them, he knew they would send in a pretty girl with no ID. No pretty girl without an ID ever got in when Xavier was at the door. Easy money.

Xavier watched the door of the deli open and the two men come out. The guy that opened the door pulled it shut behind them. There were already customers waiting to get in.

"Let's go," Paul said.

"Too many people," Xavier said. "And I told you that Serenity wants us to get them separated."

"Suppose they stay together?" Paul asked.

"I don't know," Xavier shrugged his shoulders. "I'm just doing what I'm told. Let's wait. She said to get one of them alone."

The two followed Max and Skip back the way they had come on Welch Avenue, this time on the same side of the street as the two detectives. The detectives stopped at a car. The one with the baseball cap waited while the other one got in the car and concentrated on his phone.

Xavier stopped at the corner of Welch and Chamberlain and acted like he was using the ATM there, just twenty yards from the two detectives.

"We're missing our chance," Paul remarked to him.

Xavier didn't respond. Suddenly the one standing at the passenger door walked away, leaving the other to do whatever it was he was doing on his phone. Xavier and Paul watched him take the alleyway that led to Campus Plaza.

"This way," Xavier said, pulling Paul with him down Chamberlain. "We'll go in off of Hayward."

The two hustled around the corner and came into Campus Plaza from the opposite side that Max had taken. They spotted him standing behind the Cosmic Comics building, looking around the plaza.

"Just act normal," Xavier said as they walked toward Max, who had turned and began doing something with the door.

Xavier picked up the pace, Paul at his heels. Max turned just as Xavier reached him. Xavier grabbed a handful of shirt and jacket, pulled Max forward to jerk him off balance, then slammed him backward into the brick wall with all his might. It was a move that Xavier had learned as a bouncer. In fact, it was called "the bounce." It was how bouncers took the fight out of unruly patrons. It was guaranteed to disorient the person being bounced. It was painful to an extreme, but seldom even left a mark. Cops never followed up a good bouncing, like they did a beating. It was a standing upright body slam, and Xavier had practiced it many times in the confines of the entrance to the bar where he sat checking IDs every night.

Xavier let loose of his fistful of clothing and let Max slump to the ground. As he did so, Paul stepped up and delivered a kick to Max's ribs. The move surprised Xavier, and he pushed Paul back before he could kick Max again. He glared at Paul, then leaned down, his face a mere foot from Max's.

"Time to go home old man, you got no business here," he said in the ominous voice that he used to persuade patrons who just got bounced to drag themselves outside and go home.

Xavier grabbed Paul and propelled him back in the direction they had come. He wanted to be out of sight by the time Max got his bearings. The trees that separated the parking lot on the other side of Hayward from the creek that ran along it was a perfect place to disappear. They would get into the tunnels that the creek ran through and make their way under Lincolnway and back to Friley Hall unseen.

"What the fuck? Why did you kick him?" Xavier asked Paul as he hustled him along.

"Give him a little added motivation," Paul said bitterly.

"You might have broken a rib or something," Xavier said. "Serenity said to shake him up, not bust him up."

"Fuck him," Paul said. "I hate that fucker."

Xavier just shook his head and guided Paul along the creek and into the tunnels. The water was just a trickle, and it was easy to straddle the flow as they worked their way under the street and back into the sunlight. When they got to the dorms they jumped out of the concrete channel that directed the creek to Lake LaVerne and ducked into the building. Paul got out his phone.

"Who you calling?" Xavier asked.

"Serenity," Paul answered.

"Serenity said not to call her, she doesn't want to know."

"Hey, Serenity," Paul said into his phone, ignoring Xavier. "We kicked the shit out of one of those guys for you."

Xavier was doing everything but jump up and down. Serenity had clearly said not to call, and now Paul was on the phone with her. Xavier was trying to think, but his mind was blank.

"Okay," Paul said. "Sorry, I didn't know that you didn't want us to let you know what we did. But I kicked him hard, might have broken a rib or something. He won't be coming back to Welch Avenue for a while."

"Put the fucking phone away," Xavier whispered in Paul's ear.

"Yeah, sure," Paul said, then ended the call.

"We're supposed to split up now," Paul said to Xavier.

"Fuck you," Xavier shouted back at Paul in frustration.

Chapter 14

Wednesday

"Do you think you could identify the guys that kicked your ass?" Skip asked Max, who seemed quite satisfied to sit on the trunk of Skip's car and recover.

"Fuck, I don't know," Max said. "Two big college kids."

"You sound like you're feeling a little better," Skip remarked.

"I'm fine," Max said, pulling up his shirt and poking his bruised ribs. "Nothing broke, at least I don't think so."

"You sure that you don't want to get an x-ray or see a doctor instead of poking yourself in the side and saying 'I'm fine'?"

Max slid off the trunk of the car and stood up straight. He groaned in pain as he turned his torso. "See, standing tall." He took a deep breath and let it out.

"Are you sure that you're okay?" Skip asked.

"I just got stiff sitting here for so long," Max answered. "I'm better, moving around."

"Do you think Slo-Mo and Brian really had something to do with you getting an ass kicking?" Skip asked.

"I didn't get my ass kicked," Max replied.

"Looks like you did to me," Skip observed.

"I got sucker punched," Max defended himself. "I didn't see it coming. I let my guard down; it won't happen again."

"What do you think?" Skip asked him again. "You want to go back up there and talk to them?"

Max looked at his Fitbit. "It probably wouldn't hurt me to walk a little," he said. "We need to get in some steps. I think a walk might loosen me up."

"You got any change to stick in the meter?" Skip asked.

Max dug in his pocket and came up with two quarters, which he put in the meter. The two walked to Lincolnway and stood looking across the street toward the ISU campus.

"What about the guy at Meteor?" Skip asked. "He's the first one we had contact with before the ass kicking event. He had plenty of time to set us up while we were talking to Hicks and Brian."

Max shrugged his shoulders. "What for? What's his motivation?"

"Who knows?" Skip replied. "Let's give him another visit and see how he acts."

The two detectives turned and walked west on Lincolnway toward Meteor Comics. Through the door they could see Rod standing behind the counter where he had been when they had left. Skip pulled open the door and held it for Max. As Max walked into the store, he kept a close eye on Rod to observe his reaction.

"Twice in one day," Rod said jovially, looking up from the counter where he was reading a comic. There were three customers looking at board games at the far end of the store. Rod looked that direction as well, then back at the two detectives.

"So, anything interesting happen since we last talked?" Max asked.

Rod gave him a confused look. "Nothing much," he replied. "I sold a couple of comics to some kids coming back from class."

"What did they look like?" Max asked.

"Like college kids," Rod replied.

"Two big guys, one in a red plaid jacket and the other one wearing a blue one?"

"No," said Rod. "Are you looking for someone in particular?"

"We just had a little run-in with some guys matching that description earlier, and we're looking for them to continue the conversation," Skip said.

Rod still looked confused. "I could call you if anyone comes around matching that description," he said. "I have your card and your phone number."

"We would appreciate that," Skip replied, then turned to leave. Max stared Rod in the face for a moment, then followed Skip out the door.

"Didn't seem suspicious," Max said as he caught up to Skip.

"I didn't think so either," Skip replied.

The two continued west, then turned south at Hayward.

"Brian, he's got his dream job working in a comic book store. I don't see where he profited in any way from the fire. There is no motive for him that I can see." Skip paused for effect. "Hank, on the surface it appears, had a lot to lose in the fire. Rod confirmed that he had a sizable investment in the basement, and it sure sounds like he and Hank are pretty chummy."

"And I don't picture Hank burning down the family business," remarked Max. "There's no profit in burning it down. He could have walked away from it as easily as he walked into it. He only owned a share, not the whole thing. Doesn't sound like he was in bad enough shape that he had to go to his siblings to get them to pony up. He was getting by."

"What about Slo-Mo? He's always fighting with the businesses out here," Max asked. "Did he take it to the next level?"

Skip thought for a moment. "Slo-Mo has been parking his food carts on Welch Avenue longer than most of the businesses that are there. Why start burning down businesses that piss about him now? I mean, he has his own storefront business on Welch, now. He's probably in the Welch Avenue Business Betterment Association, or whatever you call it. Besides, I can't visualize Slo-Mo burning down businesses. You know Slo-Mo, it isn't in his nature."

"He does have the Queen of the Wizards working for him," Max countered. "And she runs Campustown. Maybe there is a connection. Maybe he's not who we always thought he was. Maybe he's changed."

"You're going on what Rod says," Skip came back. "Maybe Rod's prone to exaggeration. Everyone else says that the Wizards are just a bunch of kids who read comic books and work out here. They're friends. Think about it: doesn't that make more sense than a gang of college-age comic book character impersonators in Ames, Iowa shaking down businesses and burning them to the ground if they don't pay up? I mean, that's where this is going if we go down that road."

Max shrugged his shoulders. "Faulty wiring?" he suggested.

"I say that we milk this case for a couple of more days, but honestly, at this point that's the direction I'm leaning," Skip answered. "Except for what happened to you, I don't know what to think about that," Skip said as an afterthought.

The two had circled the block and reached the corner of Welch and Chamberlain. Max glanced over at Barlow's Deli close by.

"Let's go in and get lunch," Skip suggested. "See how Brian acts when he sees you come through the door."

"Sure," Max replied. "Maybe Hicks is still there, too. See what they both do."

Skip trotted across the intersection kitty-corner, to the other side of the street. Max tried to keep pace, but the impact of his feet on the pavement caused his ribs to hurt. Instead, he held up his hands to the traffic and followed Skip's path to where Skip waited for him.

"Still hurting?" Skip asked.

"Only when I run," Max replied. "And breathe," he added.

The two detectives reached the door of the deli and entered. There was a line of a half-dozen students in front of them waiting to put in their orders. Brian was at the counter. The line moved fast.

"What do you need?" Brian asked Max as he became next in line. His face showed his disappointment that he had to interact with the two again. He looked past Max at Skip.

"I'll take a regular turkey on an onion bun, chips and a Coke. You got any rum for the Coke?"

Brian was writing the order on a pad. He ignored Max's question about the rum, handing him a paper cup and pointing to the soft drink dispenser.

"Skip will pay." Max looked around. "Barlow still here?"

Barlow looked through the window connecting the counter to the kitchen at the mention of his name. He was cooking. He gave Max a half-hearted wave and went back to work.

"Boss is in the kitchen and you're out here at the counter taking orders?" Max asked.

Brian shrugged his shoulders. "What do you need?" He turned his attention to Skip.

"Same," Skip replied. "No rum for me." He placed a twenty-dollar bill on the counter.

Brian wrote the order on the pad, handed Skip his change and a paper cup and hung the order in the window. Barlow pulled it down and went to work filling it.

"Next," Brian said, dismissing Skip.

Skip got his drink from the fountain and went to the table that Max had found in the crowded dining area of the deli. A few minutes later Barlow came out of the kitchen with two trays and placed them on the table.

"What's the deal?" Max asked him.

"Cook's coming in late," Barlow said.

"Big kid?" Max asked. "Wearing a plaid jacket and blue jeans?"

Barlow looked like he was trying to process Max's remark. "No, a skinny kid, not that tall, curly hair and I don't know what he's wearing, because he isn't here yet."

"Pretty good description," Max observed.

"Just trying to be more forthcoming with your questioning," Barlow said sarcastically.

"Max just got his ass kicked," Skip said.

"Where?" Barlow exclaimed, genuinely concerned. "You get hurt?"

"Not bad enough that I couldn't come here for lunch," Max replied.

"Who kicked your ass?" Barlow asked.

"Some college kid blindsided him in Campus Plaza," Skip said. "Got any ideas why someone would do something like that?"

While Skip was talking, Max was thinking that either Barlow was genuinely surprised or he was a good actor.

"In broad daylight on Welch Avenue," Barlow said. "I never heard of such a thing." Barlow took a seat at the table. People had taken notice of him during his exchange with Max and Skip, but he was not paying any attention to them.

"Did you call the cops?" he asked. "I mean, this needs to be reported. Stuff like this just doesn't happen on Welch Avenue."

"Come on," Max said. "Happens all the time. Kids get in fights out here. I've seen them get in fights in line at the Taco Machine."

"Those are drunks," Barlow answered. "They don't just beat people up, they argue and push each other around. This is serious."

"I'm okay," Max said. "You can calm down a little bit. You got the whole place watching us."

Barlow looked around and saw that Max was right. He lowered his voice. "I'm not kidding, you need to report it."

"We come out here this morning asking questions about a comic book store burning down, and all of a sudden someone comes up and assaults Max," Skip said in a tone to match Barlow's. "Do you think that is a coincidence?"

"I don't know," Barlow replied. "Doesn't seem so, but why would someone beat someone up for no reason like that?"

"Maybe there is a reason," Skip replied. "Maybe there is something someone is hiding that they don't want to be found."

Barlow thought for a moment. "I know that you guys are bound and determined to give whoever you are working for their money's worth, but Cosmic Comics is not the first old falling-down dump to burn out here because of faulty wiring. I mean, my thoughts on the whole thing are that you are wasting your time and someone else's money, but what the hell, everybody has to make a living. Who cares if you guys are out here playing detective? It certainly doesn't bother me, except that you keep asking me questions when I have other things to do. It is mildly annoying."

Skip sighed. "Okay, I don't know why some kids kicked Max's ass in Campus Plaza in broad daylight either, and I worked out here for years." He shrugged his shoulders. "I'm pretty familiar with what goes on out here on Welch, and I agree with you."

Barlow got up from the chair. "I'm sorry that you got hurt," he said to Max. "I really think that you need to report it. Hey, lunch is on me."

"We already paid," Skip replied.

Barlow took a moment. "Next time it's on me," he said, then went back to the kitchen.

"What do you think?" Skip asked Max as soon as Barlow was out of earshot.

"Neither of them seemed surprised to see me walking around. I thought that Hicks seemed genuine when he was acting all worried about me. I don't know. He seems more upset that it happened on Welch Avenue than anything."

"Brian didn't seem too happy to see you," Skip said.

"Exactly," Max replied. "If I had someone's ass kicked, I wouldn't be looking so disappointed at seeing them. I'd be giving them a big smirk and thinking, 'how was the ass kicking, asshole?' At least check them out to see how much damage was done."

"You're right," Skip added. "Neither one of them looked surprised to see you walking around a half hour after getting an ass kicking."

"I didn't really get my ass kicked," Max said again.

"You just said that if you were Brian you would be thinking, 'how was the ass kicking, asshole?'"

"Just drop it," Max said, irritated.

"None of them seemed at all suspicious," Skip went on. "Either they are really good actors, or it was someone else that set you up. We need to figure it out. Who the hell could it be?"

"Serenity?" Max replied.

"Do you think that one of these guys let her know that we were out here asking questions?" Skip asked.

"Could be anyone," Max replied. "Who knows? Evidently Serenity controls Welch Avenue, anyone could have tipped her off. Maybe she's got eyes and ears everywhere out here."

"How do we prove that?" Skip said thoughtfully.

"Can't," Max said. "Unless we get our hands on that big college kid in the plaid jacket, maybe we could get something out of him, but we don't have our hands on him."

"You said that you probably couldn't recognize him anyway," Skip said absently. He was thinking about all the angles that were growing out of the investigation and wondering where they were connected.

Chapter 15

Wednesday

Serenity remained at the window after her call to Xavier. She watched the front door to Meteor Comics, hoping to get a better look at the two detectives when they left. She didn't have to wait long. Serenity thought it interesting that the two were so involved in their conversation that they walked past her again, this time just four feet and a pane of glass separating them. They did not even look in her direction.

"They're old and they've gotten sloppy," Serenity thought as they walked by.

She watched them until they were out of sight and then walked away from the window. Carl was talking to some guys in suits, probably potential renters for some of the space. She did not acknowledge him, nor did he acknowledge her. She picked up a backpack from the floor and went out the door to Lincolnway. She walked the short distance to Meteor Comics and Games and went inside. Rod was standing behind the counter.

"What's with the old guys?" she asked as she walked up to the counter.

"Private detectives," Rod replied.

"What did they want?" she asked casually.

"They're investigating the Cosmic Comics fire," he said. "I think that they came in here just to see what the deal was with me and Hank. I think that at first they thought there might be some competitive animosity between us. We cleared that up."

"They ask about anyone?"

"Talked a little about Hank and Brian, that's it," Rod replied.

"Nothing else?" she asked.

"Nope," Rod hesitated. Serenity was looking at him, waiting.

"They asked me about the Wizards," Rod said.

"What about the Wizards?" Serenity asked.

"Just wanted to know who you were, what the deal was."

"Who's 'you'?" Serenity asked. "'You,' being me, or 'you' being the Wizards?"

"Both," Rod said hesitantly.

"So, what did you tell them about me?" she asked.

"Nothing," Rod replied. "I just told them that your name comes up in connection with the Wizards because you've been with them a long time."

"That's all you told them?"

"Yep, told them that the other Wizards look up to you." Rod was trying to say something complimentary.

Serenity did not reply. Rod was shifting nervously.

"Let me know if they come back in here again," Serenity said.

She turned away from Rod and walked to the back of the store, where several college age kids were going through the games that were shelved for sale there. She knew them, and they struck up a conversation. They wanted to know what she thought of the latest board games that Rod had gotten in. Serenity had played some of them. The talk was casual. She shared her opinions, listened to theirs.

The conversation went on for quite a while. Serenity wondered how they could talk about board games to such extent, but she stayed in the conversation, anyway. Two of the kids remarked that they were going to be late for class, but continued to talk. Serenity pulled her phone out of her backpack to check the time. Serenity was never late for class. Out of the corner of her eye, she glimpsed a moment of movement that she recognized through the glass in the rear door of Meteor Comics and Games. It was one of the detectives that her father had pointed out earlier. She moved closer to the door and watched him standing by himself, looking around Campus Plaza. There was no one else around. She wondered where Xavier was. It was a perfect opportunity. Her phone was in her hand. She was about to swipe the screen to call when she let her hand drop to her side. Maybe Xavier had the other one cornered somewhere. She watched the detective turn to inspect something in the charred door of Cosmic Comics. When he did, Xavier and Paul came into view. Serenity's heartbeat quickened.

Serenity watched Xavier come up behind the detective quickly. She was surprised how fast and light he was on his feet for such a big man. The detective turned just as Xavier got to him. She watched Xavier plant his feet, grab the detective and ever so quickly pull him forward, then launch him back into the brick wall. Serenity felt a wave of sexual excitement go through her body. She saw the detective's knees buckle under him and saw that for just a moment, Xavier was holding him up by the clothing gathered in his huge fist. Xavier let him go, and the man sunk to the ground. It was then that Paul stepped forward and put a boot into the detective's ribs. It was a cheap shot, and another wave of excitement swept over her. Xavier bent down and said something, then stood up and retreated toward Hayward Avenue as quickly as he had arrived. In moments, Xavier and Paul disappeared. The detective still lay on the ground. From where Serenity watched, she could tell that he was still disoriented. She watched in fascination, her breath coming fast. Within a few minutes the other detective came from the direction of Welch Avenue. He helped the detective to sit up. He kneeled on the ground to hold him steady. They were talking. The second detective was scanning the parking lot. He stood up once and started to walk toward Hayward, but turned and got back down to help the first detective to stand up. As soon as he got to his feet, he turned away and vomited. He was unsteady. Finally, the other detective took him by the arm and helped him walk toward Welch Avenue and out of Serenity's sight.

The whole time that the assault took place, the others had continued talking about board games, totally oblivious to what was going on outside. Serenity looked at the phone in her hand. She needed to get to class. Her mood was euphoric as she went past Rod without acknowledging him, and out the door toward campus. She was halfway to class when her phone rang. Serenity swiped the screen and brought the phone up to her face without slowing her pace.

"Go," Serenity said into the phone.

"Hey, Serenity," the voice that she recognized as Paul's said. "We kicked the shit out of one of those guys for you."

"Paul, I told Xavier not to call me," she responded.

"Okay," Paul said. "Sorry, I didn't know that you didn't want us to let you know what we did. But I kicked him hard, might have broken a rib or something. He won't be coming back to Welch Avenue for a while."

Serenity did not answer.

"Put the fucking phone away," Serenity heard Xavier whisper in the background.

"You two split up," Serenity said. "Go home, change clothes and stay away from each other. Lay low. Do you think that you can follow those instructions, or do I have to repeat them for you?"

"Yeah, sure," Paul said, then abruptly ended the call.

Serenity quickened her pace. She wanted to put as much distance between herself and the Campustown area as she could. She wanted to put more distance between her and Xavier and Paul. She needed to be somewhere else.

Serenity sat through class, her mind divided between the two detectives and their investigation and her calculus professor lecturing the class. It was a big class. Serenity was prone to let her mind wander during class. She knew it. She also knew that she did not want to be another college dropout working some college dropout job, so she concentrated on concentrating. Her phone was buzzing in her backpack, taking even more of her attention away from the professor who was totally absorbed in himself. Not so with the student at the desk next to hers. He kept glancing down at her backpack until it quit ringing. Moments later it made a multi-tone signal to let Serenity know that someone had left a message. She gave the guy next to her an annoyed look to match his and then tried to focus on the lecture. She was anxious to get out of class and see who was trying to call her. Usually she wouldn't care, but the circumstances of the last couple of days were overriding her usual fuck-you attitude.

As soon as class was dismissed, Serenity pulled the phone out of her backpack. They guy seated at the desk was loitering, glancing over at her as she was swiping the face of the phone.

"What the fuck do you want?" she asked him.

"Nothing," he said, getting up from the desk and gathering his books, still casting looks at Serenity and her phone.

Serenity looked up at him. "What's the problem?" she asked.

"My name is Frank," he answered.

"Okay."

"Do you understand all of that?" He pointed toward the board that the professor was erasing.

"I think so," Serenity replied.

"I was wondering if you have some time, we could go to the Union and get something to eat? Maybe you can explain some of it to me; I'm not sure I got it all."

Serenity looked at her phone. The call was from Rod. She wanted to call him back, but she also wanted to get to know Frank a little better. He looked like a puppy wanting a pat on the head. Serenity liked that. She wished that they would stay like that. It wouldn't be long before Frank would want a belly rub. Serenity sighed. "Give me a minute to call this guy back, then I'll go to the Union."

"Sure," said Frank, not moving.

"Private call," Serenity said.

Frank walked out of the classroom. The professor had already left, and Serenity was alone. She pushed the callback.

"Hello, Meteor Comics and Games," Rod's voice answered.

"What do you need?" Serenity asked.

"Hey," Rod said. "Listen, those two detectives came back in asking about two guys, one in a plaid jacket, the other in a blue jacket. They want to have a talk with them."

"Why do you think that I would be interested?" Serenity said, trying to hide the interest in her voice.

"You said to call if they came back in. One of the guys that they were describing sounds a lot like that big red-haired guy that you have with you sometimes."

"Thor," Serenity said.

"Is that his name?" Rod asked.

"Yeah, Thor," Serenity said. "Like the comic book character. Norse god. What of it?"

"I just thought that you wanted to know," Rod said, a little disappointed by Serenity's lack of interest.

"That's good, you keep letting me know," Serenity said, ending the call.

She walked out of the classroom and found Frank waiting for her in the hall. The two walked toward the elevator. "What are you majoring in?" Serenity asked.

"Mathematics," Frank replied. "What about you?"

"Mathematics, too!" Serenity exclaimed.

"I'm surprised that we haven't met before in class," Frank said, obviously excited that the two had something in common.

"Me, too," Serenity said. "What a coincidence."

"What's your name?" Frank asked.

"You can call me Serenity. What's your last name, Frank?" Serenity said teasingly. "I want to get to know you real well."

Frank gave her a confused look. "Harms," he said.

"Frank Harms," Serenity rolled it around. "I'm going to show you a secret to remember those formulas that Harris put on the board, Frank Harms, and then you'll have to show me something, and maybe it will hurt a little. But I'll like it."

Frank looked a little nervous. "Okay," he said. He wasn't sure what she was saying. It was not so much what she was saying, but how she was saying it that made him nervous. He thought that she was about the sexiest woman he had ever met.

Chapter 16

Wednesday

Max and Skip got back to Skip's car. The meter had expired and there was a parking ticket under his wiper.

"Damn it," Skip said, exasperated, looking in every direction for the parking meter attendant who had issued the ticket. He looked at the ticket and then pulled his phone out of his pocket, checking the time. "Missed 'em by five minutes," he said in the same exasperated voice.

"Damn it, damn it, damn it." Skip was actually stomping his feet.

"How much is it?" Max asked.

"Ten bucks," Skip answered.

"So just pay it. What's the big deal?"

"It's a hassle," Skip said. "They don't even have those boxes that you stick the money in anymore. You gotta go downtown to pay it."

"You can pay it online now," Max said. "It's the twenty-first century."

Skip just looked at Max.

"Make Monica pay it online," Max responded to the look. "Christ, man, why are you so stressed over this?"

Skip took a deep breath. "Because my friend just got his ass kicked, and there's nothing I can do about it. Because he doesn't even know what the guy who kicked his ass looks like. Because I was sitting out here playing with my phone while it happened."

Max chuckled. "That's sweet," he said. "I didn't know you cared."

Skip didn't reply.

"I didn't get my ass kicked," Max said.

Skip got into the car and unlocked the door for Max. Max had his shirt pulled up and was looking at the bruise on his side again.

"Get in," Skip shouted through the closed window.

Max put his shirt down and opened the door.

"What now?" Skip asked as Max got in and buckled his seat belt, grimacing in pain when he twisted his body to get through the door.

"I think that I just want to go home," Max replied.

"You okay?" Skip asked.

"Quit asking me if I'm okay," Max said. "You know, if that guy had just bounced me, I would be fine. It was the kick that is killing me right now. Why the kick?"

Skip pulled out of the parking spot and onto Welch Avenue. "What are you trying to say?"

"Just saying that you bounce someone so that you don't leave any marks. I mean, getting bounced is worse than getting punched, pain wise that is, but you recover after about ten minutes and you're fine. By the time anyone gets there to make a report, you're up walking around like nothing happened. Cops show up and you say, 'hey, I didn't do anything to him.' But get a kick in the ribs like that, that don't go away. I got a bruise the size of a football. Why would he bounce me, then kick me? That just seems counterintuitive."

Skip was thinking about it. "Good point. Who bounces people? Bouncers and cops. I suppose we can eliminate cops, so it's someone who's working or has worked in a bar."

"Considering the size of the guy, I would say that would be a pretty accurate assumption to follow up on."

"That is a whole lot of people," Skip continued. "And you don't even know what he looked like."

"I'm thinking about that, and I'm thinking that maybe I'm starting to remember a little better. I might recognize him if I saw him, maybe."

"You really remembering, or are you starting to make something up to fill the void? You know that happens," Skip remarked.

"I know all about that," Max replied. "I'm getting a clearer picture in my mind. I think that I'm getting there."

"You want to go out and walk bars tomorrow night, see if we can spot him?" Skip asked. "It's a long shot, but I'm up for it if you want."

"Maybe," Max replied thoughtfully. "I just think that if we can find him, we might be able to persuade him to tell us why he felt obliged to bounce me off a wall and then kick me while I'm down."

"Oh, I'm quite sure that I could persuade him to tell us why," Skip responded.

"That would certainly be a big break in the case," Max said.

Skip pulled into the parking lot at the G&B Detective Agency and parked next to Max's car. Monica's car was parked in her reserved spot in front of the agency.

"You know something," Max said. "I was just about ready to chalk this one up and tell Ben that there was nothing to investigate, that faulty wiring or not, there's no evidence that the fire was purposely set, and then this happened. Something isn't right with that."

"I'm with you a hundred percent," Skip agreed.

Max got out of the car.

"You going in?" Skip asked.

"I'm going home," Max replied. "I'll see you in the morning, bright and early."

"You sure?" Skip asked. "Don't come in if you're feeling bad."

"I'll be here. I don't want you guys getting in steps without me." Max went around the front of his car and got in. Skip got out of his own and went into the agency. Monica came up the hallway from the back just as he came in.

"What's up?" she asked, taking a seat at her desk.

"What's up with you?" Skip asked.

"Essie," Monica replied. "One of the kids at the daycare has pinkeye. I just went over and got her. I don't know why, the pinkeye kid went home. But they had all the kids outside while they cleaned the place down, and I just went and got her. She's in the back."

"So now we all get pinkeye?" Skip said accusingly, taking a seat in the chair opposite Monica's desk.

"I didn't think about that," Monica said in a concerned voice.

"Just kidding," Skip laughed. "I raised two of my own. Been through pinkeye, head lice, colds, Marjorie got chicken pox, we've been through it all."

Monica looked relieved that Skip wasn't worried. She had not thought about everyone in the agency being exposed. "I don't think that I've had chicken pox," she said.

"Hope you have a good sick leave package," Skip said seriously. "Because you're gonna be out a week with it."

Monica looked a little worried.

"You get them in your mouth," Skip goaded her.

"What?" Monica asked.

"The pox," Skip replied.

"That's gross," Monica groaned.

"Actually, I think there's a vaccine now. Get the shot," Skip said. "Max got his ass kicked today."

"What? How did that happen?" Monica exclaimed.

"I was sitting in the car checking out Slo-Mo on the internet, and Max went back into Campus Plaza to look around. Some big college kid blindsided him. Bounced him, then kicked him in the ribs."

"Is he okay?" Monica asked.

"I think so," Skip said. "But he got roughed up. He's feeling it."

"Where's he now?"

"He went home to rest," Skip replied.

"Did he go to the ER?" Monica asked, concerned.

"Wouldn't go," Skip answered. "I think that he was embarrassed that he let it happen."

"It's not his fault that he gets beat up," Monica replied.

"Kind of is," Skip said. "He let his guard down."

"That's cold," Monica observed. "It's not right."

"Bottom line, when the day is done, it's not who's right, it's who's left that counts."

Monica gave Skip a look.

"You've been on the streets," Skip said in his defense. "You know it's true. What did we always say? Keep aware of your surroundings. Number one rule. It won't happen again, Max getting blindsided, I mean."

Monica was not satisfied with Skip's view of the whole thing, but she let it drop.

Skip got up from his chair. "I'm going back to the office and do some internet stalking," he said.

"I'm going to do some studying, then I'm going to take Essie home," Monica said. "I checked the phone messages and the email and there wasn't anything interesting. Ben has already been over here once, but he left to go sell someone life insurance. He said that he might be back later. I'll lock the door and turn off the lights on my way out. Don't answer the door. If you need anything else before I leave, let me know."

"How's it going with you and Milton's morning walks?" Skip asked.

"Fine," Monica replied guardedly.

"Did you get team tee shirts for you and Milton?" he inquired.

"No," Monica answered. "Why?"

"I was just thinking that maybe a tee shirt would motivate him," Skip said. "You could get him a Team G&B tee shirt if you want. He's kind of part of the team."

Monica didn't say anything.

"I think that you should get some tee shirts that say, 'The Jackson Legend,'" Skip suggested.

Monica still did not reply.

"Like the legend Michael Jackson. He's a legend. You are Jacksons."

"Because we happen to have the same last name as Michael Jackson, that should motivate us to walk?" Monica asked incredulously.

"It doesn't sound so motivating when you say it like that," Skip said, dejected.

"If you need anything before I leave, let me know," Monica repeated.

"Sounds good," Skip replied. "We're walking in the morning? I mean Essie having pinkeye and all, maybe you want to skip it."

"Essie does not have pinkeye," Monica replied. "And yes, we're walking tomorrow morning."

"Maybe she'll have it in the morning," Skip suggested.

"If she does, mom will take care of her, or Milton can take a day of family leave. I'm working on a school project, so someone else is going to have to watch her if she gets sick."

"That's cold," Skip replied.

Monica gave him a dismissive look and opened one of her school books. Skip walked back to his office. When he got there, he found Essie under his desk.

"What are you doing under there?" Skip asked.

"It's my fort," Essie replied.

"My desk is your fort?"

Essie nodded.

"Can we turn it back into my desk for a little while?" Skip asked.

Essie stuck her lower lip out and gave Skip her sad eyes.

"You are exactly like your mother," Skip said. He went out the door to Max's office and sat at his desk. He looked across to his own office and saw Essie peeking out from her hideout. She was grinning.

"You think you're pretty smart, don't you?" Skip said, signing out Max from his computer and signing himself on.

Monica walked by Max's office and saw Skip sitting at Max's desk. She walked past and looked in the back room.

"Essie," she called.

Skip could hear Essie scurrying around in his office.

"Essie," Monica called.

Monica came back to Max's office door.

"You know where she's hiding?" she asked Skip.

"Maybe," Skip replied.

Monica waited.

"What all do you know about Serenity?" Skip asked.

"Not much," Monica replied. "Why are you asking?"

"She keeps coming up in this case," Skip replied. "Somehow she is connected to the Welch Avenue Wizards. Milton just blows them off as a bunch of kids. Everyone we talk to blows them off as a bunch of kids. On top of that, she seems to be the one stray in the sock drawer. Everyone else we have dealt with fits in somehow, except Serenity. Max and I think that she had something to do with what happened today."

Monica sat down in the chair next to Max's desk. "What makes you think that?"

"I don't have any concrete reasons, just what I said," Skip replied. "She is the only one who doesn't check out."

"In what way? Milton checked her out," Monica said. "He says she's okay. He wouldn't let her close to Essie if she didn't check out."

Skip shrugged his shoulders. "What does she look like? I've just talked to her on the phone, and that was briefly."

"Tall and thin," Monica replied. "Pretty girl. You would know her if you saw her. She changes her hair color from bright red to orange, and then to purple. She dresses kind of," Monica thought for a moment, looking for the word. "Provocative. She dresses like a comic book character."

Skip looked at her like he expected her to continue.

"I haven't talked to her much," she said. "Milton has talked to her several times. He says that she seems like a nice girl. He says she is very polite, and that Essie likes her."

Skip still didn't respond.

"Look," she said. "I'm thinking about running for the school board someday. I'm an ex stripper. I know as soon as I declare myself a candidate, that is the first thing everyone is going to know about me. I'll have to start digging myself out of that hole from the very beginning because to start with, that is all they are going to see. I'm going to have to demonstrate to everyone that an ex stripper can be the best candidate to watch over their kid's education and welfare. That is a burden that I carry. How can I turn around and judge someone else? You can't judge a book by the cover. Isn't that what they say? I don't like

Brian, and I don't particularly want to get to know Serenity, but to be honest with myself, I have to accept that she isn't a bad person until someone can show me differently." Monica gave Skip a resigned look.

Monica heard some snickering coming from Skip's office and looked over to see Essie peeking out from under Skip's desk.

"I'm not much of a detective, am I?" she said to Essie, who ducked back out of sight. "I should have known that Skip was in Max's office for a reason."

She got up and went into Skip's office. She had to pull Essie out from under the desk, her body limp.

"Stand up," Monica said, trying to get Essie's legs under her. Essie wouldn't cooperate. The last Skip saw of them, Monica had her under the arms and was straddling her as she dragged her down the hall.

"You are getting too big to carry," Monica was saying. "Stand up."

Skip was logged on to Max's computer. He searched Pamela Stephens and came up with pages. There were a lot of people named Pamela Stephens. He tried Facebook.

He heard Monica go out the door and Essie protesting.

"Dang," he said to himself out loud as he looked hopelessly at the pages and pages of Pamela Stephenses.

Chapter 17

Thursday

Max pulled into the parking lot at the G&B Detective Agency. Monica, Skip and Ben were on the sidewalk stretching. Max got out of his car quickly and joined them.

"You're moving pretty good, considering," Skip commented.

"Looking good," Monica encouraged him as she led them in windmills and Max came within three inches of touching his toe.

When they had done ten each side, Monica had them sit on the sidewalk and reach for their toes. "Relax your muscles," she instructed.

"I think we should do these over in the grass," Ben said, nodding his head toward the narrow band of grass that separated the parking lot from the sidewalk.

"That's a good idea," Monica said. "Tomorrow we'll do that."

When they were done stretching they stood up and twisted from side to side. Max grimaced a little at first, but loosened up quickly.

"How do you feel?" Skip asked.

"I'm feeling okay," Max said. He pulled up his shirt and turned his side toward the other three. His whole side was back, blue and green.

"Oooh," Monica groaned. "Put it back down."

Skip came up for a closer look. He took his finger as if to poke Max's ribs and Max pulled away.

"I just want to see if it is tender," Skip said, with his finger still pointed toward Max's ribs.

"It's still tender," Max said. "But it isn't as bad as I thought it was going to be." He let his shirt drop.

"Let's get walking," Monica said. "I have class today."

"Ben Ralston Agency in the lead," Ben called out as he took off at a brisk walk toward Dakota Avenue. Skip took off at a jog to catch him with Max right behind, Monica following up the rear. When Skip neared, Ben began to jog as well. Max slowed to a brisk walk. They all caught up with each other a couple hundred yards farther when they stopped at the traffic light and waited to cross Dakota. Skip looked both ways, then suddenly bolted across the street against the light. Ben went after him. Max was walking in place and watching his Fitbit count the steps. Ben and Skip continued east while Monica and Max waited.

"You're doing well," she encouraged him.

"I cheated," Max said. "I got Gloria to go around the block with me this morning after we got up. I wanted to stack up some steps before I got here."

"That's not cheating," Monica said.

The light turned and the two crossed. Ben and Skip were a ways ahead, but had slowed down considerably. Monica stepped it up in an attempt to catch them. Max stayed at her side.

Ben and Skip were waiting at the turn-around point when Monica and Max got there. The four started back together at a brisk pace. Everyone could tell that Max was hurting a bit.

"Want to kick it up a little?" Skip asked him.

Max ignored the taunt.

"I'm surprised that you even came in this morning," Skip continued to poke.

"Probably was hoping that I wouldn't come in," Max replied. "Isn't that the way your side works, it can't win, so you gotta eliminate the competition?"

"Oh," exclaimed Skip. "I suppose you expect the rest of us to slow down for you because you can't keep up."

"Right," Max shot back, picking up the pace and taking the lead.

Skip took off after him, leaving Monica and Ben, who had lost interest in competing.

"Those guys always like that?" Ben asked.

"They are," Monica replied. "They poke each other all the time like that. Any sign of weakness, the other one will pounce on it. Skip was so worried about Max yesterday that he could hardly think. Max knows it, so now he's making Skip pay for it. They are really both very sensitive guys, but they are scared to death that someone will see it, so they overcompensate."

Ben shook his head. "You are good for them," he said admirably.

"I think that I'm a bit the same," Monica replied. "I'm not sure how good I am for them, I just fit in well."

Max and Skip were waiting at the stoplight to cross Dakota. Skip was content not to bolt across the street against the light. He had already demonstrated that he could do that, and he was willing to wait. Both were chatting about Skip's swimming pool, as if they had forgotten completely their taunts just a few minutes earlier. The light turned just as Ben and Monica arrived at the intersection. They crossed together. Max and Skip continued to talk about the pool most of the way back to the agency.

"You guys need to stretch out; I need to go in and take a shower and go to class," Monica instructed. "You guys made me work up a sweat. Good job."

Monica went through the door into the agency. The three men started halfheartedly twisting and bending down, reaching for their toes.

"You ever wonder what people think about a young, drop dead beautiful black girl herding three old, fat white men down the bike path every morning?" Max asked.

"They probably think she's your personal fitness trainer," Ben suggested.

"Probably think that she is lucky to be in the company of three distinguished-looking gentlemen like us," Skip replied.

Max laughed and pushed Skip off balance as he tried to bend down and touch his toes. Ben stood up straight and leaned backwards.

"What do you guys think?" Ben asked. "I'm starting to wonder if it is all a big hang-up on my part. Maybe the fire really was caused by faulty wiring."

"I was about to reach that conclusion myself," Skip replied. "Until Max got his ass kicked because we were out there snooping around. Now I'm not convinced. I think that you are on to something."

"I didn't get my ass kicked," Max remarked.

"Well, I'm feeling bad about that," Ben replied. "It isn't worth someone getting hurt."

"Don't worry about him," Skip said. "He's a tough nut. A little ass kicking won't hurt him. Gives him character. It isn't like he hasn't gotten his ass kicked before."

Max gave Skip an offended look. "I have never gotten my ass kicked," he said directly to Skip. "I've taken a lick or two, but that's it."

Skip looked over at Ben. "Like I say, he's a tough nut. He takes a licking and keeps on ticking." Skip laughed at his own words. Max had decided to dismiss and ignore him.

"I gotta go to work, too," Ben said. "Listen, it isn't worth anyone getting hurt again. I would rather you forget it than for someone to get hurt."

"Don't worry about us," Skip replied.

Ben walked toward his office door. Skip held the door of the agency for Max. "Here, let me get that for you." Max tried to pull the door shut behind him and leave Skip outside, but he wasn't able. Monica was standing in the hall dressed for class.

"I wish you two would grow up," she commented, opening the door to a closet next to her bathroom and throwing her towel into a laundry basket on the floor.

"You say that every day," Max remarked.

"I'm leaving," she said. "Don't go in there and mess up my bathroom. You have your own."

"It isn't like you have to clean it yourself," Skip countered.

"Just use your own," Monica said sternly.

"Man," Skip mumbled. "This is like home."

Monica went toward her desk where her backpack lay. Skip went to his office to get his clothes. Max had already grabbed his clothes and ducked into the men's bathroom first. Skip heard Monica leaving and went straight into her bathroom to get cleaned up.

When he was done, Skip took his towel and wiped away any evidence that he could find that might alert Monica that he had used her bathroom and shower. When he came out, he found Max in his office at his computer.

"Why were you on my computer?" Max asked.

"Sorry, forgot to log out," Skip replied. "Essie took over my desk yesterday. I had to move into your office."

Max was intently looking at his computer screen. "Did you get anywhere with this ISU Student Directory?"

"I think that they have it restricted," Skip replied, taking a seat by Max's desk. "It isn't like the old days when anyone could get on there and look up the students."

"You remember what Milton said her major was?" Max asked. "I might be able to search her by department."

Skip thought for a moment. "Engineering," he replied.

Max was working at it. Skip waited for him.

"I'm not finding her," Max finally said, logging Skip off his computer and logging himself back on.

"Pamela Stephens," Max said. "Her dad's Carl Rogers. She his stepdaughter?"

"Maybe," Skip replied. "Probably."

The two sat for a moment.

"Give me the phone," Skip said.

Max pulled the phone from the cradle and handed it over to Skip. Skip gave Max a number to dial. Max hit the speaker button.

"Registrar's office," a voice answered.

"Hello," Skip said. "Skip Murray here, is Darlene Barton available?"

"Just a moment," the voice on the other end replied.

The phone went to elevator music for just a moment before Barton picked up. "Hello, Skip," a female voice answered.

"Hi, how are you?" Skip said.

"What can I help you with?" Barton asked.

"Do me a favor?" Skip asked.

"I suppose this is not a social call. Who are you looking for?" Barton asked.

"Pamela Stephens," Skip replied.

"With a V or a PH?" she asked.

"I don't know," Skip said, looking at Max, who held his hands up to indicate that he didn't know either.

"I have two with a V, and one with a PH," Barton said.

"What's the majors?" he asked.

"The two with the V are marketing and fashion design, the one with the PH is EE, electrical engineering."

"The one with the PH, does she live on Lynn?" Skip asked.

"Yes," Barton replied. "But I'm not giving you an address," she added.

"Don't need one," Skip said.

"Moot point," Barton responded.

"So, what have you been up too?" Skip asked.

"I'm retiring at the end of the summer, before fall semester starts."

"Good for you," Skip exclaimed. "About time."

"What about you, how's your detective agency?"

"Going good," Skip replied.

"You miss the police department?" she asked him.

"Heck no," Skip said. "Not a bit."

"Anything else you need?" Barton asked in in a conspiring tone.

"Nope, you've helped me with what I needed," Skip said. "Let me know when you retire. I'll come to the party."

"I'll do that," Barton replied, and ended the call.

"I forgot about her, your connection at the registrar's office," Max said.

"I didn't even think about it yesterday," Skip said. "Nice to know people in high places. She's the Registrar, capital R."

"I know," Max replied. "She was your middle school math teacher. You've been getting her to give you info for years. I know all about her."

Skip had a satisfied look on his face for having such a good connection at the university.

"You're going to feel a little bit inadequate when she retires," Max observed. "Who you going to call when she's not there?"

Skip shrugged his shoulders. "Worry about that when the time comes."

"Changing the subject," Max said. "We have an electrical fire and an electrical engineering student. The electrical engineering student was in the building just hours before it burned down because of faulty electrical wiring. Any connection there?"

Skip thought a moment. "Are you proposing that she goes in there and rewires the place just so that it will burn down after she leaves? I suppose you could say that would be a connection, but seriously, any building that burns down from faulty wiring after an electrical engineer happened to be in it, are you going to conclude that they had something to do with it? Because it is more than likely coincidental."

Max gave Skip a questioning look.

"Don't give me that look, I'm trying to stay realistic today," Skip defended himself. "I was thinking last night that we need to make sure that we don't jump to unfounded conclusions."

"Yesterday you were convinced that Serenity was our prime suspect," Max said.

"I know I was," Skip replied. "That's why today I'm not so sure. We're investigators. We have to go where the evidence takes us, not try to guide the evidence where we want it to go. So far all we have doesn't prove anything."

The two sat silent in thought for a few minutes. Max was swiping his computer screen.

"You have a mouse," Skip said, watching Max.

Max looked at him, confused.

"You don't have to swipe your screen and smudge it all up. You can use a mouse."

Max looked like he was annoyed.

"Just saying," Skip remarked to the look.

"I would like to go back down and look at the wiring at the breaker box again," Max said.

"What are you thinking?" Skip asked.

"I just want to look at it again. I wonder if someone could have tampered with the breaker box somehow."

"Do you think that if someone had tampered with the box, Gilmore would have missed it? That's what he does. This isn't his first electrical fire."

"No one is infallible," Max said. "I've had plenty of cases where someone came through after me and found something I missed. It happens all the time. Don't try to tell me it hasn't happened to you."

"You know it has," Skip replied.

"I would like to take another look," Max said.

"With or without Peterson?" Skip asked.

"Without."

"Can we get in there?" Skip asked.

"Yesterday the hasp was just hanging there like it was when Hank took us through. I checked it before those two snuck up on me."

"Let's do it," Skip replied.

Chapter 18

Thursday

Serenity left her apartment at eight o'clock for her eight thirty lab. It was a ten-minute walk. She cut through the Memorial Union building on her way. She pulled her phone out of her backpack to text Brian that she wanted to meet him at the Union after class, but had second thoughts. She would stop by the deli instead. She was trying to formulate a plan for her next move, and she decided that she needed to be careful about leaving any tracks that might lead to her. From here out, she thought that it would be better if her connections to Brian were not documented in her texting history. Serenity was surprised to recognize that she was feeling euphoric. Things were about to get dangerous, and she liked the feeling.

After the lab, Serenity headed straight past Lake LaVerne toward Welch Avenue. She was walking fast. She only had an hour between the lab and her next class, and she had a lot of ground to cover if she was to get back on campus in time.

Serenity got to the door of the deli twenty minutes before it opened. She hoped that Brian was there early getting it ready, but she wasn't sure of his schedule. She tried the door, then peeked through the window and didn't see any movement, but the lights were on. She knocked on the glass with her knuckles. It hurt. She tried again, banging on the door with the side of her fist. She saw Brian come out from the kitchen area. At first glance he looked annoyed, but then he looked surprised when he recognized her and hustled to the door to unlock it.

"Hi," he said, opening the door.

Serenity pushed past him into the entryway. Brian locked the door behind her.

"You alone?" she asked.

"No," Brian replied. "The cook's back there. You wanna come in and sit down?"

"No," Serenity replied. "I'm in a hurry. Do you want to come over tonight?"

"I thought you worked on Thursdays," Brian responded.

"I do," Serenity replied. "But I don't have to leave to pick up the taco cart until nine-thirty. You want to come over before that? Maybe six or seven?"

"Sure," Brian replied enthusiastically. "I'm glad you're here. I felt like you were avoiding me." He laughed nervously, hoping that was something ridiculous to think, still not sure.

"I've just been busy," Serenity smiled. "Come on over, around six. Pick up a pizza on the way. We'll eat."

"Sure," Brian replied enthusiastically again.

"Pick up something to drink, too," Serenity told him. "Mountain Dew, a liter bottle. Make it two bottles."

"Okay," Brian replied, a little less enthusiastically.

"Large supreme pizza," he said.

Brian just smiled.

"Look, I gotta get to class. I haven't been trying to avoid you, I've just been studying. See you tonight," Serenity reached down and gently squeezed his crotch while she leaned in to give him a kiss. Then she turned and tried to go out the door. Brian had locked it behind her and had to unlock it for her.

"Six o'clock," Brian said as he opened the door.

Serenity took off toward the campus. Brian watched her until she was out of his sight. He closed and locked the door. He felt better than he had for days. He had been sure that Serenity was distancing herself from him, and he was pretty sure that it was because of the investigation into the Cosmic Comics fire and the fact that he had given Monica her phone number. But it appeared that all that was forgotten. Brian was excited. Just as he turned to go back to the kitchen, his phone rang. He pulled it out of his pocket. It was Becky. He swiped the screen and took the call.

"Hey, what's up?" he answered the phone.

"Checking in," Becky's familiar voice said. "I'm heading out to work in a few minutes and I wanted to talk to you."

"I'm getting ready to open," Brian replied.

"What's the deal with the comic book store?" Becky asked. "You going to see anything out of that?"

"I doubt it," Brian replied. "Hank was way underinsured. Besides, what am I going to say that would get me anything out of it?"

"Tell him you left your backpack in there with something in it. A computer or something."

"Well, there isn't a burned-up backpack with a burned-up computer inside the burned-out store, so that isn't going to fly," Brian replied.

"Jesus," Becky exclaimed. "I mean doesn't he feel bad enough to give you some severance pay or something?"

"He doesn't have any money," Brian said, exasperated by Becky's hounding. "The money was all tied up in those comic books that he bought in Vegas. They burned up with everything else. I had it figured to make a nice pile of change off of them, and now that's gone."

"So, what now?" Becky asked.

"I'm working on it," Brian replied.

"I'm thinking of coming up there," Becky said suddenly.

"Up here?" he asked. "You got a job there in KC, there's nothing up here for you right now."

"You don't want me coming up?" Becky asked.

"Not right at the moment," Brian exclaimed. "I'm barely keeping myself afloat. I'm not keeping myself afloat. If you come up here, I don't even know where we would live."

"I'll live with you and your roommate," she said. "I'm sick of Kansas City, this place sucks. I need some opportunities and there ain't anything here for me. We're a team."

"That ain't gonna work," Brian said in a voice that he hoped would end the conversation.

"Okay," replied Becky. "I'm pretty sure that you're up there slacking, just like you was slacking the last time you were up there. Bottom line, I'm coming up to see what the hell is going on, because I don't think you are giving me the straight story."

"Look, Becky," Brian pleaded. "Give me a little time. I had a plan, I'll get another plan. I need some time to get something going here, then you can come up. I'll want you to come up then. But right now is not a good time."

There was silence on the other end.

"I don't know what you are up to, but you sound guilty of something," Becky finally snarled into the phone. "I'll give you a little time, but I'm getting sick of it down here. I need a change. So make it a fucking little time."

"I'm on it," Brian said, somewhat relieved. "Seriously, I'm seriously looking to get something going."

Becky ended the call.

Brian leaned against the wall and gritted his teeth to keep from screaming. He had come close to telling Becky to fuck off. He wondered how he ever got connected up with her. She was such a loser. She had been pulling him down with her since day one. Serenity was his ticket. She was smart, she only had another year of college, her dad had money. Yes, Serenity was his ticket. Plus, he loved Serenity. He could feel it. The only thing that he loved about Becky was fucking her, and she wasn't that good of a fuck. Brian took a deep breath. He was so happy that Serenity had stopped to see him, that she wanted to see him. He was looking forward to his day, because he knew that when he got off work he was going to see Serenity, and that made six hours of making turkey and ham subs for college kids nothing. It was just something to fill the time between.

Brian heard a car door close and looked out the plate glass door. It was Barlow. Brian opened the door for him to come through.

"Opening up early?" Barlow looked as if he was wondering why Brian was standing in the entry next to the door, instead of getting the restaurant ready to open.

"No," Brian replied. "Serenity stopped in. You just missed her."

"What did she want?" Barlow asked.

"Just wanted to talk to me about tonight," Brian explained, following Barlow toward the counter.

"What about tonight?" Barlow asked. "She's scheduled to be out with the taco cart tonight. She knows that, right?"

"Yeah, yeah," Brian said quickly. "She'll be out there."

Barlow was behind the counter putting change from a bank bag into the cash register.

"Barlow," Brian said. "Do you have anything else that I could do for you, other than making subs?"

"You want to work the Big Dicks cart?" Barlow looked up from what he was doing.

"No," Brian said. "Something that doesn't involve cooking or making sandwiches. I'd like to do something else, something more managerial."

Barlow gave him an annoyed look. "Brian, this is what I do. I'm in the service business. If you work for me, we make food. Food that the kids want to eat at a price they can afford. I feed them here between classes, and I feed them out on the street at night when they are relaxing and winding down. They expect us to be here. I'm an institution. You are a part of that institution. We are proud of what we do. People come by that were in college ten or fifteen years ago, and they come out on Welch Avenue just to get a taco or a hotdog from one of our stands."

Brian did not reply.

"It's what we do," Barlow said seriously. "People love us because we feed them."

Brian clenched his jaws and said nothing.

Barlow finished putting the change in the cash register and then slammed the drawer closed.

"Brian, you need to look at what this means to people, what we are giving them. Food, Brian, we feed them. I think if you look at it from that viewpoint you will realize how important we are to them."

Brian wanted to cry.

Barlow patted him on the back and went into the kitchen to check it out and talk to the cook.

Brian went to the door and unlocked it. Four college kids and an older woman were waiting for the deli to open. He let them in and walked past them to the counter to take their orders.

Max and Skip were making ready to drive to Campus Plaza and take another look at the fire damage without Hank to guide them.

"You packing a gun?" Skip came to Max's office door.

"I haven't been," Max replied.

"I thought that you always carried a gun," Skip remarked. "Sometimes two."

Max noticed that Skip was standing with a .40 cal Sig in his hand. "I kind of got out of the habit. You packing that, or are you just going to walk around with it in your hand?"

"I was just thinking about what happened yesterday," Skip said.

Max was unlocking his drawer and getting his Smith and Wesson .38 cal. He checked the load. "I guess it wouldn't hurt," Max said. "Wouldn't have helped me yesterday though, those kids hit me before I even knew they were there. Besides, what was I going to do, shoot college kids because they looked like they were going to be mean to me?"

Skip shrugged his shoulders.

Max got a holster out of his drawer, put the revolver in it, snapped the leather strap, then lifted his foot up on his chair. He cinched the holster up to the inside of his left ankle, then pulled his pant leg down over it.

Skip had removed his belt from the loops and was threading it through a leather Bianchi cross-draw holster. "Loaded up and ready for bears," he commented while he ran his belt back through the loops and buckled it up. "You're driving," he said to Max.

Max took his keys from his drawer along with a speed loader containing an extra five hollow point +P cartridges and his keys. "Just in case there's more bears than we expected."

Chapter 19

Thursday

Max was driving. He and Skip had left the agency and were on their way to Campus Plaza, driving up Welch Avenue from Storm Street. As they approached the intersection with Hunt Street, where Campustown unofficially started, Max slowed.

"Check it out," he said, pointing toward Barlow's Deli where a young woman with purple hair was coming out the door Brian was holding open.

"Fucking Serenity," Max commented.

The two did not try to hide their attention toward the woman who was at the moment walking on the sidewalk toward Lincolnway. She was tall, maybe six feet, and she was thin. Her long hair was purple and in pigtails tied high up on her head. In Max's cruder and younger days he would have described her as having legs all the way to her ass. She was wearing bright red short-shorts, retro looking blue mesh stockings and a pair of black combat boots. She was sporting an open leather bomber jacket and as they passed, Skip could see that she was wearing a cropped tight-fitting shirt beneath it that matched the color of her stockings. Serenity glanced his direction and locked eyes with him, but then looked away as if she was accustomed to getting people's attention, and accustomed to dismissing them as not worth returning it.

"Well, there she is," Skip remarked as they drove on down the street. "Want to intercept her, introduce ourselves?"

"For what purpose?" Max asked. "Let's stay on mission."

Skip silently agreed. Max turned into the alleyway that served as the entrance to Campus Plaza and parked the car. The two got out and watched the street, waiting for Serenity to catch up and walk past so that they could get a second look at her. They did not have to wait long.

"She stands out in a crowd," Max commented as she strode confidently past, not looking their direction.

"She has a way about her, doesn't she?" Skip remarked. "I mean, it's the first thing you notice."

Max opened the back door of the Camaro and took out a backpack stuffed with equipment that he and Skip might need. The two directed their attention to the back door of the burned-out Cosmic Comics building. When they got to the door Max carefully removed the padlock and hasp, hoping that he would not be the one to cause the screws to become so loose that they would no longer hold it in place. He pushed the door open and the two entered. Skip closed the door behind them while Max fished a flashlight out of the backpack and handed it to Skip. Max pulled a headlamp from the backpack, put it on his head, then switched it on. He clicked the switch twice, and each time the beam of light got stronger. The third time it started to blink. Max hit the switch again and the light went out. He went through the process a second time, taking it one too many times again.

"You want me to do that for you?" Skip asked, waiting patiently.

"I got it," he said, brushing off the sarcasm in Skip's remark as if it were nothing more than an offer to help him.

When Max got his light where he wanted it, the two began walking carefully through the ground floor. Enough light came through the smoke-blackened windows and the cracks where the plywood was bowed to allow them to see where they were going. The two surveyed the shelves of burned comic books and the wooden boxes filled with melted record albums.

"How did the fire get up here?" Skip asked, shining his flashlight around the store and up at the high ceiling.

"What do you mean?" asked Max.

"I mean, you have a basement and this floor, a narrow stairway and a door between the two. If the fire started down in the basement, how did it get up through the floor?"

"How would I know?" Max replied. "I'm not a fire investigator. Something to ask Gilmore, I guess."

Skip continued to shine his light at the ceiling and Max followed the beam with his eyes. There was daylight coming through in places.

"Did it burn through up there, or did the fire department chop holes in it?" Skip asked.

Max didn't know, so he didn't answer at first. He looked at the floor beneath the holes in the ceiling and did not see any debris to indicate that the ceiling had been chopped through. He noticed that Skip was looking for the same thing.

The two spent fifteen minutes searching every nook and cranny for evidence, even though they didn't know what to look for. They were counting on their common sense to lead them to something.

Skip shined the light around the store one last time. "Basement?" he asked.

Max led the way to the stairs. The fire-blackened door was closed, and Max had to use some force to pull it open.

"Did we close this door the other day?" he asked.

"Don't remember," Skip replied. "Do you think someone has been in here since we were here last?"

"I'm wondering," Max replied.

Max led Skip down the narrow staircase. He tested each step by bouncing on it to see if it would give, but they all seemed to be solid.

"You would think that if that door was open when this place caught on fire, the flames would come rushing up this stairway," Max was thinking out loud. "It would be an inferno in here. I would think that these wooden stairs would be the first thing to burn."

"Maybe," was all that Skip said.

When they got to the basement, Skip went to the boxes of comics sitting on one wall and poked them with his finger. "Got something to dig around with?" he asked Max.

Max pulled a twelve-inch screwdriver out of the backpack, which he was still carrying in his hand, and handed it to Skip. Holding his flashlight in his left hand and the screwdriver in his right, Skip stirred the charred contents.

"It was hot right here," Skip observed. "You know, sometimes when you burn magazines or stacks of papers, the outside burns but the inside doesn't. These burned clear through."

"Accelerant?" Max asked.

Skip leaned over and took an audible sniff, then another.

"Don't smell anything."

Max sidled up to Skip and took a sniff for himself. Skip shined his flashlight into the first-floor joists that were the ceiling of the basement. Plastic insulation was melted from the electrical wires attached to the inside of some of the joists. In some places the melted plastic clung to the wires, other places it was completely gone. The wires, charred black, were hard to follow in the dark recesses of the equally charred joists.

"What happened there first?" Max said as he tilted his head to direct his light to one particular place where the wires were more visible. "Did the insulation melt from the fire, or did the wires get hot and melt the insulation?"

"Likely the wires got hot and melted the insulation. What difference does it make?" Skip asked. "Because Gilmore ruled that it was an electrical fire. That's pretty consistent with an electrical fire, just saying."

That's fairly modern wiring," Max observed. "Modern in the sense that it is three wires. Why would it get hot right there?"

Skip shrugged his shoulders. "No idea. It isn't isolated. It looks like it got really hot everywhere."

Max directed his light around the room. It landed on the breaker box attached to the wall on the opposite side of the room. The two approached it.

"What do you make of that?" Max asked.

They could see that the box had been pried open and that the breakers had partially melted. The plastic had run down on the equally melted breakers below them, leaving a puddle of plastic that had taken the form of the bottom of the door.

"I would say that it was hot in there," Skip remarked.

"Why would parts of those breakers melt and other parts not?" Max asked.

"Because parts of them are made of plastic and parts of them are not," Skip answered.

"What's the parts that didn't melt made of?" Max asked.

"How should I know?" Skip replied. "Why are you all of a sudden asking fifty questions about everything?"

"I'm trying to figure this out," Max answered.

Skip shined his flashlight on the fuse box that was almost hidden between a piece of the burned two-by-four-framed panel that held the breaker box to the block wall. Max had to position his body to get his headlamp to shine into the corner. He maneuvered around a bit, then stepped back and held out his hand behind him. Skip placed his flashlight in Max's hand, suddenly feeling like he was in a very dark place without it. Max shined it toward the box.

"Can you dig a pair of pliers out of the bag and give it to me?" Max asked.

Skip found the pliers by feel and handed them to Max. Max slipped the joint so that he could get a wider grip, placed it over one of the fuses and twisted. The face of the fuse tore, leaving the part that was screwed into the socket to crush instead of turning.

"Fuck me," Max cursed.

"What are you trying to do?" Skip asked.

Max stepped back so that Skip could see. He held the flashlight on the four fuses in the box, one of them buggered up by Max's efforts.

"What am I looking at?" Skip asked.

"All of these fuses have threads showing. They're not all the way in. Why is that? Don't you think that they would be designed to be all the way in?"

"Dang," Skip replied. "Good eye."

Skip took the screwdriver that he held in his hand and wedged it between the fuse and the socket, then pounded it with his palm. Max was holding the flashlight where he could see what he was doing.

"Pliers," Skip held the screwdriver toward Max.

Max took the screwdriver, slipped the joint on the pliers back to where it was, and handed it to Skip. Skip grunted as he worked. Max could not see past his head. A minute later Skip held the pliers in the light, a crushed fuse gripped in them.

"Good job," Max remarked.

"Screwdriver," Skip said, handing the pliers and the fuse back toward Max.

Max took the pliers and slapped the handle of the screwdriver into Skip's extended palm as a nurse would hand a doctor a scalpel. Skip dug into the socket and immediately there was the sound of something hitting the floor. Max quickly shined the flashlight toward the noise. In the beam of light on the floor they both saw a penny, its edges burned and melted in places, but otherwise shiny.

"Did you know that was in there?" Skip asked.

"I was thinking that maybe it was," Max said as he retrieved the penny.

"What made you think that?" They were both scrutinizing the coin in Max's palm.

"When I was just a kid on the farm, maybe eight years old, we had a barn. It had a fuse box just like this, as did most farms. One time our neighbor's barn burned down, and all I remember is my dad saying that he probably stuck a penny behind the fuse because it was blowing out all the time, and that was a bad thing to do."

"You're kidding me," Skip said in disbelief. "Your dad mentions fifty years ago that a barn might have burned down because someone put a penny in a fuse box, and you remember it?"

"Yep," Max said in satisfaction.

Skip shook his head.

"Can you read the date on that?" Max asked. "I'm not wearing my reading glasses."

Skip squinted through the bifocal in his contact. It was hard to read in the light of the flashlight.

"What year did they quit making wheat pennies?" Skip asked.

"Don't know, the sixties?" Max replied.

"It isn't a wheat penny," Skip said.

Max shined the flashlight up into the darkness above the fuse box and both men followed the beam as it traced the wires.

"When we talked to Gilmore, didn't he say that the plans for renovations over the years showed that the old spool-and-tube wiring had been disconnected?" Max asked.

"I think he did, if I recall correctly," Skip replied.

"I'm not sure of that," Max said. "I mean, I'm not an electrician, but…" He trailed off.

"I think that we need to get Gilmore back down here," Skip said.

Max handed Skip the flashlight and proceeded toward the steps, the penny grasped tightly in his hand. Skip followed close behind. As soon as they made their way through the back door and into the daylight, Max held out his hand with the penny in it. Skip took a closer look.

"Two thousand six," Skip read the date on the coin, then looked at Max, raising his eyebrows.

"Who goes around sticking a two-thousand-six penny in a disconnected fuse box?" Max asked.

Skip pulled out his phone. He searched for the state fire marshal's number and when he found it, he touched the screen to place the call. It rang twice, then a female voice answered.

"Could we please speak to Pete Gilmore?" Skip said.

"May I ask who is calling?"

"Skip Murray, G&B Detective Agency. We found something interesting about the fire at Cosmic Comics in Ames here that we think he would like to know."

The woman asked him to hold for a minute. Max was trying to put the hasp back in place and get the screws to hold.

"Gilmore," the familiar voice came over the phone.

"Skip Murray, G&B Detective Agency," Skip said.

"Sure, what can I do for you?" Gilmore asked.

"Max, my partner, and me were poking around in the Cosmic Comics building and we found something a little suspicious. We thought that you might be interested."

"Okay," replied Gilmore.

"Well, we were checking out the breaker box and that fuse box next to it, and we decided to pull one of those fuses. We thought it looked a little wonky in there. Anyway, we finally got it out, and we found a penny behind the fuse. We think that the others have pennies under them, too, but we didn't want to mess with it anymore than we had to, because we didn't want to destroy evidence."

Gilmore was quiet for a moment. "It was pretty common practice back in the day to put a penny under those fuses to keep them from blowing. But according to the plans that I got from the city, that fuse box was disconnected in the early sixties, if I recall right. Wonder it didn't burn down before then if that's the case and it was still connected."

"A two-thousand-and-six penny," Skip said.

There was another moment of silence.

"Can you guys meet me there tomorrow morning?" Gilmore asked.

"Name it," Skip replied.

"Ten-thirty," Gilmore said.

"We can be here," Skip said.

"Keep this under your hat," Gilmore said. "I don't want anyone tipped off about this until I can get a better look at it."

"Not saying anything to anyone," Skip assured him.

"I'll see you tomorrow," Gilmore ended the call.

"Tomorrow at ten-thirty," Skip said to Max. "I think we got his attention."

"I would say that Team G&B is looking pretty damned good right now." Max was grinning ear to ear.

Chapter 20

Thursday

Brian locked up and crossed the street to the Kum and Go convenience store next door to the pizza place. He picked up two one-liter bottles of Mountain Dew and took them to the counter. He chatted with the girl working the counter. She was cute and she was friendly. The nameplate on her blouse said Carol. Brian referred to her by name numerous times during the brief conversation. When he left the Kum and Go, he went next door to the pizza restaurant to pick up the supreme pizza that he had ordered before he closed the deli.

Brian paid the girl at the counter and took a seat to wait. He had to wait almost ten minutes. Brian hated the supreme pizza piled high with everything they could throw on it. He preferred sausage and mushroom, but Serenity liked supreme. The girl at the counter called out his name. Brian looked around. He was the only person waiting. He wondered if she thought there was someone else named Parker lurking around the corner to challenge him for the pizza. Brian grabbed up his plastic bag containing the bottles of soft drink in one hand and balanced the pizza box in the other, almost losing it trying to get through the door. Luckily, two college age kids were coming in at the same time and held the door for him. Brian nodded to them and said thanks as he went through the open door. They were kids, Brian thought. He was getting old, when twenty-one-year-olds were kids. He thought about it for a moment. Serenity was twenty-one.

It was a five-minute walk to Serenity's apartment building. It was an older building, but well maintained. The apartments were expensive and housed a number of professors. Serenity lived there alone, in a fifth floor two-bedroom apartment. Brian knew that the rent wasn't cheap in that building. Even though Serenity liked to talk about how she and her father were not on good terms with each other, Brian was quite sure that Serenity was not paying her bills on what she earned working for Barlow. Brian was good with it, though. If Serenity wanted him to believe that she was doing it on her own, he would be happy to chip in a couple hundred a month to live there with her and pretend daddy wasn't picking up the rest.

Brian buzzed Serenity's apartment and heard the entry door click. He hurriedly set down the bag of Mountain Dews and jerked the door open before it locked again. He placed his foot in the door, retrieved the bag of soda and went inside. The entry was well designed and elegantly decorated, but it was a bit dated, Brian thought. He went to the elevator, hit the button and waited. It did not take long for the door to open. A couple walked out and gave Brian a suspicious look. Brian pegged them as either professors or college administrators, maybe one of each. Probably going out to supper at some swank restaurant. Brian went into the elevator and pressed the button for the fifth floor. He was a little put off that the two certainly thought that he was the pizza delivery boy. He should have told them when they looked at him that he was going to spend the evening with his fiancée in her apartment.

The elevator reached the fifth floor and the door opened. Brian made his way to Serenity's apartment. The door was cracked open. Brian opened it wide with his toe, walked in and shut it with his foot behind him. It closed with a click. Serenity was not there to greet him. He heard her in the bedroom talking to someone on the phone. He put the pizza and the bag with the soda on the kitchen counter and sat on the couch in the living room. Serenity came out of her bedroom a few minutes later and took a seat in the chair to the right and facing the couch.

"My fucking dad," Serenity said, offering it up before Brian could ask her who she was talking to. "I wish he would quit trying to run my life," she said with no other explanation. "Where's the pizza?"

Brian pointed toward the kitchen where the box was plainly visible on the counter. Serenity went to the cupboard where she took out a couple of plates and opened the pizza box. "Why don't you make yourself useful and put some ice in some glasses and pour us up something to drink?"

Brian got up and did as she suggested.

"Put those little folding tables up, too," she instructed.

Brian went to the fireplace, where the folding tables were leaning against the wall, and put them by the couch next to each other. He went to the kitchen and retrieved the drinks that he had put on the counter and placed them on the tables. Serenity came behind him with the two plates of pizza.

"You wanna move that one over by the chair?" She nodded at one of the tables.

Brian moved the table and the drink to the chair and went back to the couch. Serenity had already placed his plate on the table. She went to the chair and sat down.

"This is nice, don't you think?" Serenity said.

"It is," Brian said happily.

"What's the deal with those two detectives and the fire at the store?" Serenity asked.

"I think that they are just following up on the official investigation for the insurance company," Brian said. "I don't think it is anything more than that."

"I'm more wondering about the detectives themselves," Serenity replied. "How well do you know them?"

"They used to be cops, then they won the lottery a few years ago, I don't know. They started a detective agency, G&B Detective Agency. I don't know what the hell the deal is with them, they don't take hardly any cases. Milton told me that they just come in and dick around all day every day doing nothing."

"What about your ex, what is her connection to them?" Serenity asked.

"They used to spend a lot of time patrolling the bars when they were cops. I guess they got to know Monica when she was stripping. Anyway, she was stripping in a bar downtown, and they came in one night and offered her a job as their office manager. They said that if she would come work for them, they would pay for her to go back to school. So she went to work for them. That's it."

"They treat her well?" Serenity asked.

"Fuck," Brian snorted. "They treat her like a queen. Hell, she is the queen. She's got a huge fucking desk, sets her own schedule, she's runs the place."

"They fucking her?" Serenity asked.

"Oh, hell no," Brian laughed. "They treat her like a daughter. That cop that married her had to take them out to supper and ask them for her hand in marriage. When she married him they threw a wedding reception for her that should have been on the cover of some bridal magazine. Christ, it was something."

"You were there?"

"No," Brian said, dejected. "I heard about it, though."

"So, two ex cops and an ex stripper, and no one is fucking anyone?" Serenity said.

"They're married, and as far as I can tell, happily married," Brian replied.

"No one is happily married," Serenity commented.

Brian didn't respond.

"What about the kid?" Serenity asked. "How's the cop feel about you and the kid?"

Brian looked down at the floor. "He treats her like she was his own," Brian lamented. "Does everything a father is supposed to do. Takes her out for ice cream. Takes her down to Adventureland on her birthday, does everything that I want to do. Every time I get her, all she can do is talk about Milt."

"How do you get along with him?" Serenity asked.

"Okay," Brian said. "He's a prick, but he treats me okay. Monica makes me deal with him whenever I pick up Essie. He tries to be friendly, but I know that underneath he would like to kick my ass. She won't even talk to me. I gotta talk to the prick that gives her what I can't afford. It is like she throws it in my face."

"You sound a little bitter," Serenity observed.

"I think that you could change that for me," Brian smiled at her.

"What about the two detectives?" Serenity ignored his remark. "How do they get along with the kid?"

"Oh, my god," Brian exclaimed. "They're worse than Milton. Jesus, they give her anything she asks for. I swear, the sun rises and sets on her as far as they are concerned. I said that Monica runs the office, but that's not true, Essie runs the office. They are the never-say-no people. That agency of theirs, there's a big-ass garage in the back full of playground equipment and all her stuff. She does whatever she wants there."

Serenity finished the two pieces of pizza that were on her plate. Brian was still working on his first.

"You want to get me another piece?" she said, holding out her plate to Brian. Brian got up and took it. She gave him her empty glass as well. Brian got her another piece of pizza out of the box, dumped the ice from her glass into the sink, then put new ice in it and filled it with Mountain Dew.

"I'm guessing that the little girl is pretty important to everyone," Serenity stated after Brian had put her plate and her drink on the table.

"She sure is," Brian replied, taking his place on the couch.

"She important to you?" Serenity asked.

Brian was surprised by the question. He wondered how Serenity felt about kids. He didn't want to ruin his chances with her by saying something wrong.

"I'm her father," he said noncommittally. "I mean, she is my daughter, I got responsibilities."

Serenity didn't push any farther. His answer was enough for her. She noticed that Brian was looking at a painting on the wall above her fireplace while he was trying to formulate his answer to her question. It was new. He probably hadn't seen it before.

"Paul painted that for me," Serenity said, getting his attention back.

"What is it?" Brian was not quite sure what he was looking at. It was abstract, but at the same time it was ominous.

"It's Satan. He's crucified on a cross," Serenity explained.

Brian stared at the painting, trying to make sense of it.

"He's crucified upside down on the cross," Serenity explained, recognizing his confusion.

Brian's eyes widened. "I see it," he said. "That's something. Why did he paint it for you? Did you ask him to paint you something?"

"He painted it for me because he loves me," Serenity replied.

Serenity stared at Brian for a moment, relishing the pain in his face. Then she got up from the chair and walked to the couch where he sat. She held out her right hand. He took it. She pulled him to his feet, placed her left hand behind his neck and leaned in. She was every bit as tall as he was. She took his lips to hers. Brian could feel her breasts heaving in excitement against his chest. She held him tight in the embrace. Brian was unable to move.

While Brian was held captive by her kiss, Serenity took her right hand from his, swung it gently backwards, then brought it forward sharply, driving the back of her hand into his crotch. He grimaced and pulled away, but Serenity held him. She brought her hand back again and then bought it forward with more force than she had the first time, driving the breath from him. Brian thought that he was going to vomit. Serenity held him tight as he turned his head from her and fought to keep from retching.

"Take a breath," Serenity said softly in his ear.

She pulled his head back with her right hand, never relinquishing the hold she had on him with her left, her lips just far enough away from his to speak.

"Let's have some fun." She breathed the words in his face, pulling him into her tighter.

Brian had gotten control of himself. He quit trying to pull away. Serenity drew him backwards toward her bedroom without releasing her grasp. Brian followed her in a dance that would take him somewhere he did not know. He followed her lead, giving away any control that he had regained. "It's going to be fun," she whispered to him. "You're going to like it when we get done."

Brian surrendered himself completely to her.

Brian awoke. He was naked in Serenity's bed. She was shaking him. He focused his eyes on her. She was dressed for work.

"What time is it?" Brian asked.

"Nine," she said. "You need to get up and get dressed. I gotta go."

"I can't believe that I went to sleep," Brian said.

"That happens," Serenity replied. "I think it is just a primal response." She smiled at him.

Brian didn't respond.

"You okay?" she asked.

"I think so," Brian replied.

"Don't worry, no permanent damage that I could tell." She laughed quietly and stroked his hair.

"Did you like it?" she asked.

"Yes," Brian said.

"Maybe we'll do it again," she smiled at him. "Would you like that?"

"Yes," Brian replied.

"Get up and get dressed." Serenity stood up. "Hustle up, I need to get out of here."

"I would stay here and wait for you if you wanted," Brian said, sitting up. "I could be here for you when you come back."

"Oh, Brian," she said, still smiling. "You can't go through that twice in one night. Another time, maybe."

Brian got out of the bed and found his pants.

"Brian," Serenity said almost as a second thought, "I think that I would like to go to the mall with you and your girl on Saturday. Maybe I'll let you spend the night afterwards."

"Sure," Brian replied. "I would really like that. I know that Essie would, too."

"It's a date," she said, finalizing it.

Brian was ecstatic.

"Hustle up," she told him.

Chapter 21

Thursday

Skip drove into Max's driveway, turned off the ignition and walked to the front door. It was dark out, his way guided by the light over the door. He rang the doorbell twice and then went in. Max's house was bigger and newer than Skip's. After they won the Powerball jackpot, Skip had decided that he liked it where he was. But Max and Gloria built a new house. Skip looked around. It was tastefully done. Max's wife Gloria was a marketing consultant for a Napa winery, a job she really didn't need, more a passion. Gloria loved wine but more so, she liked the lifestyle. She was forever hosting wine tastings for the rich and famous of Ames, IA. A celebrity in her own sense. The décor reflected her taste. It looked Tuscan to Skip, even though Skip didn't know for sure what Tuscan was.

"Hey," Skip shouted. "I'm here."

After Skip had talked to Gilmore, the two detectives had gone back to the Agency. It was only noon, and Skip had wanted to order a sub sandwich from Jimmy Johns, but Max wanted to go home. He was still just a little stiff from the roughing up he had taken the day before. Skip had gone back to his office for a couple of hours, but he left early, before Monica got there after classes. The two decided that they would use the investigation as an excuse to go out on Welch Avenue for the evening. They had not been there together since they were police officers. Max claimed that he went out there all the time to get a super dog at Big Dicks, but Skip suspected that he had gone out there maybe once or twice to get a super dog at Big Dicks.

"Hey," Skip shouted. He walked down the hall toward the interior of the house. Max met him in the hallway, wearing a bathing suit and toweling his wet hair.

"Swimming," Max explained. "Loosens me up."

Max had a three-lane lap pool in the lower level of his new house. Max swam in it regularly at first, but as far as Skip knew, Max had not been in it for a long time. In fact, the pool in the basement that never got used was a topic that Skip liked to point out to him whenever he couldn't find anything else to rag on him about. Skip noticed that the bruise on his ribs had turned a dark green.

"That really looks nasty."

"It doesn't hurt that bad," Max said, twisting to look at it himself.

"Got you back in the pool," Skip remarked.

"I like this exercise kick that Monica has us on," Max said. "I'm feeling kind of good about it. I thought that a little swim would be nice. I haven't been swimming for a long time."

"Humph," Skip made a sound to show that he wasn't impressed with Max's newfound fitness kick. "Don't burn yourself out."

"Make yourself comfortable," Max told him. "I'm gonna change and I'll be right back."

"You packing tonight?" Skip asked as Max was about to leave.

"Are you?" Max asked him back.

Skip pulled back his jacket to reveal the Sig .40 cal on his waist.

Max turned and headed for a wide stairway that led to the upstairs of his house. As Max was bounding up the stairs in an effort to display his newfound fitness, Gloria dodged him coming down them.

"What's up, Skip?" she said pleasantly. "I hear that you two are going out on foot patrol tonight."

"I guess so," Skip replied, following Gloria into the next room and taking a seat on the couch.

"Want a glass of wine?" she asked him.

"I'll pass," Skip said.

Gloria took a chair opposite Skip and sat back comfortably in it. Gloria was a nice-looking woman, red hair, well proportioned. She was dressed in a burgundy satin blouse and black jeans. She was wearing a pair of shoes that, knowing Gloria, Skip guessed cost at least five hundred dollars.

"Nice shoes," Skip remarked.

"United Nude," Gloria replied.

"What?" Skip said.

"That's the brand," Gloria explained.

"Who calls their shoes United Nude?" Skip asked.

"United Nude calls their shoes United Nude," Gloria laughed. "You need to get with it," she chided him.

"What do you think about Max getting kicked in the ribs like that?" Skip asked, changing the subject.

Gloria shrugged her shoulders. "I'm not particularly happy about it," she replied. "But it isn't the first time he's come home bruised and battered. I thought that he had outgrown all of that, but honestly, when you guys started that detective agency I thought, here we go again. You two will never change."

Skip didn't reply.

Max came down from upstairs and walked into the room where Gloria and Skip were sitting. He was threading a holster holding his Smith and Wesson .38 on his belt.

"You boys looking for trouble tonight, or just playing cowboy?" Gloria asked.

"Never can tell," Max replied.

Skip stood up. "Good to see you," he said to Gloria.

"You keep an eye on him," Gloria said to Skip, nodding toward Max. "And you keep an eye on him," she said, nodding toward Skip.

The two went out of the house and got into Skip's Audi. It wasn't a long drive from Max's house to Welch Avenue. Skip parked in the small employee parking lot behind the fire station on Welch where they used to park their patrol car when they came out on Welch Avenue to patrol. Max gave him a questioning look.

"It's ten o'clock at night. They're all in there watching TV and eating popcorn. They don't care."

Max got out of the car. Skip got out and locked the doors.

"Let's go get a Big Dicks," Max suggested, taking off in the direction of the hotdog cart before Skip could even answer.

The Big Dicks cart had been a fixture on Welch Avenue almost as long as the Taco Machine. Richard Richards and Barlow Hicks had competed for the bar crowd in Campustown for close to two decades. Richard Richards had been old when he first showed up with his cart. A skinny black man with white hair and a white beard, Richard Richards was the antithesis of Barlow. He was quiet and unassuming. Barlow was young and nervous and could not stand still. Barlow parked his cart in the one-hundred block of Welch on a significant grade, where he had to chock the wheels to prevent it from rolling down the street all the way to Lake LaVerne. When he had a break in his almost nonstop taco-making dance, Barlow would check his chocks, as if a moment of rest would result in some catastrophe. Richard Richards parked his cart in the park at the corner of Welch and Chamberlain where it was flat, just off the sidewalk. He would lean on his cart and watch the kids walk by, selling them one of his four hotdog recipes if they wanted, otherwise content to watch the fellow across the street preaching the gospel and selling tee shirts to the students to make money to support the Naked Christian Church of America. That is where Richard Richards got the idea to call his hotdogs Big Dicks. One day Richards walked across the street and talked to the preacher. He wasn't interested in joining the Naked Christian Church of America, he wanted to know where he got the tee shirts made. A month later Richard Richards' cart had a sign identifying it as Big Dick's Hotdogs, and below that it said, "Wanna give her a treat? Give her a Big Dick." Tee shirt sales outdid his hotdog sales two to one. In addition to his "Wanna give her a treat? Give her a Big Dick" slogan, he had tee shirts that said, "Everyone likes a Big Dick with mayonnaise" and "Nothing better to end the night than a Big Dick." The kids couldn't buy them fast enough. Richard Richards got rich on Welch Avenue selling tee shirts and hotdogs, and when he did, he got tired of selling tee shirts and hotdogs. He sold out to Barlow and retired to Florida. He had found the American dream.

When Barlow bought out Richard Richards, he put an end to the tee shirt sales. He kept the Big Dick's Hotdogs on the side of the cart, but he painted over the part about giving her a treat. Max always wondered why Barlow didn't sell the shirts. They were Richard's moneymaker. But Barlow was always serious about his business, even if it was just a cart on the street at bar closing. Max figured that Barlow did not fancy the image of himself as a tee shirt salesman. Even back then, Barlow had standards, and giving someone a Big Dick with mayonnaise was not the image he was cultivating.

Max and Skip crossed the street to the Big Dick cart and ordered two superdogs and two cans of Coke. They sat on the wall that defined the small park that occupied the southeast corner of Welch and Chamberlain, across from the fire station. Skip looked through the windows of the station. Several firemen were sitting back in recliners watching a fifty-six-inch television on the wall. A couple were reading magazines. They looked like they were in for the night. Skip thought that the only thing they were missing were their pajamas.

"Wouldn't you love to find a fire alarm to pull right now?" Max asked.

The two laughed.

"Look over there in front of the bar," Max suddenly said.

Skip looked down Welch Avenue to the bar that was next to the fire station. "What?"

"That guy sitting on the stool outside the door, that's the guy."

"You sure?" Skip asked. "He's got his back to us, how do you know?"

"He turned to talk to someone," Max replied. "It's him."

"Yesterday you said that you didn't get a good look at him," Skip remarked.

"That's him."

"You're sure?" Skip asked again.

"Yes, I am." Max was standing up.

Skip threw what was left of his superdog into the trash can, took a big swig of his Coke and pitched the can behind his half-eaten superdog. He hurried to catch up with Max, who was already crossing the street.

Max walked up behind the kid sitting at the door of the bar. He was checking the driver's license of a young college girl. It was a Thursday night, and a dozen more college age kids were standing in line waiting to get in.

Max tapped the young man on the shoulder and he turned around. At first he did not recognize Max.

"Remember me, from yesterday?" Max said in a friendly tone.

It took Xavier a moment to figure it out. A look of recognition came to his face, reaffirming what Max already knew. Xavier opened his mouth.

"Stand up," Max calmly ordered, before Xavier could speak.

Xavier stood up and turned toward Max. He was at least four inches taller. His shoulders were wide and his biceps stretched the sleeves of his tight fitting shirt.

Without another word, Max reached up, grabbed a handful of tee shirt and tugged. Xavier leaned forward, more instinctively to save his shirt from being stretched out than because of the strength of Max's grip. As soon as he did, Max stepped in and to his right side, brought his leg up as high as he could swing it, then using his grasp of the shirt to keep his balance, brought his leg back with the force of his whole body behind it. As he did, he swung his foot out and caught the back of both Xavier's legs just under his knees. Xavier's feet came out from under him, and for a moment he felt like he was suspended in mid air. As Max's foot came through, Max threw all of his weight into Xavier's torso, driving him backwards into the pavement. Xavier hit hard. Max stepped back and did not say a word. Just as he did, Skip came in and delivered a powerful boot to Xavier's ribs. Skip stepped back, then came in with a second kick. He was about to send a third one when Max grabbed him.

"Let's go," Max said, pulling at him.

Skip looked up to see several of the kids in line taking out their phones and swiping the screens. Max had his hand over his face as he pulled Skip across the street. Skip bowed his head and did the same.

"Don't look back," Max instructed as they made it to the other side of the street.

Max let go of Skip's sleeve and made for Campus Plaza where they could get lost. Skip almost ran into the Taco Machine cart. He looked up to find himself standing directly in front of Serenity. The only thing to register with Skip, other than who she was, was the smile on her face as he stood in front of her.

"What's happening, Pamela?" Skip said, then ducked around the cart and followed Max into the plaza.

"Did you see Serenity?" Skip asked when he caught up to Max.

"Didn't stop to say hi," Max replied.

"I did," Skip informed him.

"That's nice of you," Max laughed.

They could hear sirens in the distance.

"Someone must have called the cops," Max said. "What direction?"

"Just keep moving," Skip said. "They're all going where we were and not where we are; faster we put some distance between us and them, the better chance we got."

Max led them through a walkway on the south side of the plaza that took them to Chamberlain. He crossed the street and started south in the alley, knowing that if they got caught in the alley they could bolt different directions between apartment buildings and the cops wouldn't have time to get out of their cars and lock them, then decide which to pursue.

Max was watching toward Welch Avenue, knowing that someone would eventually search that direction. He was not disappointed. A patrol car slowly came down Welch, shining a spotlight between the buildings. The two detectives hid behind a car. As soon as the patrol car passed, they doubled back the direction that they had come, away from the search for them.

"Dang," said Skip, attempting to walk without stooping and looking suspiciously like he was going to try to hide at any minute. "I didn't know that you still had it in you."

"Like riding a bike," Max laughed.

"Oh, shit," Skip laughed. "He hit hard."

"I noticed that you got in a few licks," Max remarked.

"Payback," Skip replied. "Man, this is fun, being on this side of it."

"Yeah," Max said. "I'm not going to stand around and try to explain how twelve witnesses saw me come up and put the hurt on some college kid working the door of a bar."

"You're sure it was him?" Skip asked.

"Yes, I'm sure," Max answered.

The two turned on Hunt, made a beeline across Welch, then worked their way through dark parking lots to the rear of the fire station where they got into Skip's car.

Skip drove onto the street and turned away from Welch Avenue. At the first corner, he turned right and started southbound into the residential area, driving slowly, but not slow enough to attract attention. As he was looking in his rearview mirror for any sign that someone was following, he heard Max curse.

"Shit."

A patrol car pulled in behind them from a side street and turned on the red lights. Skip slowly pulled to the side of the street and put the Audi in park.

"Make sure your gun isn't showing," Max said.

Skip was watching the police officer approach the car tentatively through his outside mirror. Skip rolled down the window. The officer came up to it but held back, shining his flashlight first in the back seat, then in the front seat. His right hand rested on the butt of his gun.

"Hi," Skip said in a friendly manner.

"Sir," the officer said, looking at Max and then back at Skip. Max was holding his hands up and smiling. "Can I see your license?" the officer asked.

"Going to have to get my billfold out," Skip said, not wanting to make the officer any more nervous than he already was.

Skip got out his billfold and held it up in the beam of the officer's flashlight while he found his license, pulled it out and handed it to the officer. The officer took it and backed toward his patrol car. Skip could see him talking on the radio. He could also see another patrol car, lights flashing, pull up behind the first officer.

"You know him?" Max asked.

"Never seen him before," Skip replied.

The second officer got out of his car and approached the first officer. They talked for a moment.

"We got another one," Skip said, not taking his eyes off the mirror. "I think he might have been on the department when we were there.

The officer in the car handed the license to the second officer. The second officer proceeded to the window. He didn't seem to be as nervous as the first.

"Hello, Mr. Murray," he said in a familiar manner.

"How's it going?" Skip asked.

The officer handed Skip his license.

"Sorry about this, but some guys kicked the shit out of one of the bouncers out on Welch just a little while ago, and we're looking for whoever did it."

"That sucks," Skip said.

"Two older guys," the officer said. "No one got a good description. Besides, the doorman isn't interested in pressing charges, anyway, we just want to talk to them."

"Well," Skip said. "Sorry we can't help you, we're the only older guys we've seen. And we're not just older, we're really older."

"They're probably long gone," the officer said.

"Probably some construction workers," Skip said. "Or some hick volunteer firemen in town for fire training and looking to impress some college chicks. That never mixes well," Skip said.

"I'm guessing," the officer agreed. "Okay, sorry again, drive safe."

The officer turned and went back to his car.

"Did he know?" Max snorted a laugh.

"Fuck if he didn't," Skip laughed with Max. "Let's get out of here and go to your place. Pop open a bottle of that expensive wine your wife has stashed in that eighty-bottle wine rack you're so proud of."

The two patrol cars pulled past Skip's car. He put it into drive and followed them down the street for a block, then turned away toward Max's house.

Chapter 22

Thursday

Serenity had seen it coming from her vantage point at the Taco Machine food cart. She spotted the two detectives coming down the sidewalk across the street. The one that Xavier and Paul had roughed up was well in the lead, and Serenity could see that it was going to be payback time. Watching him, there was no doubt in her mind that he was no newcomer to what was about to happen.

There was just a quiet moment, where the detective got Xavier's attention and he stood up from the stool, and then all hell came down. It was one of the most exciting things that Serenity had ever seen. It was exciting because statistically, by all accounts, Xavier should have cleaned house. It shouldn't have even been a fight. It wasn't even a fight, in fact, it happened so fast, and Xavier went down so hard, that it was over before it started. And the other detective got in a couple licks like the two were a well-choreographed tag team. Then they ran, and before anyone could recover from what they had just witnessed, the two detectives were gone. Xavier didn't even try to get up. He lay there in a heap, beaten. The only thing for the kids in line to record on their phones was a giant doorman laying flat on his back. And then one of them ran right past her, stopping long enough to say hi, just as calm as you please. He should have said, "Fuck you Serenity, we know who you are." It would have been the same message. She realized that she had underestimated these two. She was smiling, glad she realized that before she made a mistake.

Her next move needed to be more calculated than a phone call to a couple of her thugs.

She watched them run into the Campus Plaza, then she heard the sirens. By the time the cops got there Xavier had been helped up by a couple of the kids in line and a couple of the bar staff from inside. He was shaking his head, still in a daze when the first cop got out of the car and started questioning him. Two more patrol cars showed up, and two officers crossed the street toward her and Amy.

"I didn't see anything, and neither did you," Serenity said to Amy.

"Howdy," said one of the cops, a tall, skinny fellow not much older than Serenity.

"Howdy back," Serenity said.

The humor of her comeback was not lost on him and he laughed.

"What did you see over there?" he asked.

"I was setting up, and all I heard was a collective groan from across the street. When I looked over there that big guy was laying flat on his back, and two guys were running away."

"Any description of them?" the cop asked, looking at Amy as well.

"Tell you the truth, that guy over there had all my attention. I didn't pay much of it to anything else."

"Some of the people over there said that the two suspects ran right past you. Said one of them almost ran into you." The officer was looking directly at Serenity this time.

"Well, they're mistaken," Serenity smiled. "Because they took off and I don't know where they went."

The cop doing the talking turned his attention to Amy. The other one had left and disappeared into Campus Plaza.

"I was busy. I didn't see anything," Amy said. "I wouldn't have even known it happened if Serenity hadn't said something."

"Can I get a name?" the cop said, pulling a spiral notebook out of his pocket.

Serenity noticed that he was not wearing a wedding band.

"Serenity Stephens," she replied, thinking that she might want to let this cop get to know her a little better.

He looked at Amy.

"Amy Clark."

"Can I get a phone number for you two?" he asked.

Amy gave him the number for the phone that Barlow gave them to use when they worked the cart. Serenity gave him her own number.

"If you want to follow up in the next day or two," she said after she had given him her number, "I'll be around. You can call any time."

The officer smiled at her offer. The other cop reappeared from Campus Plaza.

"If they went that way, they're long gone. Probably ran back in the woods along that parking lot back there," he said to the officer holding his notepad.

A third officer, with stripes on his sleeves, came across the street.

"What do we have?"

"They didn't see anything," the one with the notepad replied. "No telling where they went."

"Take names and numbers," the officer with the stripes said. "The doorman doesn't want to press charges if we find them, anyway. We'll file a report in case he changes his mind, but otherwise let's get back on the streets. We're short as it is."

"Got 'em already," the officer replied, waving the note pad. "Talk to you later," he said to Serenity, then turned and left.

"That one might be fun," she said to herself out loud.

The three cops crossed the street. Another doorman had taken the place of the one who had been assaulted.

"The witnesses said it was some older guy, just walked up, tapped him on the shoulder, and when he got up the older guy did some mixed martial arts move and decked him. Then they ran off," the sergeant told them as they crossed.

"On a Thursday night?" the skinny officer commented.

"What's with the girl with the purple hair?" the sergeant asked.

"She's friendly," the officer replied.

"It's the uniform," the sergeant laughed. "Don't kid yourself."

The three were standing by the sergeant's patrol car. "Let's get back on the street. Might want to hang close and keep your eyes open in case they come back for their car or something, but stay available."

They separated and got into their cars. Welch Avenue was already back to normal, as if nothing had happened.

The bars cleared out early, as they usually did on a Thursday night. Amy and Serenity walked up and down the sidewalks picking up trash that their bar closing clientele had discarded on their way back to their dorms, fraternities and sororities. Whatever time Serenity closed down the Taco Machine, it was a signal to the people working the Big Dicks cart to do the same. She could see the Big Dicks guys picking up, too. One of the Big Dicks guys and Amy had managed to make their way to the intersection and stood talking.

Serenity walked up to the intersection and around the corner where Barlow's little pickup was parked. While Serenity backed the pickup to the cart, Amy walked back to help her hitch it up. They would pull it uphill just a block to Barlow's deli and park it in a garage that occupied the corner of his lot. The Big Dicks guys would push their cart. It wasn't that far for them, and it was flat ground.

Amy got into the truck.

"Amy, what are you doing Saturday afternoon?" Serenity asked.

"I don't have anything," she answered. "I need to do a little studying, but I don't have a lot. What do you have in mind?"

"Do you have a car?" Serenity asked.

"I do," Amy replied. "It's parked over at the Hilton lot."

"I got some Wizard work for you," Serenity continued. "You know where the Jordan Creek Mall is in Des Moines?"

Amy nodded her head.

"I'm going down there with Brian on Saturday afternoon. I need you to meet me there. I'll text you when we leave. You can drive down and text me back when you get there. I'll let you know what you need to do then." Serenity looked over at Amy. "That work for you?"

"I can do that," Amy said.

Serenity expertly backed the cart into the garage next to the Big Dicks cart. Amy would have unhooked it and pushed it in, but Serenity always liked to back it in. The guys who had been working the other cart were already hoofing it toward the dorms. Amy got out of the truck and left the door open. She went back to unhitch the cart. As soon as she did, she hit her fist twice on the tailgate, signaling Serenity to pull ahead. Amy pulled down the overhead door and locked it. She got back in the cab.

Serenity drove out of the lot. Whenever Serenity worked with Amy, she would give Amy a lift to her dorm, then bring the truck back and park it. If Amy worked with anyone else, they made her walk. It wouldn't be so bad if she lived in Friley Hall like the Big Dicks guys, but Amy lived in Hawthorn Court. It was a long dark walk at that time of the night.

Serenity pulled into the lot and parked the truck.

"Then you are good with Saturday?" Serenity looked over at Amy and asked.

"I can do it," Amy said, with a smile.

Serenity reached over and took Amy's arm and pulled her closer across the bench seat. Amy turned toward Serenity, breathing heavily. Serenity pulled her close and brought her lips to Amy's. The two kissed. Serenity ran her hand up under Amy's shirt and cupped her breast in her hand.

Chapter 23

Friday

Max rode his bicycle into the parking lot at the G&B Detective Agency. Monica, Skip and Ben were doing their stretching. They were getting into the routine. Max dismounted his bicycle, pulled it up on the curb and left it standing against the wall of the agency under the window that faced the street. He started stretching with the other three.

"Why are you always late?" Skip asked. It wasn't actually a question, more of a statement.

"I get here when I get here," Max replied. "For a guy that doesn't wear a watch, you sure are worried about what time I get here." Max emphasized the word "time."

"Does he get points for riding his bicycle?" Skip asked Monica, who was not listening to the usual morning banter, and was instead talking to Ben.

"Ben," Skip said. "Didn't get to talk to you yesterday."

Ben quit talking to Monica and turned his attention to Skip.

"Yesterday, Max and I were taking another look at the Cosmic Comics building and Max decided to start taking things apart, and guess what he found?" Skip asked, drawing it out a little.

No one responded, but Max was grinning ear to ear.

"Max found a penny," Skip said with finality.

"Okay," responded Ben.

"He found it behind a fuse in a fuse box that was supposedly disconnected a long time ago. We called up

Gilmore, the guy who investigated the fire, and he told us that in the old days people used to stick a penny behind fuses to keep them from blowing all the time. It used to be standard practice. Caused a lot of fires, though."

Skip waited for Ben to ask a question, but Ben was patiently waiting for Skip to get to the point.

"Don't you want to know what was really interesting about it?"

"It would be nice, sometime today," Ben said a bit sarcastically.

"Thing is," Skip said, ignoring the sarcasm. "It wasn't an old penny, it was a two-thousand-six penny, and it looks like there might be pennies under the other fuses, too."

"Someone stuck a penny in there to get around a fuse blowing on a circuit that is disconnected?" Ben replied.

"Yep," Skip said. "Why would someone do that?"

"I don't know," Ben said suspiciously.

"Neither does Gilmore, so he's coming up at ten-thirty to take a look at it," Skip finally said triumphantly. "We're meeting him over there, you want to come along?"

"Might be we don't have a fire caused by faulty wiring after all," Max chimed in. "Or someone caused the faulty wiring," he added thoughtfully.

"Damned right, I want to come along," Ben replied enthusiastically.

"All right," Monica said, interrupting them. "Let's walk and talk. It sounds like we all have a busy morning." She led the way. Skip and Ben took the lead, talking about pennies and fuses. Max walked with Monica. They didn't talk much. Monica was finding that it was actually getting a bit strenuous to keep up with Skip.

"Natural athlete," Max remarked.

"I guess so," Monica affirmed.

When they finished walking, Skip, Ben and Max were still busy discussing the possible people and reasons that they had come up with during the walk for the pennies in the fuse box. Monica went in, showered quickly and headed for class. The three men were still outside, sitting on the curb and still talking about the pennies. None of them acknowledged her leaving. Max's bicycle was still leaning against the building.

Max and Skip showered, changed and got ready to meet Gilmore at Campus Plaza. Max texted Ben to see if he was ready, and instead of texting back, he showed up tapping on their window a few minutes later. The three climbed into Skip's car and he headed out.

"Lookie there," Skip said as he drove down Welch Avenue toward the corner of Hunt street.

Max looked up expecting to see Serenity again, but he saw no one.

"Two cars parked at the Stomping Grounds," Skip said, nodding toward the corner.

"Gloria and Marjorie," Max commented.

"And here comes our lovely office manager, life coach and personal trainer," Skip remarked.

Skip waved as he passed Monica, but she was not looking at him. He considered honking the horn, but decided that it might be tacky.

"What do you think those three are up to?" Max asked.

"They are plotting against us," Skip said.

"For what?" Max asked.

"Just for the sheer fun of it, I would guess," Skip said. "That is what those three do. They plot against us."

Max looked back at Ben and shrugged his shoulders. "Mr. Paranoia. I wonder about him sometimes. Druggies are always paranoid." He nodded his head affirmative, then rolled his eyes toward Skip.

"If I start doing drugs," Skip remarked, "It will be because you drove me to it."

Skip pulled into the Campus Plaza and found a parking place. They were the first ones there.

It was a nice day as Monica walked to the Stomping Grounds from class. When she got there, she noticed both Gloria's and Marjorie's cars. They must not have driven together. Monica found them at a table laughing out loud. Marjory had her hand on Gloria's as if what they had just been laughing at might blow her away. Monica took a seat at the table with them.

"What's up?" she asked, knowing that whoever or whatever they were laughing at, it was probably something between the two and that they would say nothing. They were very much like their husbands. They had known each other a long time.

"Marjorie just told me about a house some friends of ours are buying, and she got a realtor to give her a tour," Gloria explained and the two laughed again. "What are you and Milton and Essie up to this weekend, got any good plans?"

"Brian has Essie on Saturday," Monica replied. "They're going to Jordan Creek shopping. Brian likes to use Essie as an excuse to go down there to that big sporting goods store. I'm surprised Milton doesn't try to go along with them. He loves that place. That, and the Bass Pro in Altoona."

The barista interrupted them just long enough to take Monica's order.

"Milton and I don't have any plans, but we really should take advantage of a day just the two of us."

"How's the school project?" Marjorie asked.

"I honestly don't know," Monica replied. "Milton is pretty easy. He just isn't motivated, you can see that. I expected that, because I'm purposely not offering him any motivation. We're jogging. I offered to let him skip yesterday, but I think that his guilt got the best of him. That surprised me. I don't talk to him while we jog or anything. I make him jog fast enough that he doesn't want to talk, anyway. It is hard, though. I mean, we used to take walks when we needed to chat about something important. I have to keep him moving fast enough so he doesn't think up something to discuss."

"Poor Milton," Gloria exclaimed.

"One interesting thing, though, he's started lifting weights again during his lunch hour. I don't know how that plays into it."

"What about the boys?" Marjorie asked.

"That is a problem," Monica continued. "First of all, the Fitbits didn't arrive until Tuesday and I wanted to start the project on Monday. I should have started it anyway, but I wanted to log the data. The first day or two, everything was textbook. My motivational tools were all working like they were supposed to. But then Ben Ralston next door decided that he wanted to walk with us. All of a sudden I had an outside influence on their behavior. I didn't know what to do with that, or how to factor it in."

"Max has been swimming, and this morning he rode his bicycle to work. He hasn't done that for a long time," Gloria added.

"Is Skip doing anything extra?" Monica asked Marjorie.

"Nope, but he does come home every day and tell me how he is kicking everybody's asses."

"That's the thing," Monica replied. "They all three are responding in different ways. Skip is all about faster, stronger, farther. Max is all about extra credit. Skip is just naturally more athletic, but Max is putting in all of this extra work."

"Maybe he thinks if he does extra work, he will get stronger and faster and pass Skip eventually," Marjorie suggested.

"That's the thing," Monica said thoughtfully. "I don't think that he plans on getting faster. Honestly, Max doesn't care about that. He doesn't think he has to keep up with Skip, because he is convinced that he's already ahead by doing all of this extra stuff. He's humoring him. He thinks it's funny that Skip thinks he's winning the game."

The three sat for a moment.

"You keep talking about Max doing extra work," Gloria replied thoughtfully. "And work is what this whole project is about, not exercise. You're just using exercise as a form of work."

"That's right," Monica replied.

"Sounds like one of them recognizes that he is working and is outworking the other one. The other one thinks that he is playing a sport," Gloria said.

"And the one playing the sport is inspiring the working man to work harder," Marjorie added. "And now we know why the Green Bay Packers are so important to working-class Green Bay: they bill themselves the working man's team. They are owned by and represent their hard-working shareholders. They make everyone work harder. That is interesting."

Monica was listening to the two talk. "I think that you two are on to something," she said. "I wonder if I should be placing more emphasis on how sports affect work production. I'm getting pretty excited about this."

"Well, you're welcome," said Marjorie. "When you become a big hotshot college professor, we will be very happy to be your consultants." The three laughed at that.

"What do you think the guys will say when they find out that all this time you've been using them as guinea pigs for your school project?" Gloria asked. The three laughed again, but Monica found her laugh to be less enthusiastic.

Serenity came around a corner and caught sight of Monica ahead of her. Serenity followed Monica for a block, staying behind her, watching her walk. Serenity had not been around Monica much. Monica avoided her. She had talked to Monica's husband a few times, but she had never talked to Monica more than to say hi. At Chamberlain, Monica turned toward the parking lot on Hayward. Serenity slowed to watch her for a moment, then kept walking straight toward campus.

When Serenity got to the drive that connected Welch Avenue to Campus Plaza, she noticed a group of men out of the corner of her eye. She made it a point to never appear curious about anything that was happening around the burned-out Cosmic Comics building, but she couldn't help herself. She slowed to look. In the group she spotted the fire investigator who had questioned her the morning after the fire. Talking to him were the two detectives. Two other men stood listening and Hank Peterson was walking away from them toward the back of the building. None of them noticed her passing. She picked up her pace.

Serenity felt a twinge of anxiety, and she seldom felt anxiety about anything. In fact, in situations where normal people felt anxiety, Serenity felt excitement. But for some reason the group behind the Cosmic Comics building was not generating any excitement for her. She had to remind herself that even if they did come up with anything, they would never have reason to pin it on her. She had even thought from the beginning that they might eventually figure it out. She was pleasantly surprised when they hadn't. She had been ecstatic that she was smart enough that they didn't notice what she had done. If they had come in and found it right off the bat, it would not have affected her in the least, but she had reveled in her cleverness and now the thought of them figuring out what she did deflated her a bit. Serenity was not happy with the feeling. She needed to shake it off, and she looked forward to Saturday when she would do just that.

Serenity hurried to class and got there ten minutes early. She had been letting her school work slide since the fire. She had been letting her mind wander. She could not afford to do that. She was a four-point student. One more year and she graduated. She intended to be the top in her class, just as she had been in high school. People noticed you when you were the top of the class. Serenity liked being noticed.

Monica got into her car and started toward the agency. She wanted to do some research online. Marjorie and Gloria had gotten her thinking. She had not originally intended to tell any of them about her project and her paper, but she had blabbed it to the two wives at one of their weekly Friday morning coffee meetings. The two had been so supportive. They said that anything that got Max and Skip out exercising was good, but Monica using them as test subjects was brilliant. Monica wasn't so sure about that anymore.

She was pretty sure that Max and Skip would laugh it off. She also knew that when they did find out, Max and Skip would jump on Milton. She didn't know how he would take that, and she was a little nervous. Milton was the best thing that had ever happened to her. She was afraid that he would feel like she used him. She thought for a moment that she would swear Max and Skip to secrecy, but then she realized that would just make things worse, because she knew that Max and Skip could not keep a secret. Besides, just the thought of keeping a secret from Milton made her feel guilty.

Monica wished she had told Milton about the project from the beginning. He would have loved the idea of making Max and Skip test subjects, controlling them like lab rats in a maze. And he would have loved the two of them having a secret from the guys. But she had needed a control for her experiment, and there had been Milton, the perfect candidate. And working out wasn't hurting him one bit. So she had used him like a lab rat, too, and now she would just have to live with the consequences.

Chapter 24

Friday

Max, Skip and Ben sat chatting about nothing in particular in the parked car as they waited for Gilmore to show up in Campus Plaza. Five minutes after they had arrived, a panel truck with "Felton Electric" painted on the side of it pulled into the lot and parked across from them. The driver was talking on his phone. Gilmore came in next, parked his car, got out, went to the passenger side of the van and began talking to the driver. He did not see the two detectives and the insurance agent in the car across from the van. Even if he had, he would not have recognized them.

A few minutes later Hank showed up and parked his car. He got out and came toward Skip's car. The three occupants got out and greeted him.

"Looks like the guy from the fire marshal's office brought an electrician," he remarked. The others turned their attention to the panel truck and the man speaking to the driver.

"That Gilmore?" Skip asked, nodding his head in the general direction.

Gilmore came around the rear of the truck and greeted Hank. "How's it going, Hank?" The driver of the truck was getting out as well.

"Mosbey and Murray?" Gilmore held out his hand, assuming correctly.

Max and Skip held out their hands and introduced themselves. Gilmore shook hands with them in turn, then Max introduced Ben.

"George Felton," Gilmore introduced the driver of the truck. "I've worked with George on a number of cases. I'm no electrician; he is, and a good one. If you ever need any electrical work done, he's your man."

Felton took a round of handshakes.

"I thought that this case was cut and dried," Gilmore explained. "But you guys finding that penny, well, I'm a little embarrassed, but I decided that it wouldn't hurt to get George here to take a look at it. I opened the case back up."

"Nothing to be embarrassed about," Skip replied. "Sometimes it just takes another set of eyes."

"You're kind," Gilmore replied.

"Just because I've been there," Skip said.

Hank had gone to the door and was removing the hasp. It almost fell off in his hands. Felton had gone to the back of his truck and was putting on a tool belt. When he got it situated, he took a large battery powered work light out of the truck and closed the doors.

"Going to be crowded down there," Max remarked.

The six men made their way to the basement of the building, led by Hank with Felton following him. Felton shined his light over every wall, across the floor and then across the ceiling. He traced wires with the beam. The others quietly tried to stay out of his way in the crowded room. Felton's light finally fell on the breaker boxes that were mounted on the wall. He moved slowly in that direction, guiding the light up to the wiring in the ceiling several times in the ten steps that it took him to get to the wall.

"This is where you found the penny?" he asked without looking away from the fuse box.

"Yes, it is," Max replied.

"You got it with you?" Felton asked.

Max fished the penny out of his pocket and approached Felton with it. He handed it to the electrician, who took it and held it in the light. He handed it back to Max. Max stayed next to Felton, feeling that he had earned the right to be in on the action. He had found the penny after all, sort of. The others stood out of the way. Felton took a pair of channel lock pliers out of a pouch and deftly twisted one of the other fuses out of its socket without tearing it up as Max had done the day before. When it came out, he inspected it in the light, placed it on top of the fuse box, then inspected the socket itself. He put the pliers back in the pouch and brought out a long narrow screwdriver.

Gilmore stepped forward with a sandwich sized plastic bag that had the word "EVIDENCE" lettered across it in red and handed it to Max. "If you can get it out of there without touching it, I might be able to get a fingerprint off of it. Just touch the edges."

Felton gave him an inquisitive look. "It got awful hot in there," he said. "I don't know how much heat it takes to obliterate a fingerprint."

"Rather find out that it wasn't evidence that we didn't destroy, than the other way around," Gilmore said.

Felton popped something out of the socket with the screwdriver and carefully removed it by holding the edges. Max recognized it as another penny. Felton held it in the light.

"Twenty-eleven," he remarked.

Felton dropped the penny in the bag that Max was holding open, placed the screwdriver in his pouch, took out the channel locks and pulled another fuse. There was another penny. He dropped it into the bag, put the fuse on top of the box next to the one he had taken out previously, then went after the fourth and last fuse. He dug out another penny and deposited it in the bag.

"I need something to stand on. I have a stepstool in the truck, if someone wants to get it," Felton said, looking up into the recesses of the wall above the fuse box.

"I got one right here," Hank said, walking to the far wall and coming back with a charred stepstool, the rubber on the steps melted off. It creaked as he opened it.

Hank looked at it when he got into the light. "Maybe I better go up and get the one out of the truck," he said.

"Put it down," Felton said. "Let's see if it will hold me."

Hank put the stool down and Felton moved it into place with his foot. Hank stayed next to Max, thinking that he too had earned the right to be close to the action.

Felton tested the first step. It felt solid. He moved up on the first step, tested the second, and moved up higher. He pulled a flashlight out of his tool bag and held it up, pushing it and his head into a space where Max was pretty sure he was going to get stuck. "Lordy, lordy," they heard his muffled voice.

Felton continued to stand on the second step of the stool with his head stuffed up in the charred joists. Everyone stood silently, allowing him to do his inspection without distraction. Finally, he stepped down. The sides of his face were black from the burned wood.

"Come here, Pete," he said.

Gilmore went to the corner. Max and Hank moved back out of his way. Felton handed Gilmore the flashlight. "Climb up and follow the wires. It's hard to see, but you'll see it. This fuse box is wired in."

"According to the plans of the remodel in eighty-four, it was disconnected," Gilmore said as he climbed the stepstool with the flashlight.

"Maybe it was, but it isn't anymore," Felton said.

"Lordy, lordy," they heard Gilmore's muted voice in the same tone as Felton's when he said the same words.

Gilmore came down from the stool. His face was smeared black, same as Felton's.

"Wouldn't be the first time that the plans were wrong," Gilmore remarked.

"Someone wired it back up," Felton said.

"You think so?" Gilmore replied.

"I'm positive," Felton said.

"How's that?" Gilmore asked curiously.

"Because someone wired two-twenty out of the box. They put two one-ten wires together in a series to make two-twenty, then they put pennies in there to keep the fuses from blowing, because those fuses were going to blow immediately, as soon as they turned on the juice to it." Felton pointed to the lever on the side of the box that turned on the electricity and was in the on position.

"Jesus," Gilmore responded. "Wouldn't it have been instantaneous? I mean, the fireworks?"

"Don't know," Felton said. "I've never done it before. But it wouldn't have taken long for it to start cooking."

Gilmore looked straight at Hank. "Who would have come down here and done that?"

"Not me," Hank said in desperation. "I don't do electricity." He looked around at everyone for a sympathetic response.

"It was someone who knew what they were doing," Felton remarked. "It wasn't an amateur job."

"How about an electrical engineering student?" Max piped up.

"Not unless he had some wiring experience," Felton replied. "Whoever did this has done some commercial wiring. This was a wiring job. They don't teach electrical engineers how to wire up a building, they teach them theory."

"Brian?" Max asked Skip.

"I doubt Brian is much of an electrician," Skip said thoughtfully. "If he was, would he be selling comic books for Hank or making subs for Slo-Mo? I don't see Brian being smart enough to do something like this."

They looked at Hank again. "I'm an IT man," Hank pleaded. "Come on, I don't know anything about one-ten two-twenty."

Felton was up on the stepstool again. He was holding his phone up into the joists along the wall. Everyone was watching and they could see the flash as he took a series of pictures. When he was satisfied, he climbed down from the stepstool and took a couple of pictures of the fuse box.

"I'll send these to you," he said to Gilmore.

Gilmore led everyone up the stairs and outside into the light.

"George," he addressed Felton. "Do you have a drill driver and some construction screws? I want you to toenail some screws into the jamb and make sure that back door doesn't come open."

"Can do," Felton replied.

"Front door, too," Gilmore said as Felton turned toward his truck.

"Listen up, gentlemen," he addressed the rest of them. "I'm going to tape this place off with crime scene tape. Nobody goes back in. I'm going to tear out that wall if I have to. This case is back open. I don't want anyone here talking about what we found today." He looked each person standing around him in the eye. Each nodded affirmative. He gave them each another look. "Listen, thanks for bringing this to my attention, that I missed that fuse box. I let things get routine."

"It happens," Skip quipped.

"Right, but that doesn't make it set any better," Gilmore said.

Felton stopped on his way to the door with his drill driver. "If you hadn't told me that you found that penny, I would not have taken the time to climb up there for a better look," he said.

"You're kind, too," Gilmore said.

"It was someone small with long arms," Felton said. "I'm short and fat. I couldn't have gotten that far up the wall to wire that in. Unless he's a contortionist, I don't think he could have, either," Felton nodded toward Hank.

"Serenity," Max suggested again.

"I'll put her on my list of suspects," Gilmore said. "I'll talk to her. I'll have to wait until Monday and take those pennies down to the DCI lab and see if they can get any prints off them first. I'll go from there."

"I'm still not thinking that some college kid did it," Felton said, turning toward the door to secure it.

"Who else?" Skip asked.

"I don't know," Gilmore said. "The case is open again and we will have to see where the evidence leads us. I'll bring in some more specialized people and see what they find."

The four didn't reply. Gilmore shook hands around. "I'm out of here," he said. "I will try to keep you guys updated on what I find. I really appreciate it."

Gilmore turned and went to his car. Felton came back. "Nice to meet you," he said, handing them each a business card. Skip dug out a G&B Detective Agency card and exchanged. Ben gave Felton one of his. Felton went to his truck.

"What now?" asked Hank.

"I don't think this is going to have much effect on you either way," Ben said. "Unless you burned the place down, and I don't believe that you did. But the insurance carrier will pay you out whether it was accidental or intentional, it's all the same to us."

Hank breathed a sigh of relief. "If you guys need anything from me, call me up. I would really like to see this all get settled. I got a good offer from Rogers Enterprises, and I'm ready to sign on the line. This whole thing is really weighing on me. I swear to God that I had absolutely nothing to do with the fire, but my brother and sister act like it was all my fault. I just want to pay them off and move on with my life."

Max raised his eyebrows to Skip.

"I see what you're doing," Hank said. "I was more than happy to keep that store up and running, if only for the sake of my parents and grandparents. But what's done is done, and I'm just as ready to wash my hands of it at this point. I didn't burn the place down."

"Just shitting you," Max said. "I don't think that you burned the place down, but I'm still wondering about Brian and Serenity, I don't care what Gilmore and Felton say."

"I don't see why or how they would have done it, but I'm not going to argue with you," Hank replied. "But I am telling you, Brian was pretty happy there and he was crushed when the place burned. It was like he lost something, too. Just saying."

Max and Skip shrugged their shoulders and turned to Ben. "Let's go back to the office," Skip suggested.

The three got in Skip's car and headed toward Mortenson Road.

"I guess we're done," Max turned in his seat toward Ben in the back.

"Done?" Ben asked.

"You said that you had a gut feeling the fire was something more than faulty wiring. You wanted us to investigate and prove that. We did. You owe us two hundred bucks," Max said.

"Aren't you going to investigate it to find out who started the fire?" Ben asked.

"That wasn't the deal. The deal was to show that it wasn't faulty wiring. Besides, that's Gilmore's job. We aren't going to step on his investigation. You got what you wanted. Two hundred bucks, and that's cheap at half the price." Max gave him a smug look. "We can put you on a payment plan if you don't have it, but we'll have to charge you interest."

"I got it," Ben said in a resigned voice. "How much for you to stay on the case until Gilmore identifies the perp?"

"Not interested," Skip called back over his shoulder. "We weren't interested in it in the first place, but we figured Max owed you for going around handing out your cards and introducing himself as you."

"Gilmore's a good man, he'll find out who did it," Max added. "He just got caught up in the routine. It happens. He's on it now, and he'll be twice as all over it."

Skip pulled into the parking lot at the agency and parked across the lot under the tree. Monica's car was in her reserved space.

"I'll go get a check for you," Ben said as he got out of the car.

"I'm heading across the street to Filo's," Max said.

"I guess that I'm going to brief Monica on what we found and where we are at on the investigation," Skip said.

"Tell her that we're done with it and to expect a check," Max reminded Skip. "In case Ben tries to get us back into it."

"Done," Skip reassured Max.

Skip walked into the agency. Monica was at her desk absently staring out the window.

"What are you thinking about?" Skip asked.

"Brian," Monica replied absently.

"You're supposed to be thinking about Milton like that, not Brian," Skip teased.

"I'm not thinking about Brian in a loving way," she laughed.

"Good girl," Skip replied. "Don't start."

Chapter 25

Saturday

Brian parked his car in front of Monica's townhouse at eight o'clock sharp. He had Essie from eight in the morning until eight in the evening. He got out of his car and went to the door. Milton met him.

"Hey," said Brian.

"I'll help you put the booster seat in your car," Milton said pleasantly.

"I probably ought to get one of those of my own," Brian said, feeling like he was borrowing both the seat and his child for the day. Following Milton into the garage, he wondered if he would feel more like a father if he had his own car seat for his own daughter.

Milton got into the rear of his Jeep Wrangler and struggled with the seat. "They don't make these things easy to get in and out," Milton was saying. "The setup's okay, but the damned buckles on the straps fight me every time."

Brian wasn't listening, he was admiring the Jeep. Monica's late model Nissan Sentra was parked next to it. Brian thought about Monica and Milton. They were everything he was not. He wondered how it had happened, how Monica had gone from stripping in a bar to wife of a police detective, living in her own townhouse, driving a nice car, going to college and working for a detective agency run by a couple of rich cats who probably gave her paid vacation, paid holidays, paid everything. A wave of jealously come over Brian. It wasn't quite fair. Milton emerged with the seat.

"I'll take it," Brian said, reaching out.

"Let me do it," Milton said. "It's tricky."

Brian didn't argue. They had the same conversation every time.

"So, you're going down to the mall, I hear," Milton made conversation while he was installing the seat in the back of Brian's Saturn Ion.

"Later we're going down," Brian said, standing behind him and holding the door open as if it somehow assisted with the installation. "We're going to Dunkin' Donuts first, then I don't know what. We have to wait for Serenity, she's going down with us. She worked last night," Brian explained.

"Going to Bass Pro while you're down there?" Milton asked between grunts, as he wrestled with the straps that held the seat in. It was always hard to get them to hook into the seat.

"Doubt it," Brian replied.

"Monica loves that place," Milton said, removing his body from the car and standing up.

"She loves Bass Pro?" Brian asked incredulously.

"Yeah," Milton said. "She took up fly fishing. We take Essie with us sometimes. I used to be big into fly fishing, and last summer we got back into it. Monica thought that it looked like something wholesome that we could do as a family. I'm thinking of getting a boat."

"I would have never thought of Monica as someone who liked fishing." Brian rolled it around in his head.

"One of these days, if you have the time, maybe you can have Essie for a long weekend, and Monica and me can go down to Missouri to go trout fishing."

"Jesus," Brian thought, "he actually winked at me, like we're in this together." Brian didn't reply.

"Okay, let's get the little lady," Milton said.

When they got to the door, Monica was waiting. She had Essie's backpack in one hand, and Essie was holding the other.

"Hey," Brian said to Monica.

"You taking her down to the mall?" Monica asked.

"Later," Brian said.

"Serenity going with you?" she asked.

"She worked late last night," Brian replied. "Waiting for her to get up, then we're going down. Hopefully have lunch at Joe's Crab Shack."

Monica didn't say anything.

"I'll have her back before eight," Brian said, reaching toward Essie.

Monica didn't say anything back.

"Have a good one, then," Milton interrupted the silence. He waved Essie down the stairs. Monica handed Milton the backpack and he followed Brian to the Saturn.

"Need help getting her strapped in?" Milton asked in a helpful tone.

"I can get her," Brian said.

When he was done getting Essie into the car seat, Milton passed him the backpack, which he placed on the floor below her feet.

"Have fun," Milton called to her as Brian shut the door.

Milton watched Brian get into the car, back out, then drive out of the lot. He turned toward the door of the townhouse where Monica still stood.

"They're fine," he said to her.

"You sure?" she asked.

"No," Milton replied, "but what are you going to do? You going to tell Brian that he can't have Essie because your bosses have a feeling that his girlfriend had something to do with a fire?"

"I have a feeling about her," Monica said.

"So do I," Milton agreed with her.

"You don't act like it," Monica replied.

"Monica, I'm not happy about Essie spending time with Brian. I don't even like the guy or his girlfriend, but the court gave him visitation, and there isn't really anything we can do about it."

"He's behind in his child support," Monica remarked.

"You wanna take him back to court?" Milton replied. "Because that's fine if you do. I'm sure that the lawyers would be happy."

Monica went back into the house. Milton followed her, wondering what he had done to cause such discontent.

Brian drove to Dunkin' Donuts and parked. He got Essie out of the seat and held her hand while they crossed the parking lot. When they got inside, Essie immediately wanted a big girl donut with sprinkles. Brian wanted to get her the Munchkin donut holes, which were cheaper and he could share. He knew she would have a fit if he cut her donut in half. Milton and Monica spoiled the hell out of her. They would probably buy her whatever she asked for and throw away what she didn't eat. And those two guys that Monica worked for, they would probably just buy her a donut shop of her own.

By the time they sat down, Essie had forgotten about a whole donut of her own and seemed happy to munch on the Munchkins, sharing them with Brian.

"How is Grandma Shawna?" Brian asked.

"Good," Essie answered.

"What do you and Grandma do while Mommy is at work and going to school?" he asked.

"Go fishing with Mommy and Papa Milton," Essie said.

Brian was stung by the reference to Papa Milton. "I mean when Mommy and Milton are at work," Brian asked her again.

"We go to the park," she answered.

"What do you do at the park?" Brian asked.

"Play," Essie answered and took a big bite out of one of the Munchkins.

"What do you like to play on at the park?" Brian pressed.

"The slide," she answered.

Brian was becoming frustrated with the conversation. He was hoping to build some kind of relationship with his daughter, but Essie didn't seem interested. He watched her eat the Munchkins. She took a drink of water from the straw and smiled at him. He smiled back. Maybe when he and Serenity got together things would be different. Maybe she would see them as she saw her mother and Milton, as a father and a mother, instead of just Brian, the person she had to go with every other Saturday. He could only hope.

Brian was not content to sit there and divide his attention between Essie eating Munchkins and the traffic going by on Lincolnway. He was wasting the time that he had with her, waiting for a text or a call from Serenity. He knew that she would not be in any hurry, and that aggravated him even more. He hoped that it would all be worth it in the end. One thing was bothering him, though. Serenity had not had him use protection when they had sex the other night. The last thing that he wanted was to knock her up. He didn't need two kids to support. That was aggravating him, too. He told himself that Serenity was a smart girl, but then so was Monica. It wasn't fair that girls didn't have to take any of the responsibility.

Brian caught Essie looking at him. She had finished her Munchkins. He looked at crumbs scattered all over the table, and his glance went to the floor. "You make a mess," Brian said. "You're old enough to not make such a mess."

Essie just looked at him and smiled.

Brian got a text. He looked at the screen. It was Serenity. "About time," Brian thought. He pulled up the text. "B a couple hrs," it read. "What the hell am I going to do for a couple of hours?" he thought. He wondered what she was doing. It bothered him even more that she didn't call and talk to him, she just texted that it would be a couple of hours. She knew that he was waiting for her.

"Essie, what do you want to do?" Brian asked.

"Go fishing," Essie said.

At first Brian was angry at her answer, but he calmed down. "Let's go to Lake LaVerne and walk around," he said. "You wanna go look at the swans?"

Essie was nodding her head and getting out of the booth. "Finally," Brian thought. "She wants to do something I suggested."

Brian left his car in the lot, walked with Essie down Lincolnway to Welch and waited for the light to turn. They crossed to the other side of the street that separated Campustown from the ISU campus itself and the pond named Lake LaVerne. It was a warm morning and Brian slowly walked his daughter around the lake, letting her run ahead of him, taking his time, waiting for Serenity to text or call again.

When they got to the east side of the pond, Brian took Essie into the massive Memorial Union building. They walked the halls that were almost silent at that time on a Saturday morning. They went through to the north door and back out into the sun, the Campanile standing tall in the grassy area facing them. Brian cautioned Essie not to step on the zodiac design in the floor at the entryway. Brian didn't need any more bad luck than he already had.

Outside they went to the fountain and Essie stuck her hands in the water, splashing around and almost falling in. Brian grabbed her just in time. He was quite sure that Monica would not appreciate him bringing her back home to change clothes before they went to the mall because he let her fall into a fountain. Essie was content for the moment to walk around the fountain inspecting the four statues of Indian maidens that occupied the four points of the compass around the concrete bowl. Brian's phone sounded that he had a text. He fished the phone out of his pocket. It was Serenity. "ready," was all it said.

"Gotta go, Essie," Brian said.

Essie ignored him and he had to chase her down and take her hand. They started walking back toward Dunkin' Donuts. Brian was in a hurry to pick up Serenity, and Essie was slowing him down. He didn't realize how far from his car they had wandered.

"Wanna piggyback ride?" Brian asked her.

Essie didn't seem to know what he was talking about. Brian lifted her up and tried to get her to hang onto his back, but she didn't know what to do.

"Haven't you ever had a piggyback ride?" he asked in an irritated tone. "Doesn't Milton give you piggybacks?"

"He lets me ride his shoulders," Essie answered.

"Okay, you want to ride on daddy's shoulders?" he coaxed.

It took a bit of wrangling to get her on his shoulders, but they finally succeeded. Essie was heavier than Brian expected. He set out at a brisk walk toward the car. Essie was bouncing on his shoulders.

"Quit bouncing like that," Brian told her.

She stopped for a moment, but then started again.

Brian finally reached the car and clumsily deposited Essie on the ground, hanging on to her hand so that she wouldn't run out into the drive-up traffic while he unlocked the door of his car. He breathed a sigh of relief when he got her in the car seat, got the straps buckled up and pulled snug. He went around to the driver's side of the car and got in. His phone sounded the tone for a text again. He pulled it from his pocket. It was Serenity. All it said was "READY!!!!"

Brian backed the car out of the parking space and pulled out of the lot onto Lincolnway. He drove the three or four blocks to her apartment building and parked in front. He took out his phone and typed, "In front." He looked toward the door for Serenity. He had hoped that she would be waiting for him to arrive.

Serenity got the text that Brian had arrived and was waiting for her. She went to her kitchen counter where her purse and two phones were sitting, one her personal cell phone and the other her work phone. She put her personal phone in her purse and went out the door. On the elevator she got on the work phone, went through the contacts to find Amy. She pushed the call. It rang once.

"Hi," was all Amy said, just as Serenity was getting off the elevator. She could see Brian's car through the glass entry door.

"We're heading out," Serenity said. "I want you to drive down to Jordan Creek Mall and hang out. We'll probably get something to eat first, so you've got time. I'll give you a call when we get there. I'll call you. Under no circumstances call me on my personal phone. I'm using the work phone today. Okay?"

"Okay," said Amy.

"I'll let you know what I need you to do when I get there. You just hang out. Go shopping, I don't care, just be there and be ready when we get there," Serenity instructed. "And do not text me on either phone. If you absolutely need to, call me on the work phone." Serenity ended the call without waiting for a response.

Brian saw Serenity in the entryway of her building. She was on her phone, and she stopped when she got to the door. Brian waited impatiently, but there was nothing he could do. Finally she came out the door to the car and got in.

"Hey there, little cutie," she said as she buckled her seat belt, turning toward the back seat where Essie was sitting. "How are you today?"

Essie smiled.

"We're going to the mall," Serenity said in an excited voice. "You'll like that. Maybe we can go to Build-a-Bear and you can get a teddy."

Brian winced. He wondered how much a stuffed bear cost. He wasn't flush with cash for this trip. He maybe had enough money for lunch. He let it go. He was sure that Essie wouldn't remember by the time they got to Jordan Creek.

Chapter 26

Saturday

Max got out of bed and went into the bathroom to brush his teeth. He had felt Gloria get up an hour earlier, but he had stayed in bed thinking. He was bothered about the case and had to keep telling himself to let it go. It was in Gilmore's hands now. G&B had done what they were hired to do. But still, the bounce on Wednesday, and everything else that had happened since he and Skip had started investigating the Cosmic Comics case, weighed on him. Nothing about it had been routine.

Max went through the house looking for Gloria. He finally found her in her office where he had expected to find her in the first place, even though it was the last place he looked.

"What are you doing today?" Max asked her.

"Late lunch at the country club with a women's group, then they want a wine tasting. Want to come along?" she asked.

"I don't think so," Max said. Gloria often asked Max if he wanted to go to tastings. He didn't know if she asked him because she thought that he might like to come with her, or just to tease him.

"What are you thinking about?" she asked.

"I just have a feeling," Max said pensively. "I talked to Monica and Skip yesterday after we were at Cosmic Comics with Gilmore. Brian has Essie today, and they are going down to Jordan Creek Mall this afternoon. They are taking Serenity with them. I'm thinking about going down there and seeing if I can get an eyeball on them. See what they're up to."

"Isn't that a little creepy?" Gloria asked. "Following Brian, his daughter and his girlfriend around the mall?"

"Well, when you put it that way, it does seem a little creepy," Max said. "But I'm thinking about doing it anyway. Monica doesn't feel real good about Serenity being along with them, what with all that's been going on."

"Monica doesn't feel good about it, or you don't feel good about it?" Gloria asked.

"Both, I guess."

"What do you expect to uncover at the mall?" Gloria asked.

Max pondered. "If Brian and Serenity were some way involved with the fire, and we're breathing down their necks, maybe they plan to take off with her," Max said. "I don't know, I have a feeling."

Gloria didn't respond.

"What time do you think you'll get home from your tasting?"

"Around three or three-thirty," she replied.

"I'll be back by four," Max reassured her.

"I'll not make any plans for the evening," she replied, smiling.

"I'm serious," Max said.

"So am I."

Max came up behind her and kissed her on the head, more to reassure himself than her, then left the room.

He went down to the basement and opened his gun safe. His Smith and Wesson was locked up at the office. He pushed some larger pistols around, the huge Beretta .40 cal and a Smith .357, before he found what he was looking for. He pulled a stainless Walther PPKS and two magazines filled with hollow point bullets out from under the bigger guns. He shoved one of the magazines into the gun, pulled the slide sharply back and let it snap forward. He found a paddle holster in a box on the floor of the safe, slid the gun into it, then put it over the belt and waistband of his jeans. He found a light nylon pullover and put it on to conceal the pistol. He was surprised that what had felt so routine at one time felt so odd now.

Max went out and got into the Camaro. He was questioning himself, wondering if he was following a gut feeling or if he was letting his paranoia take over. He drove out the driveway and toward Dakota, which would take him south out of town. Max quickly left the city limits and was surrounded by corn fields on one side of the road and soybean fields on the other. When he got to the small town of Slater, ten miles south of Ames, he stopped at the Casey's convenience store to fill up with gas. It was a fact that gas was always five cents a gallon cheaper in Slater than in Ames. While he filled his tank he thought about going back to Ames and spending his Saturday relaxing or raking the yard or anything instead of going on what was in all likelihood a wild goose chase.

After he got gas, Max drove west on State Highway 210 to Madrid, then south on Highway 17. It was the back way. Max almost always took the back way. An hour after he left Ames, he pulled into the parking lot at the Jordan Creek Mall in West Des Moines. It was not quite noon. Max drove around to the back where a couple of restaurants sat away from the mall and around a small artificial pond. He parked, got out of his car and headed toward Joe's Crab Shack. He thought that he might have a bite to eat before he went into the mall in search of Brian. As he came into the entry to the restaurant a young lady behind the counter was picking up a handful of menus for the couple ahead of him.

"I'll be with you in just a minute," she said to Max, leading the couple out to the dining area.

Max looked out across the tables and caught his breath. Brian, Serenity and Essie were sitting at a table not thirty feet from him. Brian and Serenity were caught up in conversation. Essie was looking directly at Max and waving. Max waved back, abruptly turned around and scurried out the door.

Max hurriedly walked across the street to the food court at the mall. He grabbed a quick piece of pizza and a Coke, then took up a seat where he had a clear view of the door but was far enough away that he would not be noticed by a casual observer coming through. It was the closest entrance to the restaurant, and Max was pretty sure that eventually the other three would come through it. He waited patiently.

A half hour later he was rewarded. Essie came through the door and started rubbernecking around. Max put his hand over his face before she could catch sight of him. She would make a good detective someday, he thought. Brian was talking to Serenity, who looked like she was thinking about something else. As they passed the food court, Max got up, threw his paper plate and plastic cup in the garbage and started a loose tail.

Max saw nothing that looked suspicious by any stretch of the imagination. It appeared that Brian and Serenity were shopping. It certainly did not look like they were planning to abscond to parts unknown with Essie. Max followed them through the second floor as they went from one store to the next. A couple of times Brian took up a bench outside the store and entertained Essie while Serenity was inside. Other times he went inside with her. When they came to the Build-a-Bear store, all three went in. Ten minutes later Serenity came out by herself, went to the railing overlooking the first floor and made a phone call. A few minutes later she went back into the store. Twenty more minutes passed and they came out, Essie holding a purple bear that matched the color of Serenity's hair. It looked like Serenity was putting a receipt in her purse. Max thought it was interesting that Serenity bought the purple bear for Essie. Essie put the bear under her arm and took Serenity's hand with her free one. Serenity looked down at her, smiled lovingly and squeezed her hand. Max admitted to himself that maybe Brian and Serenity were a better fit than he had first thought. Essie appeared to be having a good time.

Max followed them to the end of the mall outside of the Scheels sporting goods store. The three stopped for a moment and talked, then Brian went into the store. Serenity took Essie's hand and led her to the escalator. They went down to the first floor. Max stood at the railing and watched them come out below him, where he saw Serenity lead Essie to a large play area. She let Essie run, and took a seat with the rest of the adults who were supervising their wards. Everything appeared perfectly normal.

Monica had many times told Max and Skip how long both Brian and Milton could walk around Scheels and buy nothing. It was the only thing Monica would admit that the two had in common. Max decided that it was time to get a cup of coffee. Leaving Essie and Serenity in the play area, Max hurried to the food court and Starbucks to get a cup. The line was long and Max was impatient, but he reassured himself that nothing was happening and he had plenty of time to get a cup of coffee. He was even questioning the value of continuing the surveillance. Even if Brian came out before he got his cup, he was sure he could pick up the tail again. It might even be good to be out of sight for a little while. And if he lost them, it was probably no big thing. He was close to convincing himself that his gut feeling was nothing more than paranoia after all.

Max watched people stroll past the Starbucks. Max often went shopping with Gloria. Not that he liked shopping, but he was an inveterate people watcher and could while away an entire afternoon sitting on a bench watching people go by.

"May I help you?" The young barista caught Max's attention.

"Just a fresh brew, light," Max replied.

"What size?"

Max looked up at the sizes. He was used to Filo's, where they had small and large. Starbucks was weird, he thought. The barista waited patiently.

"A grande," Max said to her.

"Name?"

"Max."

The barista wrote his name on the cup and put it on the counter next to the cup for the person ahead of him. Max paid and waited.

"You can wait over there," she pointed toward the end of the counter.

Max took a quick look out the door as he went to stand with the three other people waiting for their drinks. He caught his breath. He thought that he had seen Essie walk by with a young woman who was not Serenity. Max dashed to the door and looked. He did not see some stranger with Essie, or even a young woman with a child. Max looked over the rail toward the play area at the other end of the mall, but he could not make it out. He ran toward that direction, looking over the railing the whole way. When he got in sight of the play area there was no sign of Serenity or Essie. They were gone.

Max panicked. He didn't know whether to run back the way he had come in the hopes of catching up with whoever it was he thought he had seen, or if he should go into Scheels and see if perhaps Serenity and Essie had gotten tired of waiting and went looking for Brian. Twice he started the direction of Scheels, and twice he turned around. He told himself that he needed to make up his mind. He ran to the entrance of Scheels and looked inside, hoping that he would catch sight of Brian, Serenity and Essie walking together in the store. Then Max went into police mode. He had a fifty-fifty chance, and the odds got worse every second he waited. He turned and went back the way he had come, made a fast tour of the perimeter of the upper floor, looking through the door of every store, glancing down over the railing to the lower level as he made the round. When he got back to where he had started, he checked the play area again. Essie and Serenity were still nowhere to be seen. Max was convinced from his vantage point that he had covered the interior of the mall the best he could. Turning away from the interior, he went straight out to the parking lot, then turned toward the direction that he had seen the woman and child walking. Better than a fifty-fifty chance that they were on this side of the building, he told himself. His hunch told him that if someone had Essie, she would go out the side that she had been walking on. Max quit thinking about his chances, they were becoming smaller and smaller every second. He had to concentrate on what he was doing. Max was finding it hard to breathe, even if he had been working out for almost a week.

Chapter 27

Saturday

Serenity had a nice lunch with Brian and Essie. Essie was well behaved, waving at everyone. Brian was giving her a pitch, selling himself, trying to rationalize why he and she would be right for each other. She had heard it before. She had no intention of settling down to domestic life with Brian Parker, or anyone else for that matter. She wondered why people were like that. "Why do they always want to get hitched together in the same harness?" she thought. "What fun is that?" She hardly listened to him talk, but he was cute when he pleaded like that. When he was in that desperate condition, she knew she could do almost anything she wanted to him. She gave him an occasional smile to fuel his enthusiasm, the rest of the time she watched the geese through the window behind him, standing around the pond shitting on the concrete.

Their food came and they ate. Essie needed some help. She thought she was too big to wear a bib, so Brian spent a good part of the meal just coaxing her to put on the bib and then eat something. Serenity waited. She did not want to hurry things, they had to unfold at their own speed if her plan was to work.

Finally, Brian asked the waitress for the bill. The first credit card that the waitress ran through was rejected, so Brian dug in his billfold for another. He looked up at Serenity as he did so. She wondered if he was embarrassed or if he was hoping she would bail him out. She did not respond. She was waiting. It all had to look natural.

Brian's second card went through. Serenity casually watched him sign the receipt. He gave the waitress a two-dollar tip for a twenty-eight-dollar bill. Serenity laughed silently, thinking how pathetic he was to think that she would want someone who had such a hard time just buying her lunch. Brian got out of his seat, wiped Essie's hands with a wet wipe, then got her out of her high chair and stood her on the floor. "Let's go to the mall," he said enthusiastically, smiling at Serenity and then at Essie.

"Christ," Serenity said to herself. "The dumb shit thinks that the little girl is going to win me over and make me want to be with him." Serenity laughed out loud thinking that just the opposite was the case; he was lucky that his ex had her most of the time. Serenity had no interest in being tied down by a kid, not her own, and certainly not Brian's.

Brian was still pitching himself while they walked the block from the restaurant to the mall. He was so absorbed with talking to her that she actually had to keep an eye on the little girl so that she didn't run out in front of a car. When they got inside the mall Serenity made it a point to go into almost every store as they walked toward Scheels. She knew that was where Brian was headed, and she was setting the stage. No hurry, take her time.

When they got to the Build-a-Bear store Brian tried to get past it without Essie seeing, but Serenity had plans.

"Hey, here's the bear store," Serenity said, grabbing Essie's hand and pulling her inside. Brian reluctantly followed.

They walked down the aisle of bins that contained the deflated carcasses, a stuffed example on a shelf above each one, a picture on the outside of the bin. Essie immediately grabbed one and held it up to Brian.

"Let's look at all of them," Brian suggested, taking the bear from Essie and putting it back in the bin from where she had taken it.

As they worked their way around the store, they came to a bin that held purple bears. It was the one that Serenity had been looking for.

"How about this one?" Serenity asked, pulling the bear out of the bin and holding it up for Essie to see. "It's the same color as my hair, see?"

Essie squealed and reached for it. Serenity let her have it.

"How much is it?" Brian asked quietly while Essie was waving it around.

"You don't need to worry about it," Serenity said to Brian. "It's on me."

Serenity turned her attention to Essie and ignored Brian. She got the attention of a young woman who worked there, who helped them through the bear-building process. Serenity's phone rang just as they were getting ready to stuff the bear.

"It's work, I gotta take this," Serenity said, holding up the phone. "You can finish this up. I'll come back and pay for it." She went out the door without waiting for a comment. Brian took over. He felt good about it. He would help Essie make the bear, and then she would always associate the bear with him.

Serenity hustled outside and answered the phone.

"You in the mall?" Serenity asked.

"Yep," Amy replied.

"Okay, here's what we're going to do," Serenity continued. "I'm at the Build-a-Bear store, you know where that's at?"

"I can see you up there, I'm on the bottom floor," Amy answered.

Serenity looked down and saw Amy looking up at her. She took a step back, away from the railing and out of Amy's sight.

"We are about done here," Serenity said. "Brian's going to want to go to that sporting goods store at the end of the mall over there."

"Scheels," said Amy.

"I'm going to take the little girl to that kids' playground on your level," Serenity said. "When I get in there, I want you to come in and sit down next to me. I'm going to give you the little girl. You're going to walk her out to your car nice and natural-like. I'll tell her she's going with you, so I think she will go with no problems. Then you put her in your car and take her over to Valley West Mall. You know where that's at?" Serenity waited for an answer.

"Yes," Amy said dubiously.

"Don't be thinking," Serenity said. "Just do what I tell you. You think about it, you're going to fuck it up. Understand?"

"Yes," said Amy more positively.

"That's my girl," Serenity said.

"I want you to take her to the Valley West Mall and drop her off inside," Serenity instructed. "Get her close enough to security that they'll notice her alone, or push her in some store, but make sure you see someone find her. You understand? We don't want anything bad happening to her. We're just getting someone's attention."

"Yes," said Amy.

"Then get the fuck out of there and drive back to Ames," Serenity said. "And do not breathe a word of this to anyone."

Amy did not say anything.

"Are you up to this?" Serenity asked.

"Yes," Amy replied a little less enthusiastically. "I don't have a car seat for her."

"Don't worry about that," Serenity replied. "You just take her over there. Drive straight there. It will take you ten minutes. Make her lay down or something. Use your head, just do it."

"Okay," replied Amy.

Serenity ended the call and went back into Build-a-Bear. The salesgirl was just getting the bear registered for its birth certificate. Brian looked relieved to see her. He was worried about paying for it, no doubt.

"What are we naming this bear?" Serenity asked.

The salesgirl was poised expectantly, waiting for a name.

"Let's name it Penelope," Serenity suggested. "That is a good name for a bear."

"Okay, Penelope," Brian said impatiently, ready for Serenity to pay for the bear so that they could leave. "Wanna hit Scheels when we're done here?"

"If you want to, you can," Serenity said. "I think that Essie, Penelope and I might go down to that kids' play area down there while you're in Scheels."

Brian happily shrugged his shoulders. "Suit yourself."

When they left the store, Brian and Serenity parted ways at the escalator.

"Take your time," Serenity told him. "I know that you like that place. You've spent your afternoon waiting for me, I'm in no hurry. We'll have a good time down there in the play area. It will be fun for both of us," she said in a blissful tone.

Brian went into Scheels. Serenity took Essie's hand and led her to the escalator.

"Essie," she said.

Essie looked up at her.

"Do you like your bear?"

Essie smiled.

"I like your bear," Serenity said. "I wanted you to have that bear because I like you, too."

Essie hugged the bear.

"Essie, your daddy and I are going to go to another mall in just a little while. But your daddy wants his friend to take you there for him, and then he will see you when he gets there. Her name is Penelope, just like your bear, and she is a very nice girl. You will like her. She likes your daddy. She likes your bear, too. So that is what your daddy wants you to do. She'll be here soon to take you. We'll play until she gets here."

At the bottom of the escalator Serenity led Essie to the play area and let her go. Serenity took a seat with the other bored adults. She purposely did not look around for Amy, contenting herself with watching Essie play. Serenity had perfect faith in Amy. First of all, Amy was in love with Serenity. She professed her love every time the two had sex. The other thing was that Amy wanted Brian. Amy had often remarked that if Serenity ever got tired of Brian, she would like to have him. Amy wanted Brian because he belonged to Serenity and having Brian would be like having a part of her. Serenity assured Amy that when she tired of Brian, Serenity would give him to her. But Serenity would never give Brian to Amy. People like Amy and Brian were valuable because they were vulnerable. At one time she had considered them for a threesome. That might have been interesting. But not anymore. She could never let Brian and Amy get close enough to reveal their roles in what was about to happen. She would make sure that they never talked about it.

Amy sat down next to Serenity. Serenity took her hand and put her head on Amy's shoulder. "I'm going to get up and leave in a couple of minutes," she said quietly. "She's the little girl with that purple bear, see her?"

"Yes," replied Amy. "Do you think that she will go with me?"

"I don't know," Serenity said. "She is the most innocent creature I've ever seen. Her name is Essie."

Serenity was silent for a moment.

"I told her that your name is Penelope. Tell her you are Penelope and Daddy wants her to go with you. I think she'll go. I'm going to get up, but I'll stay close enough that if she makes a fuss I'll come back."

The two sat for a moment.

"Give me a little kiss," Serenity said.

Amy gave her a surprised look.

"We're a couple," Serenity explained. "A little kiss."

Amy turned and kissed Serenity. Serenity got up and walked out of the play area. Amy watched the little girl play for a few minutes. Amy was scared, but she loved Serenity and would do anything for her. She took a deep breath and then stood up and approached the little girl.

"Hi, Essie." Amy stood next to Essie. "I'm Penelope. Your daddy wants me to take you to another mall. He had to go there, and he wants you to come there and be with him."

Amy held out her hand and smiled. At first Essie didn't respond, but then she took Amy's hand and Amy led her out of the play area, up the escalator and toward the other end of the mall where she had parked behind the bookstore. Essie walked along beside her as if she were taking off on another adventure.

The two walked past the food court and through the book store. They passed a table full of children's books on display. Essie wanted to stop to look at them. Amy tried to pull her away, but Essie started to pitch a fit. Amy let her look, but kept urging her on. She did not want to make a scene and draw attention to herself, but she felt an urgency to leave the mall and get it over with.

"Come on, little girl," she said, not remembering Essie's name.

Finally, Essie lost interest in the books and walked with Amy toward the door and the parking lot. Amy was fighting the urge to run.

Chapter 28

Saturday

Serenity was going to give Amy five minutes. As soon as Amy left with Essie, Serenity marked the time on her phone. She knew better than to fly by the seat of her pants. While she waited, she thought about how her little end play was going to take everyone's attention away from Cosmic Comics and the fire. It would certainly spook them, hopefully convince them that further inquiries into the fire might not be in their best interests. At the least, it would give her stepfather time to make a deal with Peterson and tear the place down before they got back to it. When the five minutes were up Serenity ran into Scheels Sporting Goods.

"Have you seen a little girl, four or five years old, wearing a pink sweatshirt with a green cat on the front of it, blue jeans and a teal colored nylon jacket?" Serenity breathlessly asked the cashier at the door. "She was just outside in the kids' playground, and I turned my head for a second. Now she's gone. Her dad is in here. I thought maybe she came in looking for him."

Serenity prided herself on always being in control; it was key to her role as leader of the Wizards and cemented her control over the others. Still, her plan hinged on her ability to sell herself as the panicked girlfriend who just lost her boyfriend's kid.

"No, I haven't," the cashier replied, looking into the store, out the door towards the play area, then back to Serenity, not knowing exactly what to do.

Serenity took several quick breaths, sliding herself into hysterics.

"Oh my god," she let her voice waver. "Oh my god," she said again, liking the sound of it.

Another man, older than the cashier, came up and asked what the problem was. Serenity started to repeat what she had told the cashier, but could not remember the clothing description that she had used. She looked at the name tag on the older man's shirt. His name was Gary, and he was an assistant store manager.

"What is the name of the father?" Gary asked.

"Brian Parker," Serenity answered quickly.

Gary picked up a phone, punched some numbers and asked for Brian Parker to come to the lower level mall entrance immediately. His voice boomed over the loudspeaker. Gary put down the phone, picked it up again and punched a new set of numbers into it.

"Do you have a description?" he asked Serenity. Serenity did not answer immediately. She still couldn't remember what she had said before.

"Green sweatshirt with a kitty on the front, blue jeans and a teal colored windbreaker," the cashier piped up, giving Serenity a sympathetic look, thinking that she was in shock.

"All associates," Gary said into the phone. This time it did not go over the loudspeaker. "We are looking for a small girl, four or five years old, green sweatshirt, blue jeans, teal colored windbreaker. She may be in the store and she may be with her father. Be on the lookout and report to me if you spot anyone with that description. Team leaders, station someone at all store exits." Gary turned to Serenity. "I just hit the alert button for mall security. If you can stay put, they will want to talk to you."

Serenity did not reply. Her heart was racing. She wasn't sure she liked the feeling. She did catch that the cashier had described Essie as wearing a green sweatshirt. Serenity did not remember saying that it was green. She watched the confusion grow, satisfied with the events that she had set into motion.

Brian arrived at the entrance. He looked worried. "What's going on?" he asked Serenity. "Where's Essie?" He looked around like he expected to see her close by, but didn't.

"She got away from me," Serenity said, giving her best show of concern.

'What the fuck is that supposed to mean, she got away from you?" Brian confronted her.

Brian had never talked to Serenity like that, and she didn't like his tone. Later she would make him pay for talking to her like that, but for the present she had to stay in her role.

Two mall security guards showed up. One of them was blatantly giving Serenity the once-over. He smiled at her. She smiled back.

"What's wrong?" the other security guard asked.

"Kid went missing," Gary said. "The woman here thought that he might have come in here."

The guard looked at Serenity.

"There was some kind of ruckus over by one of the stores," she said defensively to the guard. "It got my attention, it got everyone's attention. When I turned back I didn't see Brian's little girl anywhere. I got up and looked around for her, to see if she was behind something, and when I couldn't find her, I came in here."

Everyone's attention was on Serenity. "I thought that maybe she came in here looking for you," Serenity looked at Brian, feigning fear. Brian did not know what to say, he was helpless. Gary had pretty much taken over the show.

The security guard took the transmitter to his radio from his belt and asked Gary for a description.

"Four or five years old, green sweatshirt, kitty on the front of it, blue jeans, teal sweatshirt." He gave it a tone of finality when he finished.

"Hold it," Brian interrupted. The security guard had keyed the mic to speak, but he let it go and turned his attention to Brian. "That's not her description."

Everyone looked at him, confused.

"Four-year-old little girl. She's dark complected, mixed race, with curly dark brown hair, really curly and really dark brown. She's wearing a blue cotton dress, black leggings and a purple North Face zip-up fleece. She's wearing Chuck Taylors, I mean the tennis shoes. You know what I mean?"

Brian looked at Gary, then back to the security guards. Everyone was waiting for him to go on.

"She is dressed very fashionable," he added. "And she is carrying a purple stuffed bear."

"Where did you get green sweatshirt?" Brian asked Gary, while the security guard was calling in the description.

"The lady," Gary said, nodding toward Serenity.

"I was scared," Serenity said in her defense. "I couldn't remember what she was wearing."

"So you made something up?" Brian said incredulously.

"No, I didn't make something up," Serenity shot back.

Brian turned his attention back to the security guard.

"Okay, we got all exits covered, and we're calling the West Des Moines PD. They'll be here as quick as they can get here. I got people out in the parking lot." He looked at each person. "You all just sit tight until they get here," he said when no one responded. "We're going to comb the store."

The two security guards left Gary, the cashier, Brian and Serenity at the entrance.

"What ruckus?" the security guard who had been doing the talking asked the other. "I didn't hear about any ruckus. And what's with the description that she gave? Did that conversation just seem hinky to you?"

"She's something to look at," the other guard remarked. "I'll bet she could fuck your eyeballs out."

"We got a little girl missing," the first security guard admonished. "Get your mind out of the gutter and back on task. We gotta find this little girl. You take the right, and I'm going left. Meet you upstairs in the middle. Check out anyone with a kid under ten, I don't care what they're wearing or what they look like."

Max was moving fast, scanning the parking lot and the sidewalks. As he approached the entrance to the book store he spotted the woman with the little girl that he had thought that he had seen before. He was quite sure it was Essie with her. She was wearing the same clothes. He knew it was her, but his years of experience told him to get close enough to get a facial recognition before he did anything else. As he got closer, the little girl turned her head toward him. He instantaneously made the positive identification. She smiled at him and waved the bear clutched in her hand.

"Essie," Max shouted.

Essie tried to pull away from Amy, who tightened her grip and turned away from Max, walking hurriedly. She spotted a mall security guard coming toward her, his eyes turning toward Max who was yelling at her to stop.

Max was running now, just a dozen steps away from Amy, who was about to also be intercepted by the guard.

"That man is nuts," Amy told the mall security guard. "I don't know what is wrong with him, but I don't want him near me."

The security guard turned toward Max. Amy kept walking.

"Sir," the security guard stepped into Max's way. He held out his hand, barring Max from dodging around him. "Sir, hold up here."

"She is getting away! That is not her little girl, that is Essie Parker, and that is not her little girl," Max was screaming.

It took a moment for it to register in the guard's mind that he was looking for a missing little girl, and not some nut running around the parking lot. He turned his head toward Amy and Essie, who were putting distance between them.

"Ma'am," the security guard shouted. "Ma'am, stop," he ordered.

Amy picked up the pace.

"Sir, don't move," the guard told Max. Max held up both hands. The guard turned and ran after Amy. When he got to her, she tried to keep walking, but the guard blocked her path. Max could see him talking on his radio, then turning his attention to Amy. Each time he talked on the radio, Essie looked back at him. She waved at Max. The gesture was not lost on the security guard. He turned and motioned for Max to come to them. Max was tempted to run but decided that might be alarming to everyone involved. He walked briskly to where they stood.

"Hi, Essie," he said. Essie smiled at him.

"Sir," the guard said. "Just stand there, I have West Des Moines PD on the way here. Until then, we all just stay quiet and wait."

"This man is crazy," Amy said.

"Ma'am," the security guard replied. "I asked you to just stand here and wait."

Amy started to walk away. Max dodged around the guard and grabbed Amy by the arm.

The guard grabbed Max. "Sir, unhand the lady," he said.

"Not until the PD gets here," Max shot back.

The guard was trying to decide where his authority rested. He breathed a sigh of relief as a West Des Moines patrol car came wheeling around the building toward where they were standing.

"Fuck, fuck, fuck," Brian said in exasperation inside the Scheels store. He felt like he had been waiting for hours for someone to arrive. He wasn't even sure who they were waiting for. One of the security guards they had talked to came rapidly toward them.

"Sir, one of our mall security and West Des Moines PD has a man, a woman and a kid matching the description of yours stopped out in the parking lot. If you will come with me, we'll go out there and see what they have."

"Let's go," Brian said, heading out into the mall and realizing that he had no idea where they were going.

The West Des Moines patrol officer had his notebook out and was questioning Amy. Max was locked in the back of his patrol car. The mall security officer and Brian arrived, with Serenity and Gary right behind them.

"That's my little girl," Brian shouted as they approached.

The three turned and looked at him. Essie waved.

"Amy, what the fuck are you doing?" Brian said when they got there.

Amy opened her mouth to say something but closed it when she saw Serenity shaking her head. Brian turned and looked at Serenity. She was standing stoicly beside Gary. Brian looked back at Amy.

"Sir," the officer said. "Is this the child that you reported missing?"

"Yes, this is my daughter Essie," Brian replied.

"This woman is saying that she is the babysitter and that she has permission to have her," the officer said.

"That's bullshit," Brian said. "Essie was playing in the kids' play area in the mall and my girlfriend was watching her. She got distracted and when she looked back Essie was missing. I don't know why Amy has her."

"You know this woman, then?" the officer asked, pointing at Amy, who was still holding Essie's hand. Essie, in turn, was looking at Max, who was peering out the window of the patrol car trying to get Brian's attention.

"Yes, I know her," Brian said. "Her name is Amy, and she works with my girlfriend." Brian followed Essie's gaze to the patrol car. "And that's Max Mosbey you've got in your car," Brian said. "He's a private investigator and my ex works for him."

The officer was looking confused. Another officer was pulling into the lot and parking next to his patrol car.

"Stay here and don't anyone move," the officer said. He walked to the patrol car that had just pulled in. The driver was getting out. He had sergeant's stipes on his sleeve.

"Amy, let go of my daughter," Brian said.

Amy looked at Serenity. Serenity nodded and Amy let Essie go. Brian was watching Serenity. Essie ran to Brian and hugged his leg. She did not seem to be the least afraid, though.

"What the fuck is going on?" Brian asked Serenity.

"I have no idea," Serenity replied. "I'm sure that the authorities will get it sorted.

"Why is Amy here?" Brian asked.

"I said, I have no idea," Serenity replied again. "Quit asking questions and let the authorities do their job."

"Fuck that," Brian said, but did not speak more.

The two officers came back to where everyone was standing.

"I need everyone's ID," the original officer announced. "Do you have custody of this child?" he asked Brian.

"I do not," Brian said. "Her mother has custody. I have visitation. I have her today."

"Where is the mother right now?" the officer asked.

"I'm assuming she is in Ames, that's where she lives with her husband," Brian replied. "I live in Ames, too."

"Does she know where her child is right now?" he asked. "Does she know that you brought her down here to the mall?"

"Yes, she does," Brian replied, glancing toward the only person he trusted at the moment, Max, who was still trying to get someone's attention. "That man in your car, Max Mosbey," Brian said. "He is an ex Ames cop. He owns a private detective agency. He is Essie's mother's boss. He can help, if you let him out of the car."

"I know who he is," the officer replied. "I've checked him out, and he'll get out of the car when I'm ready to let him out."

Brian didn't argue.

"IDs everyone, and I'll need a phone number for the mother," the officer said. "I need to check some things out here."

The sergeant had come up and was listening. When the officer was done talking the sergeant took Amy by the arm. "Ma'am, I need to put you in the back of my car."

As the Sergeant was leading Amy away, Brian heard him giving her the rights to remain silent. Brian turned to Serenity. Gary was still on the scene, but was not standing beside her anymore.

"Do you have something to do with this?" Brian asked.

"I swear to god that I have no idea what is going on," Serenity answered. For the first time she was feeling real fear.

Chapter 29

Saturday

Monica and Milton were the last to arrive at the West Des Moines Police Department. Even Skip beat them. From the looks of the expressions on their faces it was not a good conversation on the way down. Monica ran to Essie and grabbed her up. Essie seemed to be totally unfazed by everything that was happening around her, even her mother's emotional embrace.

Milton took a seat in the waiting area next to Max.

"Rough trip?" Max remarked.

"Don't ask," replied Milton.

Monica directed her attention to Brian.

"How did you let this happen?" She glared at him.

"I have no idea how it happened," Brian replied, resigned that he was going to get all the blame.

"The cops are sorting it all out," Max took charge, even though he was an emotional wreck himself. The difference was that he had been in the center of this kind of situation before. "No one knows what happened or why. They're questioning Serenity right now, and some gal that she works with. They seem to have concocted some scheme, but we don't know for sure what it was or why they did it. The officers talked to Brian and determined that he was not aware of any of it. That's what we know, so let's just all try to stay calm and wait."

"Serenity was behind this?" Monica was glaring at both Milton and Brian. "I thought you checked her out!" Monica directed her attention to Milton.

"She checked out," Milton replied.

The West Des Moines police sergeant came out into the waiting area.

"Mrs. Jackson?" he addressed Monica.

"Yes," she replied. "This is my husband, Milton Jackson," she introduced Milton.

The sergeant shook hands with Milton. "I believe our paths have crossed," he said, recognizing him.

The sergeant pulled up a straight back chair and sat down. He glanced over at Skip. "Mr. Murray, I believe our paths have crossed as well."

Skip nodded, recognizing the sergeant, but not being able to place when or where they had met.

"Here's where we are at," the sergeant began. "Pamela has lawyered up and she is not saying anything to us. We have charged her with accessory to kidnapping, and she is in holding, waiting for bail. The other woman, Amy, is very open. She seems to have a thing for Brian and wants him to be aware that none of this was her idea. She is telling us that Pamela had a plan to have Amy take the little girl to the Valley West Mall and dump her off there to throw a scare into Brian. She says they did not intend to keep the little girl or hurt the little girl. She does not know why Pamela wants to scare Brian, but that is what she thinks was Pamela's motivation."

"I think that it isn't Brian that she wanted to throw a scare into," Skip piped up.

"How's that?" the sergeant asked.

"We've been working on a case for an insurance agent in Ames, following up on a fire investigation of a comic book store that burned in Ames a month ago, where Brian worked before it burned down. Things have been contentious from the beginning. Just Wednesday a couple of guys accosted Max and physically assaulted him, warning him to stay away. Yesterday it was determined that the fire was not accidental, and the case was re-opened. Serenity was our prime suspect."

"That explains a lot," the sergeant commented. "Just to let you know, Pamela's stepfather is on his way here to bail her out. She grew up here in West Des Moines and comes from a very well-to-do family."

"What does that mean?" Monica asked.

"It means that she is going to get bailed out this afternoon and she is going to get a good lawyer," the sergeant replied.

No one commented.

"Amy isn't going to be so lucky. She's being charged with kidnapping and we'll be holding her."

"Any questions?" The sergeant looked from one to another. "Okay," he said. "I think that Mr. and Mrs. Jackson can take their daughter home. I'll ask Mr. Mosbey and Mr. Parker to hang around for a while, just in case we have more questions. We are right now in the process of obtaining a no contact order against Pamela so that she cannot make contact in any way with the Jacksons or Mr. Parker when and if she gets out." The sergeant got up from the chair and left the room.

Monica stood up with Essie in her arms. Milton stood up beside her, and she handed Essie to him.

Skip stood as well. "I'm going to walk these two out, and then I'll be back," he said.

The four of them left the waiting area.

"Listen," Skip said as they walked out of the building. "This whole thing is scary, but I think that it is important to realize that it is not Brian's fault, or Milton's, and that it is something that is not going to happen again."

He didn't get an answer.

"I'm just saying, let's not let it take over our good judgement."

"I'm just saying that I'm not sure that it is worth it to put my family in jeopardy over the G&B Detective Agency." Monica stopped walking.

"Come on, Monica," Skip replied. "This is not about G&B Detective Agency."

"What is it about?" she asked him.

"It's about crossing paths with a whacko."

Monica did not answer.

"I realize that this whole thing is extremely frightening," Skip said, touching Monica's arm. "But we are not your enemy. Milton is not your enemy. Brian is not your enemy. We are all family. It is frightening for us, too. We need each other, so remember that."

Monica did not say anything for a moment as she stood looking at Skip. "Well, Brian's got a lot of explaining to do before I believe that," she finally said.

"Let's talk in the office Monday morning," Skip said. "We're done with the Cosmic Comics case. We proved what Ben wanted us to prove, and as far as G&B Detective Agency is concerned, case closed."

"It just bothers me that someone targeted my daughter over this case," she said in parting.

"It bothers me, too," Skip said. "It bothers everyone. But I don't know how we would have seen it coming and prevented it. Other than not taking any cases."

"I thought that was what we were doing, not taking cases," Monica replied.

"We'll talk about it Monday," Skip said. "Please."

Milton had been silent throughout the conversation. As Monica turned toward the car, Milton had an urge to shake Skip's hand. He transferred Essie to his left side and held out his free hand. Skip took it. Then Milton followed Monica to the car.

Skip went back into the station and to the waiting room. Max and Brian were in conversation. "Monica is really shook up," he said when the two looked up at him coming into the room.

"I don't blame her," Max replied. "I'm shook up, too."

"Yeah, well you handle being shook up a lot better than her," Skip noted.

"I'm pretty shook up," Brian said.

He got no sympathy from either of the other two.

Skip sat down.

"We've been talking," Max said. "Brian here was getting pretty knowledgeable about the vintage comic book and vintage record business when Cosmic Comics burned down. We were just talking," Max stopped for a moment. "Just talking, nothing more, but I wonder if we might want to invest in relocating Cosmic Comics somewhere else on Welch Avenue and getting Brian here to be the manager?"

"What about Hank?" Skip asked. "Hank lost his family business; Brian lost his job."

"Like I said," Max replied. "We're just talking. Maybe Hank would want to invest his insurance money in it as well, and we'd be partners. I don't know. Lots of details to work out. I'm just suggesting that maybe investing in a store in Campustown might be a good thing for everybody. At least it would get Brian out of the deli and into a job with a future. He's up for it."

"I would really appreciate the chance," Brian piped up. "I really thought that I was getting a feel for the business. I think that I could make a go of it if I had a little financing. I mean, Hank was doing his best, but that vintage comics promotion that I was planning was going to give that place a shot in the arm. It was just bad luck that it didn't happen."

Skip did not look convinced. "I'll think about it."

"He'll come around," Max said to Brian.

The sergeant and the arresting officer came into the room. "Mr. Parker, I think that we have all we need from you for now. You are free to leave. But I would like Mr. Mosbey and Mr. Murray to stick around. We need to talk."

Brian looked at the two detectives. Skip nodded. Brian stood up and took a business card that the officer handed him. "If you hear anything or think of anything that might be related to this case, give me a call. Under no circumstances have contact with Miss Stephens."

Brian nodded.

"Any questions?" he asked.

Brian shook his head.

"You can head out, then," he said.

Brian gathered his things and left the room. Max and Skip waited expectantly, wondering why the officer wanted to talk to them. The sergeant was standing by the door.

The officer waited until he was sure that Brian was out of earshot. "First of all, my brother grew up with Pamela and works for her dad. I talked to him on the phone, and I talked to the fire marshal's investigator, Gilmore, to see if the comic book store burning might have anything to do with our case. The thing is, Gilmore said that you guys suspected Pamela because she is an electrical engineering student. He said that an authority on electrical wiring told you all that the wiring that caused the fire was not something that an engineering student with no actual experience in wiring would be able to do."

He stopped and looked at the two.

"There was an electrician there that said that," Max said. "When they discovered that the fire had been started intentionally."

"Right," the officer continued. "Before he was a big-time commercial developer, Carl Rogers was an electrician. Pamela has been pulling wires and wiring up commercial buildings since she was old enough to go to job sites with her stepdad. They are real close. He adopted her when she was just a little girl. Her mother never changed her name from Stephens, but she and her stepdad are thick. My brother said that she most definitely would know how to short out a circuit."

"Okay," said Skip. "That is a twist."

"I'm telling you this in confidence, because it is all just conjecture, and I don't want to see my brother lose his job over conjecture, but he says that he thinks Pamela is in cahoots with Rogers to pressure some businesses up there in Ames to sell out to him. He says she has some thugs that paint shit on the buildings, break windows and throw trash in the doorways of places at night to make the owners have second thoughts about the profitability of not selling out."

"When the Cosmic Comics building burned, Serenity's dad got right in there to put in an offer to buy it," Max said. "Evidently he had tried before. You think that Serenity took advantage of Brian to get in there and burn the place down so that her stepdad could come in and buy it?"

"That's what I'm going to tell Gilmore to take a closer look at when I call him back," the officer replied. "I'm not letting her go until I talk to him again. He might want to add an arson charge to the kidnapping. She might not make bail."

Max pondered what he had just learned while the officer was talking.

"She didn't take Essie to throw a scare into Brian, no reason to do that," Max said. "She did it to throw a scare into us, didn't she?"

"To scare you, and to get your heads out of the investigation. Give you something else to focus on for a while, something with a higher priority," the officer replied.

"Hoping that her stepdad could get in there, buy the building, and then either tear it down before we could get back to it, or at the very least, keep us out," Max reflected.

"Sounds as good as any other explanation for what went on," the sergeant said, chiming in for the first time since the younger officer had started talking. "This is an ongoing investigation," he continued. "We are sharing it and our thoughts about it as a professional courtesy. None of this gets out."

"Goes without saying," Max assured him.

"You guys got anything else?" the sergeant asked.

Max and Skip both shook their heads.

"Have a nice drive home," the sergeant said.

"Can you keep us abreast of where this goes?" Max asked.

The sergeant thought for a moment.

"If you happen to think of it," Max said.

"If I happen to think of it," the sergeant replied.

"Appreciate everything," Max shook the sergeant's hand, then the officer's. Skip did the same.

The two walked out to the parking lot. Skip had parked his car right next to Max's Camaro.

"Do we go back to Ben with all of this?" Skip asked.

Max thought for a moment. "We just told Monica that the case was closed. This case was closed as soon as we determined that the fire wasn't accidental. That's what Ben hired us to do. We don't owe Ben anything more. I say we let Gilmore run with it and we mind our own business."

"I think that is a good plan," Skip agreed.

Brian was driving up Interstate 35 back to Ames. When he got out of the metro area north of Ankeny, he fished his phone out of his pocket and held it up where he could scroll through the contacts and watch where he was going at the same time. He found the number and pushed call with his thumb. It rang five times, and he was sure it was going to voicemail when Becky answered.

"Hey, you won't believe this," Brian said, not identifying himself.

"Brian?" he asked.

"Who else would it be?" Brian asked casually. "Listen up, get ready to pack your bags. I think in a week or two I might be able to get my own place and you can come up here."

"What changed?" Becky asked.

"Monica's bosses want to go into business with me. They want to invest in a comic book-slash-record store and make me manager. I'm thinking I see money in this arrangement."

"No shit?" Becky said excitedly. "About time."

"Yep, you wouldn't believe how it came about, but I'm seeing a wide-open door to the bank vault, and I'm going through it."

Becky laughed out loud.

"I knew that I would catch a break sooner or later," he said. "Listen, I'm in traffic right now, but I'll call you later. I just had to let you know."

"Love you," Becky said over the phone.

"Love you, too," Brian replied and ended the call. Things were looking up.

Chapter 30

Monday

Monica got up at six o'clock and started putting on her clothes to go walking. Milton was already up and brushing his teeth. Her mother, Shawna, and Essie were still asleep. Monica went into the bathroom and pushed Milton to one side with her hips as she reached for her toothbrush. She was anxious to get walking. Today, instead of jogging with him she was going walk, so that she could tell Milton about her research paper and how she had been secretly using him as her control subject. She was not sure how he would react to her treachery. She had wanted to keep it from him for a month, to give her time to get her data compiled and her observations recorded, but she couldn't keep her secret from Milton. She should have picked someone else in the first place. She should have used Shawna.

"We need to get one of those places that has two sinks in the master bathroom when we buy a new house," Milton said.

"That would be nice," Monica replied. "It wasn't a problem when you were working patrol. I mean, we were never in here at the same time."

"You want me back on patrol?" Milton asked seriously.

"No, I like you in detectives," she said. "We'll get a house with two sinks in the master bathroom. You stay on Detectives."

"We need to get serious about looking for a new house," Milton said.

Milton and Monica made it out the door and Milton started to jog. They had been doing it in the mornings regularly for a week now.

"Milton, let's just walk today. I have to talk to you about something," she said as they started out in the morning sun.

"You want to quit the agency. This thing that happened with Essie has you spooked," Milton said.

"No," Monica reflected. "I think I got past that. I think that was something that no one could have predicted. It was so random. I mean, someone could try to take her from a playground, anywhere. It is something that all parents have in the back of their minds," she paused for a moment. "It's like being married to a cop and having it in the back of your mind that he might not come home some night, it's something you have to live with. I can't live my life in fear that I'm going to lose one of you. I can't live my life in fear that someone is going to try to take Essie again."

"What then?" Milton asked casually as they rounded a corner.

Monica tried to collect her thoughts. "I've been doing a term paper and research project for one of my classes," she began. "It's about motivating people to work. How society and the working class is manipulated by the social-industrial complex to produce more products, and how the social-industrial complex manipulates the consumer to buy them."

"Are you turning into a commie on me?" Milton replied.

"No, it is something we are studying," Monica said. "It doesn't have anything to do with commies. I'm doing a project on motivating workers. I'm using exercise as a form of work, because most people do not like to exercise, especially the subjects in my project."

"So, all of this walking and jogging is to gather data for your paper?" Milton asked, still in a casual tone. Monica was thinking that things were going better than she had expected.

"Yes, and I feel bad, but I wasn't really thinking about the unintended consequences. I am using Max and Skip as my test subjects. I'm using several techniques to motivate them to exercise, like giving them rewards, developing an illusion of team, encouraging competition."

"And they got no idea that you are doing this to them?" Milton asked, this time more engaged. "Oh man, this is precious."

Monica paused before she went on. "You are my control subject," she said.

"What's that mean?" Milton asked.

"I'm not motivating you, I'm just making you go out walking with me and I'm not using any motivational techniques on you. Then I measure their progress against yours," Monica replied, waiting for a reaction from Milton.

"So you are doing all of this stuff to Max and Skip, but I'm just going along and doing our thing, normal like?" Milton remarked. "You want to see if I do anything different than they do?"

"Yes," Monica said.

"You just blew your research," Milton said.

"I know," Monica said.

"Because you know I'm going to slack off to make those dorks look like you're really leading them around by the nose," Milton laughed. "I'm motivated now. Let's turn around and go home."

"Please, Milton," Monica pleaded.

"Oh my god," Milton laughed.

"Don't tell them," Monica replied.

"Oh, I'm not going to tell them, but that won't stop me from laughing my ass off every time those two go acting like they are really into being fit and healthy, which is something they've been talking about all week, acting all righteous and flashing their Fitbits around. And all week if they aren't talking about their 'arson' investigation, they're talking about how fit they are getting."

Monica did not reply. She was starting to wonder if she should have said anything at all. Milton did not seem to be at all disturbed by the fact that she had been using him as a test subject without telling him.

"What about Ben?" Milton asked. "What did you do to motivate him?"

"Nothing," Monica replied. "He just came out and wanted to join us. I think that he likes the comradery. He likes hanging out with us."

"There's an interesting slant to work into it," Milton said. "Can we go back now?"

"Why not?" Monica said, shaking her head and wondering what she was going to do now with her project.

Max liked staff meetings at G&B Detective Agency. He had never been a fan of meetings before, and the only purpose he had ever seen for them was so that those higher up on the chain could listen to themselves talk. But not so, he told himself, at the G&B Detective Agency. At the G&B Detective Agency a staff meeting was a collaboration. Of course, the G&B Detective Agency staff consisted of just three people. Skip had called a staff meeting for Monday morning, and it was Monday morning.

Max pulled into the parking lot and parked next to Monica's car, which was parked in her reserved space directly in front of the door. Max and Skip did not have reserved spaces, but there was never a lack of spaces available. The property manager had allocated them eight. Monica was coming across the street with a cardboard box containing two mugs of coffee, one for her and one for Max, and a latte for Skip.

Max waited for her. "What's up?" he asked when she got closer.

"Nothing," she replied.

"Where's Skip? I thought he called this hootnanny," Max exclaimed.

Monica shrugged her shoulders and led the way into the agency. She placed the cardboard box on her desk and took one of mugs out, handing it to Max, who took a seat in one of the chairs facing her desk. She sat down with her own coffee.

"Coming in the parking lot right now," she remarked.

Max turned to see Skip parking his Audi on the other side of the lot, as far from the door as he could park it. Max always wondered why he parked clear over there. Whenever he asked, Skip asked back, "Why not?"

"We going to walk?" Max asked.

"I think we should," Monica replied.

"I think we should," Max said.

Skip was walking toward the agency when Ben Ralston came into view. The two started talking. Skip was doing some stretches in the middle of the parking lot, glancing up at the windows wondering where Monica and Max were.

"Might as well," Monica said, feeling a bit down after her talk with Milton. She felt like her project was falling apart. She had planned for it to go differently.

"What's bugging you?" Max said. "One week and you are already turning into a slacker. Look at us. Don't you want to get fit?"

"Come on," Max was getting up.

"Coffee is going to get cold," she commented.

"We'll heat it up in the microwave," Max said, holding the door.

"Gross," Monica replied, walking past Max and out to the parking lot where she was greeted by Skip and Ben.

Monica followed Skip's lead through the stretching.

"We all loosened up?" he asked, not waiting for a reply.

"What's on the agenda for the staff meeting?" Max asked.

"I thought we should talk about what happened on Saturday. I was thinking that one of our staff might want to express her views on it. Maybe we need to make some changes to address what happened and make sure it doesn't happen again. She is too valuable to us to lose her," Skip replied.

Monica was listening.

"That's the agenda," Skip said.

"I'm over it, and I'm moving on," Monica replied. "I don't want to talk about it anymore."

"Cool," Max quipped. "Staff meeting cancelled. I hate staff meetings."

Skip glanced at the two while he walked. He looked over at Ben, hoping for some support, realizing that Ben had absolutely nothing to do with it and was not even listening to them.

"I think that we need to have a staff meeting anyway, talk over other issues."

"Like what?" asked Max

"I'll think of some things by the time we get back."

"I think you just want to hear yourself talk," Max chided.

"Better than listening to you talk," Skip shot back.

Monica listened to the two going after each other. She felt good, better than she had felt all weekend.

Epilogue

Four months later

WHO News: Ames. Daughter of Campustown Developer Found Guilty in Story County Court of Kidnapping and Arson. Sentencing Date Not Yet Set.

Made in the USA
Monee, IL
12 November 2020